The Qualities of Sand

The Qualities of Sand

by Alison Blanche

For my parents, my husband and my son

*"Do not follow where the path may lead,
Go instead where there is no path and leave a trail."
Ralph Waldo Emerson*

You all taught me this in your own way

Prologue
1984

The pain ripped through her body rendering her unable to breathe. She didn't scream, she barely moved, just allowed the pain to course through her knowing that it would stop. It left as swiftly as it had arrived, like a train heading out from the station intent on another destination. She looked to the front of the car and stared at her father's hands as he gripped the steering wheel. He was so thin she could make out the map of veins through the almost translucent skin. She stared at them as they branched off into different directions, returning the blood. She didn't know if he had a heart.

She turned to look out of the window and watched as the world passed by. The trees were a lush green, leaves shining after the recent summer showers. The sky was a rich royal blue with hardly a cloud to disrupt it. Green trees and blue skies – life continued as normal. She looked at the veins in her own hands. The little blue lines, like roads on a map their destination clear, her immediate destination was obvious; it was the rest of her life that would now change.

She attempted to stifle a scream as another pain assaulted her body; she felt she was being torn in half. She grabbed her swollen stomach as she saw him glance in the rear-view mirror, had she seen a flicker of concern cross his face or was she just hoping that she had? The pains were regular now with the respite in between almost imperceptible. She felt suddenly afraid that they wouldn't make it to the hospital in time. She felt afraid that they would.

She looked to the front of the car once more, her father was steadfastly silent. They hadn't exchanged a single word during the seemingly endless journey. When she looked back on the day all she would remember was the awful pain and the pendulum swing of the rosary beads which hung from the rear-view mirror.

Another pain came, this time she screamed – unable to hold in her anguish any longer. The car swerved into oncoming traffic and angry motorists blasted their feelings as her father regained control of the car. The journey continued in silence, the echoes of her pain hanging in the air between them.

She thought back to the day several months ago when everything had changed. She had known in her heart even before she had sat in the chair opposite the GP. He had confirmed her worries with a short sentence delivered without care or compassion. He couldn't have judged her more harshly than she had judged herself, but he still peered over his glasses as though he was a superior being. There had been a boyfriend of some months who had told her he loved her, she had been confident to tell him of their predicament. It had soon become painfully clear though that it was in fact her problem and he wanted no part in whatever she decided to do about the situation. She didn't mourn the loss of him because it was obvious he wasn't the man she thought he was. He left the university abruptly a week after she told him she intended to keep the baby, so the man who had initially promised her the earth then disappeared to the other side of it. She hadn't told her parents about him, knowing they would disapprove of the age difference. It made the admission of her pregnancy all the harder. Her mother had raged and demanded she have an abortion as her father watched in silence. This had been the pattern of their lives for the last few years, her mother would shout and scream as her impotent father looked on. Her world was littered with ineffectual men.

Her mother had booked the abortion for her in a clinic on the outskirts of the town where they wouldn't be recognised. The hypocrisy of the situation had astounded her. They were a God-fearing family, they attended church more regularly than the priest, but apparently her parents hadn't been listening to the text of the Bible. She had thought about running away but with no money to support her let alone a baby, she became resigned to her fate. She stopped eating properly and then dropped out of university unable to take part in the life around her; she couldn't see a way out for her or the growing baby. The night before the abortion she had taken to her bed too weak from lack of food to leave the toxic environment that she was living in. There had been a gentle knock on the door of her bedroom and her father had walked in. He looked smaller and she realised then that he too had lost weight. He had sat on the side of her bed and

3

grabbed her hand. He had told her then that he had cancelled the abortion. She had been overjoyed, she had sobbed, hugging him, telling him that she would get a job to help to pay the bills. Perhaps she could continue her degree part-time and the baby could go with her to the university as they had just opened a crèche. It would all work out, she had felt the belt of sorrow loosen and she could breathe properly for the first time since she had discovered she was pregnant. He had looked at her as though she was a little girl, then he had held her in his arms as he told her that an adoption had been organised. Her mother had reluctantly agreed after he had called the local priest to talk to her about the sin an abortion would leave on her soul. He had held her tight as he told her it would be the best thing for them all. She had slumped in his arms as he talked, like a balloon that slowly deflates. The fight seeped out of her – the more she wilted the harder he held on to her until she wasn't sure if it was him who was squeezing every last bit of fight out of her.

She began to eat better, a little each day for the sole purpose of feeding her baby. She slept and ate as the pregnancy progressed. She left the house only to go for her antenatal checks avoiding eye contact with the happy, smug mothers. She didn't look into the eyes of the sympathetic nurse who asked if she was feeling OK as she drew blood from her arm. Her mother had spent more and more time praying for the soul of her harlot daughter, telling fellow parishioners that her daughter was ill but she was receiving treatment and the prognosis was good. She was confident her daughter would be back to full health in a couple of months.

A few days before the birth, her father had come into her room. It was a Sunday morning and unusually he had stayed home from church. He didn't say a word just handed her a newspaper that was folded in half, she waited for him to say something but he had smiled sadly and left the room. She looked at the paper – it had been opened and folded and an article had been circled. The article was about a bereavement group who were advertising a recent name change. They were now called Sands, there was a phone number and various testimonials from people who had been helped by the Stillbirth and Perinatal Death Association (SPDA) as it was previously called. She looked at the empty doorway.

Less than two days later she was safely delivered of a baby boy weighing in at exactly 8lbs. He had cried as soon as he had entered the world. Maybe he knew. She held him in her arms and then he was gone, whisked away to a better life, to a loving home with two parents. She had whispered to him that she loved him and that maybe one day they would find each other again.

She had found the newspaper that her father had given her, under her bed a few weeks after the birth. She had rung the help number and then replaced the receiver without waiting for anyone to answer. Over the weeks, she had gone as far as listening to one of the group asking if they could help her as she sat in her cold house, the phone cradled in her hands as tears ran silently down her face. She didn't think she would ever recover from the loss, her arms ached with the memory of holding him and on some nights she awoke convinced that she had heard him cry.

Sands – The Stillbirth and Neonatal Death Society –explained that it was there to help anyone who had lost their babies whatever the circumstances, but she had given hers away.

John
October 2014, Wales

History is a child building a sandcastle by the sea
And that child is the whole majesty of man's power in the world.

Heraclitus

The beach was busier than John had anticipated as they walked down the small shingle lane that led from the rented cottage straight onto the expanse of golden sand. Even at this early hour there were several families setting up for the day. Seth, his eight-year-old would have stayed in bed reading or playing on his PSP. Peggy however had led the mutiny to relieve her father of his much-needed sleep. At the tender age of six she was a born leader.

They had made pancakes in the tiny whitewashed kitchen. Seth had helped John to weigh out the ingredients while Peggy had sat on the high stool pretending to be in charge. The FM radio blasted out the local radio station. Popular songs rang out to which the three of them sang along, interspersed with some quite bizarre Welsh adverts. With bellies full and a rather shabby attempt at clearing up the batter splashes made when Peggy had decided to help, they packed their bags for the beach.

John paused for a brief moment. The scenery was breathtaking, and he felt his emotions unravel. In the early sunlight the sands glistened, the larger pebbles gave way to smaller ones that eventually blended with the golden sand which was then swallowed up by the sea. The sea was not the mystic aquamarine of the Mediterranean, but slate grey like the roofs of the surrounding cottages. It was fringed with a lacy white frill as it broke on the vast shore.

He pulled himself together as they looked for a place to decamp. They found a spot fairly close to the little café on the beach. It would be handy if John needed a couple of shots of espresso to keep him going after the early start. He set about disgorging the contents of his rucksack which contained a miscellany of plastic beach toys, balls, blankets and the ubiquitous stripy wind break, the staple of the British seaside. He placed the cool box in the shade afforded by the wind break. It was crammed with a plethora of pasties, sandwiches, salad and fruit. It was more than enough to feed the entire occupants of the beach and was wholly unnecessary since the walk back to the cottage was less than ten minutes. But Peggy had insisted. She wanted to stay on the beach until it was dark, the sun was to go to bed before her, she had declared.

John watched as his children settled on the blankets he had spread across the sand as if he was some nineteenth century gold rush prospector staking his claim. He opened the tube of sun-cream and called to Peggy. He covered her fair skin with the sunblock; it was mid-October and the sun weakening but he didn't want to take any chances of her burning. She was often referred to as little Annie with her pale skin and titian curls, which never failed to infuriate her.

"What do you want to do Peg? Shall we go crabbing?" asked Seth.

"No," screeched Peggy. "They'll pinch me and it will hurt and Daddy will have to take me to the hospital and I might lose all my fingers and…"

"OK Peg, I'll think of something else," said Seth.

John breathed a sigh of relief. Peggy was enough of a drama queen without adding crabs to the mix.

"Daddy, that's enough cream, I look like a snowman. Why is Seth allowed to put on his own cream? I want to do my own next time."

"You're not old enough, Peg. Remember what happened when you did your own hair for school last week?"

Much to John's surprise she didn't argue. Maybe the trauma with her hair had been a good thing even though it hadn't felt like it at the time. It had taken both him and Martha nearly an hour to remove the offending clips and even then, a pair of scissors had to be involved.

Seth seemed deep in thought, possibly considering the options of beach activities that would be safe enough for his sister. John worried constantly that the boy took on too much where Peggy was concerned. It was as though he wouldn't let her be unhappy, not even for a second. Maybe the trip to Wales hadn't been such a good idea after all. He knew though that the alternative was no better. Either way seemed wrong.

"I know, Peg," said Seth, instantly – so animated that it made John question his doubts once again.

"Let's build a sandcastle, one that's the biggest and best that Swansea has ever seen."

John relaxed.

"Yes," shouted Peggy. "Let's make it the best in the whole of the world and the stars and everywhere else."

Peggy loved one-upmanship regardless of the recipient. Or especially if it involved her older brother. John was an only child, sibling rivalry was an alien concept to him.

"OK Peg, whatever you say."

They began by designing the castle. Seth took this seriously using a discarded stick that had more than likely been carried onto the sand by some enthusiastic dog. He marked out the shape of the base in the damp sand further down the beach from where they had settled and where John was pretending to read. They had insisted they would design the sandcastle and once that was done they would allow John to help.

"A castle for a princess," said Seth.

"Which one?"

"What?"

"Which princess, Seth?" asked Peggy. She spoke slowly enunciating every word as if Seth was the six-year-old, "Snow White, Cinderella… which one?"

John tried not to laugh as Seth stared at his sister in disbelief. Peggy was standing refusing to do any more work until the current issue was resolved. He didn't want to interfere as it was so nice to see them like their old selves again. He sighed, his mind always took him back to why they had come here in the first place. He put the book that he had been trying to read on the blanket. He couldn't have told anyone what it was about if his life had depended on it. His mind refused to allow him any respite from the pain. When he had asked the head of the kids' school if he could take them out of school before half-term she had said it was a marvellous idea. On reflection she found most things marvellous. However, she had waived the fees and told him to have a good time whilst giving him that "look". It was the same one he received from the other teachers, the mums on the school run and his colleagues at work. He guessed it was inevitable when you became a widower at the age of thirty-three.

"Seth, you have to decide which princess because they all have different castles."

A valid point thought John pleased at his daughter's argument, maybe she would be a lawyer when she grew up. Seth had also stopped working now that his entire workforce was working to rule. Seth stared at the ground for a few seconds and then reached down and scooped a handful of sand. John watched as the boy let the sand fall through his fingers; he felt his heart ache. Jeez he was so stupid. Seth knew the significance of sand, it made John feel closer to her but maybe it upset Seth.

"It's for a very special princess," said Seth. "This princess had the most beautiful castle throughout the whole of the world."

"And the stars and everywhere," added Peggy.

"Yes Peg, and everywhere. In fact it was a well-known fact that Cinderella was very jealous of it."

"Whose castle, Seth?" asked Peggy.

"It is the castle of Princess Peggy of Port Eynon."

"Me?" she asked.

"Yes, you Peg, who else?"

At this, John watched as Peggy ran across what would eventually be her castle and threw herself at Seth. She rained kisses all over his face until he was almost puce with embarrassment. John chuckled to himself as he saw Seth look around to see if anyone else had noticed the overt display of affection. When he had been growing up he had missed not having a brother or a sister. You weren't supposed to be able to miss something that you had never had but somehow, he had.

He watched as his children settled back to the task of building what was now Peggy's castle. In the kitchen that morning while Peggy was putting anything in his rucksack that wasn't nailed down, Seth had asked about local pirates. They had been to Cornwall a few years previously and Seth had loved the stories about the real-life pirates. He mentioned that he had seen a sign on their journey down to the cottage that seemed like somewhere pirates would live. Seth was growing up fast but the young boy inside him was not quite ready to leave. He loved the idealised picture of friendly pillaging pirates, but he was growing up and recently he had started questioning most things. What was the point of the tooth fairy? What did the fairy do with all the teeth? Why did Father Christmas have to be fat? Surely that wasn't a healthy way to live; he was practically morbidly obese. Evie had been great at this sort of thing. John had tried to think how she would have answered Seth, especially with Peggy listening intently. He said that the tooth fairy was one of the first to engage in recycling and used the teeth to make removable ones for the grandmas and granddads who had lost theirs. As for Father Christmas being so fat, it was for insulation to protect him from the heat of all the chimneys. And in January like most other people he went on a strict diet. So, for most of the year he was actually quite slim. Seth had thought over his answers and seemingly happy with his explanations had then gone on to ask why pirates wore an eye patch. This one John did know – it was apparently to get one eye accustomed to darkness in readiness for a night-time raid. Seth had tried it out in his bedroom and declared it was the best trick ever. John felt Evie would have been proud of him that day. He looked at his children immersed in the task at hand. The sun was shining and the sea sparkling as though the stars from the night sky played in the sea during the day. He felt such an immense sadness inside him that he had to swallow to stop the tears that threatened to engulf him.

Tom

October 2014, Wales

If you came to me with a face I have not seen,
With a name I have never heard, I would still know you.
Even if centuries separated us, I would still feel you.
Somewhere between the sand and the stardust.

Lang Leav

Tom rubbed his eyes, they felt gritty and sore. He stretched his arms behind his back until they clicked. His ex-girlfriend had told him he would get arthritis if he kept doing it; he was sure there was a bit of devilment that made him still do it. He looked at the huge pile of files on his desk leaning precariously towards him – he doubted he would be able to have much of a social life until 2020 at the earliest. He yawned again. Jeez, why was he constantly so tired? He knew that the workload didn't help but he was a young man, well youngish, only mid-thirties. Surely that was still considered young even in today's youth-obsessed society. He scanned the open file on his desk wondering if it was simply the workload that was getting to him. There was a sharp knock at the door, and Shirley popped her head in.

"Tom, the partners meeting has been postponed until tomorrow."

"Great, thanks Shirley. At least now I may get home before midnight!"

"You and me both," she said as she returned to her office.

Shirley was like the mother of the firm, short and a little overweight, enough as she liked to say, to fill out her wrinkles. His mother referred to her uncharitably as the troglodyte. Susan couldn't understand any woman who didn't know the assistant on the Chanel counter by her first name.

Susan had noticed his recent tiredness and had threatened to make him an appointment with the GP. He looked at the recent photo and letter on his desk from his father. The photo was taken in some exotic destination, each one much the same as the last. Both Tom's dad and his dad's second wife – he couldn't bring himself to refer to her as his stepmother – looked tanned and healthy, they made a handsome couple. Neither had bags under their eyes, not even a small piece of hand luggage thought Tom wryly. Susan would merely say that why would they, her ex-husband and his secretary, now wife, had left their problems for everyone else to sort out. He admired his mother's pragmatic approach to the cards that she had been dealt.

Still feeling exhausted, he closed the file he had been looking at and decided to leave work early for a change. He turned off his coffee maker and grabbing his coat from the hook on the back of the door he left his office. He called goodbye to the remaining staff and walked out from the cool interior into the warm evening. He often felt the aged offices had some sort of dimmer-switch effect, outside was always warmer and louder and more alive. The offices were brutally cold during the winter months and they didn't really warm up much during the summer. However, at least during the winter months the central heating was on. The partners refused to have it on during the summer, regardless of the fact that it was still quite cold. That was one of the problems working with lawyers; they could argue their case well.

He drove home in next to no time, the traffic much lighter, rush hour was still a few hours away. There would be a couple of hours of daylight left so, as he parked his car on the road opposite his house, he decided to take Febus for a walk to the nearest beach which was only a short drive away. He regularly used the services of a local dog walking service to take Febus out twice a day on the days he worked. They were essentially a group of students run by someone whom he figured would turn out to be the next Richard Branson. They had quite a bit of free time on their hands and needed the extra money and had fairly flexible hours. Febus loved them all and quite often when Tom was walking him, Febus would spy one of his "walking friends" and charge up to them dragging Tom behind him.

Tom let himself in to his large Victorian semi which had cost him an arm and a leg just over five years previously. Stepping into the bright hallway he called out to the dog who Tom hoped had been snoring in his basket and not causing destruction in some other part of the house. The dog as always greeted him as though he hadn't seen him for years, there were lots of cries and hugs and that was just from Tom. He picked up the lead and poop bags and, with an even more excited dog, they left the house.

The dog stayed close to heel as they made their way across the soft sandy surface, the lead dangling redundantly by Tom's side. The day had now cooled considerably, but even so he was glad to be out in the fresh air. Febus was examining every inch of the beach using his nose to guide the way, sniffing his route haphazardly across the sand. He was picking up speed, his tail proudly waving in the air like one of those bumper car antennae in a travelling fair. He raced towards the sea almost as if he had just realised that it was there. Tom followed behind making his way to the water's edge. The dog was never happier than when he could swim. Tom often joked that Febus could swim the Channel if he smothered him in lard and told him he would meet him the other side. The dog launched himself into the shallow water and swam in time-honoured doggy paddle towards the horizon.

Alice
October 2014, Wales

It is impossible to walk on the beach without making an imprint in the sand
and taking some of it with us. Life is very much the same.
If we noticed this we might
be more aware of our actions and words.

An Inspired Approach

Alice crossed the road from the vets to the small car park at the rear of the building where her truck was parked. She should have intervened, she knew that she could have saved him but she had stood by like a mute, her mouth sealed by her reluctance to confront the elderly vet. The dog had whimpered unable to make more noise as the muzzle prevented him from doing so. She knew the vet wouldn't have listened to a lowly nurse but still she should have at least tried. She had removed the muzzle and had watched as he had euthanised the dog while she stroked his coal-black fur and silently apologised that she hadn't tried to save him. She couldn't look into his dark brown eyes, not because she would see any blame directed at her, but because she knew she wouldn't. She had stayed until he had slipped away and then she had locked herself in the toilets and cried for them both.

She wasn't sure how much longer she could do this job. She couldn't stand back and watch while the elderly vet compromised the care of the animals in his care. She would have to walk away once more.

She could feel the warmth of the late evening sun on her face and instantly felt a little better. She often wondered if she had lived somewhere like Australia she would have been happy all the time. But that was before. Now she couldn't shake the constant feeling of wanting to be somewhere else; she guessed it was just a symptom. She had moved to Wales because she couldn't stay in London but found that her problems had simply followed her, taking the shortest route. She was never without them for long. "Before" was almost three years ago now.

She drove the few miles in her pick-up truck from work to her little cottage by the sea. The first day she had seen it she had fallen in love with it. The beautiful little fisherman's cottage with the cobbled path and the peeling paint on the front door and windows had looked as though it just wanted to be loved. She understood that. She had bought it in an instant. It had looked so dramatic in the driving rain she had pretended to be Rebecca when she viewed Mandalay for the first time. The first night she spent in it, she lay awake as usual but then the sound of the sea as it moved to the melody of the moon had filled her sleeplessness. She took walks in the first few days getting to know the area. She loved the rocks with their verdant verges raised high above the icy water. The cliffs with their dramatic rock formations with a crown of trees perched precariously on the top of them. In the winter months the trees appeared to huddle together to keep warm, in the summer they looked like gossiping friends. It had helped to salve her, it still did.

She arrived home parking the car a few metres away. She felt unsettled as she walked up to her front gate; the weather was still warm and she was reluctant to shut herself away in the cottage for yet another night of little sleep. As she walked up the cobbled path she decided to borrow her neighbour's two spaniels and take them for a walk on the beach. She often borrowed the dogs from Hannah as she desperately missed having her own. It was a good arrangement and Hannah had subsequently become a good friend.

She put her key in the door, picking up the mail as she stepped into the hall. She looked through the letters, there was nothing with a London postmark and she let out a small breath. She dumped them on the small shelf above the radiator, pulled out her favourite cardigan from the cupboard under the stairs and tied it around her waist. At this time of year, the evenings cooled quickly, and she may need it later. She slipped her keys in the pocket and pulled the door shut behind her.

She knocked on Hannah's door and then heard the gentle barking of Hedy and Belle as they galloped to see who the intruder could be. She then heard Hannah's gentle reprimand as she opened the door.

"Hi Alice, come in."

Hannah was tall and willowy with a tendency to stoop in an apology for her height. She had mid brown hair which she allowed to run riot; she didn't believe in hairdressers.

"Hi Hannah, can I take them to the beach for an hour?"

"Yes, of course. Come in while I grab their leads."

Alice followed Hannah. The cottage was a carbon copy of her own, but a mirror image. However, that was where the similarities ended.

Hannah rummaged in the under-stairs cupboard and pulled out two leads at which point the dogs went into meltdown. Laughing at the noise, Hannah clipped a lead onto each of the dogs' collars and handed them over to Alice.

"Thanks Han, I need a walk tonight."

"No problem, you're doing me a favour actually, I didn't have time to take them out earlier. My deadline is looming and I'm starting to panic!"

"You'll get there, don't worry. Look, if you need a break, meet me for a coffee at the little café later."

"OK, I'll see how I get on, thanks. Are you OK? You look a bit down."

"I'm fine. It's just that Selwyn had to put a Gordon Setter down today, and well, you know my feelings on him and his quickness to euthanise."

"You should report him."

"I know, but he isn't really doing anything wrong; it's just that nowadays there are more options."

"Try not to take the worries of the world on your shoulders. I will see if I can get this section finished and meet you for a coffee later, OK?"

"Thanks Hannah."

With that, Hannah disappeared back into the dark cottage. Alice walked up the path as the dogs weaved in and out of her legs as though they were on an agility dog trial. She closed the old wooden gate behind her hoping Hannah would be able to meet her later since she could do with the company. She loved her because she was the only person she felt totally at ease with. She sometimes wondered if she should tell Hannah everything but something always stopped her at the last minute regardless of how many bottles of wine they had drunk. She would never have told her London "friends". She had found out the hard way that they were anything but. If it had been their dogs she was walking they would probably have charged her – not the other way around.

The dogs had calmed considerably now that they were on the beach and they trotted happily beside her as she made her way to the waters' edge. Neither dog liked to get wet, but they were more than happy to venture close to the foamy edge, then run away barking as if the sea were some liquefied foe. The day was now cooling and she shivered. She hated the saying "like someone walking over your grave" but it still came to mind.

She pulled the cardigan from around her waist and slipped it on. She had picked it up at a jumble sale at the local church on the cliff, where she had ventured one Saturday afternoon a week or so after she had moved in. The church grounds were bustling and she had felt a little uncomfortable since she wasn't a churchgoer and was ready to leave when a kindly old lady passed her explaining that they were holding a sale to raise funds for the local lifeboat. She thanked the woman and looking at the choppy sea below felt obliged to pop in and buy something. She knew she could have just given a donation at the door but felt that would have been the wrong thing to do. The small church had been crammed with old pictures, brass candlesticks and a few clothes stalls. She had walked through, pausing at each stall and saw the "knitted stall," never imagining how many things could be made simply by putting two needles together. There were knitted people, boxes, toilet roll holders, even knitted flowers and of course cardigans and jumpers. There was even a knitted swimming costume – she wasn't sure how that was going to work out. Then she saw the cardigan. It was beautiful so she asked if she could try it on, thinking that it would be rough against her skin. It wasn't, it had felt soft and as soon as she put it on she felt that it belonged to her. When she paid for it, the stall owner delighted in explaining its provenance. It had been knitted, as had most of the other items on the stall, by a closeted order of nuns. It had struck her looking at the vast array of woollen items that the nuns seemed to be taking the harsh realities of life and re-making them into softer versions. Or maybe it was just her state of mind. Either way she had loved the cardigan even more because of where it had come from. She had been so taken by the story that she hadn't asked where the nuns lived but preferred to imagine them, huddled together around an open fire and only the sound of the clicking needles breaking the silence, somewhere on the Isle of Arran.

She continued her walk glad to be out in the fresh air until she was almost adjacent to the little café which was just thirty or so feet away. However, her usually uninterrupted view was obscured by an enormous sandcastle. It was spectacular, almost breathtaking. As she stared at it, wondering who had built it, she heard excited voices coming from the path that led from the holiday rentals. As they grew nearer she could see a young boy with unfashionably long blond hair followed closely by a younger girl with colouring similar to her own, except the little girl's curls were tighter. Lastly, a tall man in his mid to late thirties hurried behind them. He handed the young boy what looked like a camera, a proper one with a zoom lens. She watched as they set about recording their masterpiece. Initially the young girl seemed reluctant to take orders from the boy who Alice assumed was her brother. In the end, he managed several shots including one with the girl standing at the side, possibly to indicate scale. She smiled at them and moved on; it wasn't her happiness.

She continued with her walk, following the shoreline. The dogs still battled against the sea happily barking when once again it retreated. Initially she had wanted to follow the path to the cliffs but already the day was preparing to hang the closed sign outside its door. It would soon be dusk and mother-nature was preparing for bed. She loved this time of day, it was more subdued, softer and less harsh than the brilliant sunshine of the full day. There was a magical quality to it. It was like looking at the world through rose tinted glasses, something Noah had accused her of time and time again. She felt more at peace than she had for a long time and welcomed it with open arms. It had eluded her for so long she almost hadn't recognised it.

She turned to make her way back along the shorter route in case the light went altogether. It was only then she saw the furry mass hurtling towards her. It was a blur of white, like a huge smudge running across the landscape. Water cascaded off it in every direction as it moved. She heard shouting just before the impact.

She landed on her bottom much to the distress of her charges, who barked their absolute displeasure at the large white mass whilst maintaining a safe distance. She realised now that it was a dog, a big hairy white and brown Pyrenean mountain dog. Again, too late she watched in horror as it began its very own spin cycle. Enormous droplets of water were thrown off the dog directly onto her as he came to the end of the cycle. Unlike her, the dog was now almost dry.

A hand appeared in front of her offering to help her up. She accepted, since she had little choice given that she felt wetter than if she had taken a dip in the sea fully clothed. Her brief new-found peace seemed to evaporate.

"I am so sorry. I couldn't stop him in time. I should have kept a closer eye on him. I am so sorry. He has herding instincts you see, he … may have wanted to round you up, you know, like sheep."

Alice looked at him in amazement. Had this man just told her that his dog thought she was a sheep? Was he stark raving mad? He didn't look like he had escaped from the local asylum; quite the contrary in fact he had an air of stability about him. He was tall with dark-brown hair that curled slightly at the end, olive skin and green eyes. His cheeks were very red and she wasn't sure if that was because of the situation or his normal complexion. Either way, he was handsome. She guessed he was roughly the same age as her, or perhaps a year or so older. Completely spontaneously, she started to laugh hysterically at the ridiculousness of the situation. Once she started laughing, she couldn't stop.

"Are you OK? I am so sorry, you must have had a bit of a shock," he said.

At this she laughed even more, the poor man was trying so hard. As always, after her life had changed, her emotions were a fine balancing act which, like the scales of justice, could tip either way. She felt her mood plummet; the tears of laughter would soon turn into something darker. It was time to leave. She was cold and wet and now she just wanted to go home and have a hot bath.

"I really can't apologise enough, you look soaked through. Of course, it goes without saying I will pay for any dry cleaning etcetera. That cardigan looks expensive. I'm Tom, by the way."

He once again extended his hand, this time in a formal handshake. She liked that, granted it was a little old-fashioned but there was something endearing about him. She recognised the warning signs; she just wanted to get home and dry off.

"It's fine, I don't live far from here. I can go home and dry off. Thanks anyway."

Alice slipped off the soaking wet cardigan and hung it across her arm; she turned to go. She felt more than a little embarrassed now that she had calmed down. Her dogs who had sat quietly through the whole exchange began to walk back to the cottage with her. They started barking again, she looked down at them, all three of them.

"Sorry, sorry. I'll put him on the lead now."

It crossed her mind that it would have been a good idea to have done that before but she remained silent. She watched as he clipped the lead to the sturdy harness. With the dog safely secured the man nodded to Alice, she smiled back and walked away from them.

"Would you like a coffee or something? We could grab one at the café?" he asked, calling after her.

She turned back to face him. The dog sat obediently at his heel looking like he would never cause any trouble. Alice knew better than anyone that appearances could be deceptive. She hesitated for a second; it would be so easy to have some company, it wouldn't mean anything, but walking away was what she was good at. When she didn't, that was when the trouble started. He was handsome and seemed kind but he was someone else's potential friend. She walked away from him gently shaking her head. As she did she felt a warm breeze skirt round her as though it was in a rush to be elsewhere.

25

"No worries, it was just a thought, although I should give you my number in case you incur any costs from dry cleaning or therapy."

She turned around to see him smiling; he was teasing her but he hadn't realised how close he was to the truth. She would go home. The breeze returned from wherever it had gone in such a rush. It was even warmer than before, she felt her cheeks flush.

"Go on," he said. "One small coffee can't hurt."

They looked at each other in silence. The day went quiet, even the seagulls stopped screeching at each other. She felt the beach was waiting for her to make her mind up. In her heart she knew it would be the wrong decision but she had felt something, it was unquantifiable but she had still felt it, however, it always resulted in heartbreak, she needed to start learning lessons. So, she was surprised when she heard herself agreeing to one small coffee.

They walked towards the café chatting easily as they made their way past the sandcastle. They decided to sit outdoors to make the most of the dry weather. Tom went inside to order the drinks and to ask for a blanket – the café had them hanging in the porch if customers needed them. Alice assured him that she was now almost dry but Tom insisted. Alice settled the dogs on the warm wooden decking and in a few seconds the three dogs were huddled together fast asleep.

"Excuse me."

Alice found herself looking directly into the huge brown eyes of a young boy.

"Would you mind taking a photo of us by my sandcastle?"

She looked to the enormous sandcastle that she had admired earlier.

"You made that magnificent castle?"

The boy blushed with delight and nodded.

"Well in that case I would be delighted."

She guessed that if Tom came back and she was gone he would be unlikely to think she had run off especially considering she had left the dogs behind. And anyway, there was something about the young boy that tugged at her heart strings. She recognised a kindred spirit, there was always that kind of look – it was one she herself wore every day. She could see his sister and his dad and guessed the mum had either left or died.

She chatted to the boy mainly about the magnificent castle as he beamed with pride. He introduced his father and sister. She introduced herself then saw the little girl pointing to the decking.

"I think your boyfriend is looking for you."

Alice turned around to see Tom looking across the beach. She waved and he responded with a wave of his own.

"Is he your boyfriend or your husband?"

"Peggy!"

"Sorry Dad, is he your partner?"

"I was telling you off for being so nosey, Peg."

"He's just a friend, and what about you Peggy, do you have a boyfriend?"

The little girl giggled, obviously delighted to have been asked such a grown-up question.

"Not yet, at the moment I am not keen on boys but I know that in the future I probably will be, so I will have to come back to you on that one."

Alice laughed out loud.

"Excuse my daughter. She has a very mature head on those young shoulders."

The young boy, Seth, handed Alice the camera. She took several photos of the sandcastle with the family standing proudly in front and alongside it. They looked slightly out of kilter as though they hadn't quite worked out how to re-group as a family when one of their founder members was missing. She knew then that the mother had passed away and not left; it was the gaping hole that she left beside the sandcastle.

They thanked her and she left them to gather up their belongings. She re-joined Tom, who looked relieved that she had come back. She told him about the family but she didn't say that she knew the mother had died, most people didn't understand, she was observant and perceptive – it wasn't as though she dabbled in the dark arts or anything.

The drinks arrived, a hot chocolate for her and a black coffee for him. She took a sip of the warm sweet chocolate and felt herself relax once more. The dogs began chasing rabbits across the sand dunes, their legs twitching in their sleep.

Alice watched as the family walked up the path towards the holiday cottages. Peggy looked tired and had dropped behind Seth and John. The boy turned around to see his little sister near to tears; he hesitated then handed her the camera. Alice watched as the child very carefully lifted it and began to take some more photos. Alice waved to them both as they made their way to the path. The girl once again lifted the camera and took one last photograph. Alice nudged Tom who turned around and smiled at the camera.

Martha
October 2014, England

The more sand has escaped from the hourglass of our life
The clearer we should see through it.

Niccolo Machiavelli

Martha settled the dog under the table so that he was out of the way. She wasn't worried about him, he was a darling dog but he was getting older and sometimes too much fuss wore him out. She came to the Italian coffee shop at least twice a week but it was the first time she had brought him with her. She was looking after him while John and the kids were away in Swansea; she hoped it had been the right decision for them to go since, after all, she had been instrumental in suggesting the trip.

The smell of the coffee in the air was intoxicating and even though she usually drank tea, and as John said not even proper tea but that relaxing stuff, whenever she came here she had one small cup of coffee. She ordered a weak black coffee and a Danish pastry from the hovering waitress and opened the newspaper. Finding the crossword she laid it out on the small marble table in front of her.

She took a sip of the hot coffee knowing that she was bound to be reflective particularly today of all days. The coffee was rich and smooth – if coffees were graded like fine wines this would be a good vintage. They had taken the bold step of putting a sign on the door to say that it was the best cup of coffee in town and indeed she was inclined to agree with them. She looked out of the window, the town was full of people going in every direction. Everyone was in a rush to be somewhere else instead of just enjoying where they were. She chuckled to herself because she had been going to mindfulness classes and had become something of a convert. She had gone initially to combat the loneliness that descended on her from time to time. She had been surprised to find that it had helped her immensely particularly on days like today.

She looked at the clues, scanning to see if she knew any of the answers without thinking too hard. She wondered if John and the children were enjoying their time in Swansea. Tomorrow would be the first anniversary – it had been an incredibly difficult year for them all. She tried to concentrate, dwelling on things never helped – another mindfulness gem. She tried the crossword again, 1 across: a Chekhov play written in 1901. She wasn't a fan but at one time she had known all his plays. She tried to remember them, she knew that there were twelve, but couldn't even bring half of them to mind. She was just too distracted – so much for mindfulness.

The table next to her filled up with a harassed mum and her three small children. The chairs screeched on the tiled floor as she attempted to seat them all. Then it came to her – *Three Sisters* that was it, she filled in the letters carefully in black ink. Happy to have had her mind taken off other things she smiled at the young mum.

"How old are they?" Martha asked.

"Six, four and almost three, I must have been mad to have them so close together."

Martha looked at them, they were beautiful children. The older two were a boy and a girl; they were bright as buttons with blue eyes and blond curls. The youngest, another girl, had dark wavy hair with huge brown eyes. Despite the difference in their colouring you could tell that they were siblings. They spotted Darwin under the table, the two oldest asked politely if they could stroke the dog. Martha nodded and gently encouraged Darwin from his hiding place, he was only too happy to oblige. The children were delighted and sat on the floor stroking him.

"What's his name?" asked the boy.

"It's Darwin."

"That's a nice name. Does he like it?"

"Yes, I think that he does. He's a beagle, so my son named him after the famous explorer Charles Darwin who had a ship called the *Beagle*."

"Does he like exploring?"

"He loves exploring especially in the countryside."

"Then he has a good name. I like my name, it's Ethan and it means strong, I am even stronger than Marcus in my class and his dad works in a gym."

Martha smiled, he reminded her of Peggy.

"You have beautiful children and they are very polite," said Martha.

"Thank you. It doesn't cost anything for manners; my mum drummed that into my sister and me when we were growing up and I hope I've done the same."

"My mother was the same."

31

Martha was surprised at herself for bringing up her mother and then for saying something favourable about the woman she disliked so much. But she couldn't argue with the fact that she had made sure that Martha was polite at all times. She tried not to think of the possible reasons why. The young mum was still talking.

"I wouldn't be without them of course. It's just that sometimes it's like having a minor weather system in tow. We cause disruption wherever we go. We completely disturbed your concentration, sorry."

"You did nothing of the sort, actually you did the opposite. I was struggling with the answer for my crossword and your lovely children helped me remember."

"What was the answer?"

"*Three Sisters*, though of course I can see Ethan is a boy."

"Actually, a lot of people mistake him for a girl. It's the curly hair and the huge eyes."

They continued to chat for a little while then Martha returned to her crossword but her heart was no longer in it. She scanned the rest of the clues uninterested in continuing. Darwin sighed – Evie had always said that the dog was psychic. It was as if he had a deep sorrow because it was a year since his beloved mistress had died. She needed to take her mind off everything so she looked once more at the clues. One caught her eye – "What was the name of the film starring Will Smith, based on a true story about Chris Gardner?" She knew the answer to that one so filled in the squares in her black pen with neat precise letters, and wondered why some things were so hard to bear.

John
October 2014, Wales

Writing my love for you in the sand,
So the waves can wash it away,
And I can write it over and over.

John looked at the children, both fast asleep, exhausted from their day on the beach. Peggy had managed to catch the sun even though he had regularly re-applied suncream throughout the day. She had small, red circles that had blossomed on her cheeks. Lying asleep she looked like a beautiful porcelain doll. Evie was missing so much that it physically hurt him. It was almost a year, a few hours and then it would have been a year. Looking back, he didn't know how he had survived it. It was only the children that had made him get out of bed in the morning and not drink himself into an early grave. He pulled the quilt over Peggy who had kicked it off doing her impression of a bed angel, arms and legs outstretched. The memory of Evie had gradually faded for her, but not for Seth. John reached up to the top bunk and settled the quilt on Seth. The boy had taken to sleeping in the foetal position since he had lost his mum. He pushed the long hair out of Seth's face. He had asked him again whilst they were on the beach if he could trim his hair but again Seth had refused. He was so compliant about everything else that John was loath to push him. He would leave it for another day.

John crept downstairs feeling incredibly low. Tomorrow was the first anniversary of Evie's death. He hadn't been able to face being in the house where she had died. He needed to be near a beach but away from home. In the end, it had been his mother, Martha, who had suggested Swansea; she had known someone years ago who had lived there. It had seemed as good a place as any for them to go to, she had understood his need to get away. The three of them had loved Swansea from the minute they arrived. Especially today on the beach John had felt a salve to his wounds, the Welsh were exceptionally friendly; no-one had passed them without making some comment about the sandcastle in their lilting Welsh accents.

The kids had returned to the cottage tired out after the long day. Peggy had been near to tears, refusing to have a bath even though she was covered in sand from head to toes. She had sat by John as he lit the fire too tired to move. It had turned cold as the evening bled into the night. He promised her that if she had a very quick bath they would be allowed to toast marshmallows in front of the fire. It had the desired effect and she ran up the tiny staircase which creaked even under her tiny frame. It was the quickest he had ever managed to bathe her. Less than fifteen minutes later, she was in her pyjamas, hair washed and dried sitting in front of the now roaring fire. Seth ran up and had a quick shower rather than a bath and then sat by his sister's side. It was a picture of domestic bliss and it broke John's heart.

He remembered when Evie had been gone for only a few weeks and he had been reading Peggy one of her Disney stories – *Sleeping Beauty* – she had been tired and a little confused as to where exactly her mum had gone to. She had asked John if her mum was like Sleeping Beauty and whether she would wake up again after a hundred years. John had felt as though she had already been gone for a hundred.

The fire crackled, spitting tiny flares of orange and red into the chimney. The children had sat on the inglenook seats holding their toasting forks aloft laden with mallows of pink and white. Even though the handles were long and made of plastic, John had wrapped a tea towel around the handle of Peggy's just to be sure. It was always prudent to take the more cautious approach when dealing with his daughter. She waved hers in the air as though it was a magic wand and she was casting spells. She would put it near the heat until it softened and then force feed John the sickly sweet treat. John feared he may be in danger of developing Type 2 diabetes.

"Peg you have some now, I've had enough," said John.

"But I don't like them, I'm just cooking the march mallows for you to eat," she replied, thrusting the fork in John's direction again.

"They are marshmallows Peg, not march mallows," giggled Seth.

John watched as his mischievous daughter lifted the toasting fork onto her left shoulder imitating a rifle and started to march up and down the little white room. He had felt the memory of what happiness had been like.

As he now sat in the pretty floral armchair by the fireside, he felt the heaviness return. The fire had almost burned itself out but the room remained warm. He glanced at the old-fashioned clock on the wall to the left of the fire, it was nearly twelve. The arms of the clock would join briefly under the Roman numerals XII, then the day that he had dreaded would dawn. They would have survived all the "firsts" then – birthdays, Christmases and ordinary days, ones where the pain almost swallowed him whole.

He moved to the sideboard which was snuggled in the tiny alcove; it was finished in the same white wash that covered the whole interior of the cottage. The two-door unit looked bespoke, fitting the space perfectly. Evie had fitted him perfectly. He opened one of the narrow doors and inside, as he had hoped, he found a few bottles of spirits. There was a full, unopened bottle of Jack Daniels and a few bottles of vodka and rum that were only half full. At the back was an empty bottle of cognac, as he lifted it to the light he could see that there was a drop in the bottom. He didn't need much. He walked to the kitchen keeping an eye on the time as he ducked his head under the low beam. In the kitchen area he pulled a tumbler from the cupboard above the sink and poured the remnants of the bottle into the glass. He checked the time, three minutes to go. He took the drink back into the lounge and sat back down in the floral chair.

The two arms embraced and the clock chimed the dawning of another day. He raised the glass, the amber liquid glowed from the reflection of the burning embers. He toasted the girl he had met at fifteen who had sat with her friends on the wall opposite his house. She had sat there every day after school for two weeks until he had plucked up the courage to ask her out. He toasted the young girl he had proposed to, lifting her up on the same wall, then kneeling down to propose realising too late that they were too far from each other for him to place the ring on her finger. He toasted the woman who had borne him two children after being sick for every day of both pregnancies. He toasted the woman who he was supposed to grow old with, the one who had said she demanded that they still would hold hands even if they couldn't remember each other's names. And finally, he said a toast for the woman who had begged him to find someone else to love but just not as much as he had loved her.

He wiped away the tears that flowed silently and freely following a well-trodden path. Without taking a sip from the glass he walked through to the kitchen and poured the contents down the sink. He washed the glass, dried it and returned it to the cupboard. He turned off the lights and slowly made his way up the narrow staircase to an unfamiliar bed in which he knew he wouldn't be able to fall asleep.

Evie
England, 2012

She made broken look beautiful
And strong look invincible
She walked with the universe on her shoulders
And made it look like a pair of wings.

Ariana Dancu

Evie waited patiently in the queue. The woman in front of her – a short, stout woman of indeterminate age kept fussing. She fussed about where her elderly companion would sit while she stood in front of Evie waiting to be served. Then she fussed about what drink she should order for the companion who was now out of earshot having made for the seat she was instructed to sit on. Evie had always been a kind and patient person, particularly with the elderly. She had figured she would get old one day, it seemed she may have been mistaken about that. She felt a scream building but it settled at the back of her throat ready to be used at a moment's notice. The woman decided on two cappuccinos and Evie sighed with relief. Then the barista asked if she wanted chocolate on top and a whole new problem presented itself.

Evie eventually sat down. Her hands were shaking so badly that she had spilt some of the tea from the spout of the china teapot. She had watched as the dark brown liquid sloshed across the plastic tray. She picked up a paper napkin from the table and wiped away the spilled tea, poured milk into her cup and then added the strong tea. She didn't usually drink tea, she was more of a coffee drinker. She wasn't even sure how she liked it so she added a spoonful of sugar in case. The sugar was also good for shock. That's what people drank when they had experienced a shock, hot strong sweet tea; it was supposed to make you feel better. She took a sip and swallowed the tea, she didn't particularly like the taste and she didn't feel any better. She needed to tell John; she hadn't even told him about the hospital appointment, had she assumed it would be nothing? She hadn't wanted to worry him, even though she had lain awake last night staring at the familiar ceiling. It was as though she was looking at it properly for the first time, noticing tiny hairline cracks; why hadn't she noticed them before?

She was stirred out of her thoughts by a commotion on the far side of the busy café. There were raised voices and as they became louder the chatter in the room quieted. Evie looked across to where the shouting had come from and immediately recognised the woman from the queue. She was staring at one of the waiters, a young lad who looked close to tears. The companion was silent but was rocking back and forth in the seat, tears ran unchecked down her lined face. Now that the shouting had stopped the other customers began chatting once more, Evie could see that whatever had caused the problem hadn't been resolved. She sighed and walked up to the table, where no-one was moving.

"Is everything OK?"

It obviously wasn't but she was at a loss how else to help.

"It's all my fault, I'm sorry. Dorothy has dementia and gets quite confused. She thought that this young lad was her husband. Sadly, he has been dead for over ten years. It's the uniform, it reminds her of when she and Harold first met. I should have explained the situation better, I'm sorry."

She directed this last apology at the waiter who had now regained his composure. To the surprise of all three women, he sat down at the table opposite Dorothy and proceeded to chat to her. Once he had sat down, Dorothy visibly relaxed and the old lady and the young boy chatted as though they had known each other for years. Evie sat down opposite the "queue" lady and introduced herself.

"Are you OK?"

"Yes, thank you, I am now. I'm Theresa and this is my Aunt Dorothy. Thank you for coming to our help, everyone else just chose to ignore us. I just wanted to disappear, I hate a scene but sadly since her diagnosis this is what we have to deal with on an almost daily basis."

"Do you have any help?"

"My husband was good but he passed away last year about the same time as she came to live with us. I joke sometimes that he took the easy way out. Anyway, the kids help when they can but they have their own lives to live. There are some groups but I struggle with my own situation so I don't want to listen to anyone else's and then feel guilty because apparently they have it so much worse than me."

"I'm so sorry Theresa."

Evie felt guilty for being so impatient, she hadn't had a clue what was going on in her life. She looked around the café, the buzz of conversation had returned to normal after the mini drama. She wondered how many of their lives were filled with honey.

"Why on earth do you feel bad? You came to help while everyone else stared at us as though we were an exhibit in the local zoo or pretended we didn't exist."

"Because to be honest, I was one of those people – I judged you without knowing what you were going through."

Theresa grabbed her hand and squeezed it.

"Since we are being open and honest I did the same to you."

"What do you mean?"

"I thought that you were a stuck-up bitch who couldn't even wait for two minutes for me to get Dorothy settled and order my drinks?"

Evie laughed at the woman's candour.

"I can't argue with the bitch bit. I'm not sure about stuck-up, people usually just refer to me as being posh."

The two women smiled.

"So? Are you going to tell me what has happened to you today to upset you so much?"

"Is it that obvious?" said Evie.

Theresa simply nodded. Both women looked towards Dorothy who was happily chatting to the young waiter whilst sipping her chocolate-free cappuccino. So, Evie told a complete stranger what she hadn't had the courage to tell her husband or anyone else. She related it all from the very beginning, before she was worried to when she was concerned to when, today, she had had all her fears confirmed.

They parted with mobile numbers secured in their phones. It had taken Theresa a little while as she fussed about whether to put Evie's surname in or not. Dorothy waved goodbye to the waiter promising to meet him at the dance hall that Friday. She then declared to the whole café that she would be wearing her red dress, there was a muted cheer. Evie knew that she had made a friend for life for however long that would turn out to be.

She made her way home to tell John and then they would both go together and tell Martha, his mother. She crossed the road feeling a little less anxious about delivering the news. Thinking about Martha, she remembered that she had to post a letter she had written a few days ago and had completely forgotten about it in all the drama. As she paused at the red letter box, the term "can of worms" came to mind. She hesitated, her hand still clasping the crisp white envelope. She had been

41

unsure as to whether she should even write the letter, let alone post it. The funny thing was that because of her bad news she felt compelled to follow it through and the reservations that she had originally had no longer seemed important. She dropped the letter into the slot before she changed her mind again. She walked away as the letter to Mr Nathan Devore, 221 The Grove, Greenwich, London, fell to the bottom of the large red royal mail box.

Several weeks later John wasn't handling her illness well. From the very first day they had reacted differently. John was overly protective to the point of smothering her. When she had mentioned that she needed a little more space he had stormed off telling her she could have as much space as she wanted. She wondered if that was why she had been reluctant to tell him in the first place. She sat upstairs fuming, which was, at least, a change to feeling scared so she carried on raging against his insensitivity. John poked his head around the bedroom door – she paused waiting for his anger.

"There's a cup of tea for you downstairs. I've made camomile," he said softly.

"OK, I'll be down in a second."

She watched him go, she was fuming again. The bloody cheek of the man, camomile was what his mother drank to calm her. Was that his not so subtle message that she needed to calm down. If that was the case he needed to have it intravenously.

The dog nudged her hand, she stroked the top of his head. She felt calm with the dog, he was better than a hundred cups of camomile tea. He whined and looked up at her with his big brown eyes. They were all trying too hard, that was the problem.

"I know Darwin," she said to the dog, "you understand. I just wish we could make John see it from our perspective." She called to the

dog who obediently left the room and followed her downstairs. It was funny, Darwin had always been John's dog but since her diagnosis he had stuck to her as though her life depended on it, maybe it did. John looked up from the kitchen table, she noticed for the first time the dark rings under his eyes and the fine lines that had appeared on his face. It reminded her of the ceiling in their bedroom. Sometimes you can look at something every day and not see what is in front of your eyes.

"Sorry," he said.

"Me too."

"I've had a cup of camomile as well but to be honest love it tastes like crap. I don't know how mum can drink it."

She walked over to him and hugged him because in that moment it was the two of them against the world.

Sand: Sedimentation

(the process of settling or being deposited as a sediment)

Even castles made of sand
Fall into the sea eventually.

Jimi Hendrix

The tide pushed its way up the beach and then retreated. It repeated this process pushing its way further up the sands, it still fell back but it had made progress. It continued in this pattern back and forth, back and forth. Each time it crept closer to the magnificent sandcastle that stood proudly in the black night. Back and forth went the ocean again and again and little by little it moved further and further. It reached the sandcastle only barely touching it before it pulled back. The next time it lapped the walls before it went back, then the walls softened. The moat filled with the sea water as if in its last minutes, it could fulfil its true purpose. The sodden walls crumbled dissolving into liquid around them. The whole structure shuddered as it finally fell into the water. Finally, the sea's relentless progress cleared the remains of the sandcastle. In the morning, it would be as though it had never been there.

The sea had reclaimed the sandcastle with its last grain of sand.

Alice
November 2014, Wales

The prettiest smiles hide the deepest secrets.
The prettiest eyes have cried the most tears.
The kindest hearts have felt the most pain.

Unknown

Alice wondered why she had let things get this far with Tom. As she brushed her hair sitting at the small Queen Anne dressing table, she knew that it was her own fault and knew that the cup of coffee on the beach was going to lead to something more; they had both felt the spark of something between them. Her auburn hair shone as she continued to brush. They were going for afternoon tea to the best hotel in Swansea, his mother wanted to meet her or more precisely had summoned her. When Tom had suggested it, she had tried to talk him out of it but he hadn't listened mistaking her reluctance for something else entirely. The problem was that in a different world she would have been delighted to go, yes, she would have been nervous – Susan sounded like a force of nature, but that would have been normal.

She looked in the dressing table mirror as she continued

to brush her hair, she had developed dark rings under her eyes again. The strain of sleepless nights wracked with guilt and terror were painted under her eyes for the world to see that she was hiding secrets. Sometimes Tom looked so deeply into her eyes she was sure that he saw the horrors within her but the deeper he looked the more he loved her, maybe he needed to look even deeper still. He was starting to become a little curious though, he had been asking too many questions about her family, past boyfriends and other things that normal people would discuss. She shouldn't have let it get this far, she knew better than anyone else. Only last week he had jokingly asked if she was in witness protection. She had laughed it off, he hadn't been serious but it wouldn't take him much longer to demand answers, and she couldn't give them to him. She gently rubbed concealer into the dark, delicate skin under her eyes in a circular motion, she watched as the skin took on the tone of the little pot. She looked much better on the outside.

She looked at her reflection. She had a pretty woollen pinafore dress in black and cream over the top of a cream, long sleeved t-shirt, thick patterned black tights and boots. It was perfect for meeting Susan but she felt all wrong. She usually avoided meeting the families; after what had happened before, it made sense. Up until now she had kept to it but Tom had been different in every way and it made her want to be different as well. Tom had shown her what normality looked like, he had made her feel as though anything was possible, then she went home and the doubts crept in, one by one they waited in line to bestow their gifts. She would finish it now, text him to say she didn't feel well but she knew that it was too late for that, she had no choice but to go with him and meet his mother. The

47

best outcome would be for Susan to hate her on sight, then the problem would be solved, but the mothers never did, for some reason they always loved her.

She looked at her watch, she still had an hour to go before Tom was due. She decided to go for a quick walk along the beach, wrapped herself up in her red padded jacket adding cream gloves and a long, knitted cream scarf, then opened the front door. The sun pushed its way into the hall casting a soft golden hue over the tiled floor. At this time of the year it was weak but it still valiantly carried out its role, she felt an affinity with it. She pulled the door closed behind her.

The beach was almost empty but there were a few dog walkers and several joggers enjoying the dry weather. She walked on the damp sand nearer the shore and walked until her cheeks were glowing due to a combination of the brisk exercise and the even brisker wind. At times like this, she could almost feel a peace, as long as she kept moving and realised that psychologists would have a field day with her over that. She walked towards the sea and even though the day was bitterly cold, she wanted to be near the waters' edge. She looked at the horizon – the perfectly straight line stretched out in the distance beyond the expanse of water. A perfect straight line, she knew it was an illusion, the geometrical horizon, but even so it made her feel that the impossible was possible. Could the same be true for her too, could the seemingly impossible happen for her, could she be happy with Tom, could she tell him the truth about Noah? She stopped fantasising – of course she couldn't because he would simply stop loving her if he ever found out the truth. She looked at her watch, he would be picking her up soon so she decided to go back otherwise she would be late for him.

She arrived back at her front door just as Tom was pulling up onto the rough ground at the end of the road. She recited her mantra in her head, she could do this, she was worthy of this but, as always, Noah came into her head.

Tom waved to her as he got out of the car, he was dressed in jeans, a blue shirt and a purple jumper.

"Morning gorgeous, walking again!"

It was said as more of a statement. It had become a bit of a standing joke between them. He seemed to accept her need to walk off her problems, well the ones he knew about anyway.

"You know me."

She said it as a joke, a throwaway comment but it stilled her. Tom didn't know her, he didn't know what she was capable of.

"Are you ready? Mum said she'd meet us at the hotel – she was having coffee with Edward first."

Alice had heard a lot about Edward, in fact they had almost met him a few days ago when they had gone to the theatre but Edward's date had been taken ill at the last minute much to Alice's relief. As for Tom's father, she didn't know that much about him, but she knew enough to steer clear of the subject in the company of Susan.

"Of course, I'm really looking forward to it."

"So is she. She can't wait to meet the girl who my dog swept off her feet."

Alice laughed, Tom always made her laugh. He made her feel like the best Alice there could be, the best version of herself which Noah wouldn't have recognised. She had to tell Tom now that she was a fraud, that she would hurt him. Instead, she kissed him and wondered how she was ever going to make this right.

Martha
November 2014, England

But someday I will find my way back
To where your name is written in the sand.

Taken from 'Summer Paradise' by Simple Plan

Martha picked up her daily paper from Pam's Papers; she could have had it delivered like her neighbours but she liked the walk and a gossip with the shop's namesake and owner. They were good friends and went to the local leisure centre once a week for a surprisingly competitive game of badminton. Martha had enjoyed the walk but it had been cold enough for her to go back for her gloves and scarf. At the shop, Pam remarked on the changing weather after the long, unseasonably hot dry spell. They had both joked if that was the effect of global warming then that was fine with them. They heard a grunt of disapproval from the front of the shop. They smothered a laugh as they looked to the source of the sound. A young lad was leafing through the magazines. He had scruffy jeans and a threadbare jumper, dreadlocks in his hair and enough piercings on view to make Martha worry what would happen if he stood in the rain for too long.

She winked at Pam.

"Do you know what I heard last week about this global warming thing?"

"No, what?" asked Pam playing along although she wasn't sure where she was being led.

"Apparently it's all down to cows letting off wind. Yes, it's all because of the farting Friesians. They are the real culprits. It makes you think that it's a good job we eat red meat, imagine what it would be like if we were all vegans. It would be like the ninth circle of hell."

The boy slammed down the magazine that he obviously had no intention of paying for and stormed out of the shop.

"Sorry Pam I may have just lost you a valued customer."

At this, both women burst into fits of laughter which Martha thought was unfortunate for the poor old man from across the street who had come in for his paper. She laughed even harder as she saw him check his flies.

After picking up some shopping for tea she returned home. Still laughing from the encounter, she dumped the shopping on the kitchen counter and set about making tea for John and the children. She chopped onions and sautéed them in a little butter and oil. While they were browning she put the shopping away. As she emptied a packet of minced beef and a packet of minced lamb into the now golden-brown onions, she thought about how much better John and the children were since they had come back from Swansea. The meat sizzled as she used the wooden spoon to make sure all the meat browned. She was glad that she had suggested it, although when they were away she had fretted as to whether it was the right thing to do. She was relieved – in particular that Seth had been more animated since being away. Peggy was Peggy and she was so glad of that; she didn't worry so much about her, Peggy would weather any storm.

She had even had a conversation with John about him dating again. She added turmeric, cinnamon and smoked paprika to the meat and stirred, then added tomato puree, a little brown sugar and stock. As the meat mixture bubbled on the stove she remembered that Seth had printed out some of the photos from their break away. Even though she had looked at some of the ones on John's phone, Seth wanted her to look at the ones from the digital camera so he had asked John to print them out; he was so proud of the sandcastle that they had built. Evie would have been so proud of them both, it made Martha's heart ache for her. She put the timer on the cooker for thirty-five minutes, popped the button on the kettle and dropped one of her camomile tea bags in a mug. She went over to the bureau and picked up the large envelope with the photos, made her tea, leaving the tea bag in as she usually did and sat down to look through the pictures.

Sitting at the small oak table in the centre of her kitchen she took a sip of tea. The rain continued to throw itself at the window unabashed. She opened the fat wallet of photos and sifted through them, most of which she had already seen when they had been on the camera. Some showed exceptionally pretty scenes, the coastline was quite breathtaking, they had been really lucky with the weather, the sun shining in all of them. Then there were ones that Martha guessed that the children, particularly Peggy, may have taken, featuring headless bodies and then heads without bodies. The rest were obviously ones that John had taken, pictures of the children looking happy and relaxed. There were very few of John, just one or two presumably taken by the children. He looked happy but behind the smile she could see he was struggling. She gathered the photos together, she would get on with the tea and look at the rest later. As she shuffled them into a large pile, one or two slid off the top of the pile and onto the floor. She bent down and picked them up, intending on adding them to the pile when something caught her eye. She looked at the one in her hand; it wasn't of John or the children but of a couple sitting at a café with what looked like two small dogs and a huge hairy beast at their feet. On looking more closely at the couple in the picture, she noticed that the woman had the same curly red hair as Peggy but her complexion wasn't as fair. She stared at the man. On looking closer, her heart raced ahead of her thoughts and then seemed to stop as if to give her total silence to concentrate. She couldn't make any sense of what she was looking at. The young man in the photo was a man she hadn't set eyes on for over thirty years.

Evie
November 2012, England

Evie stood in the shower allowing the water to run down her hairless body. It hadn't taken very long for the ravages of the chemo to take hold. The cold cap had been useless. Although she had hated losing her long blonde hair and thick eyebrows, it was her eyelashes that had caused her the most distress. Her once pretty eyes looked smaller and less vibrant, she likened it to having a painting and not framing it. There were times when people had remarked on her eyes, no-one did anymore and she was surprised at how much it hurt her. She had never thought of herself as vain, she knew she was attractive, possibly beautiful even, she had been complimented all her life and had been faintly embarrassed by it. She had wanted to be taken seriously in her work as a sedimentologist not singled out for her looks. Now, however she missed it; it shouldn't have mattered, she was fighting a battle for survival, but it did. She felt she was ebbing away. It was as if she had forgotten to turn off some

54

invisible tap and her life was trickling away drop by drop. If only she knew where it was she could turn it off, stem the flow somehow.

She slowly rubbed the towel across her shoulders gently drying her skin. She needed to pull herself together; it was less than four weeks until Christmas but she didn't want to endure the feast of a birth when she felt she was dying. Celebrate Christmas was the term tossed about but she had little to celebrate and just wanted to close her eyes and pretend it was a different year. The irony of wishing time away when she knew in her heart of hearts that she had little left wasn't lost on her. Irony was a constant companion to her. She threw the towel on the floor, suddenly angry by the constant Christmas-related advertising from the small independents to the large supermarkets – everyone was urging her to have the best Christmas ever.

After they had had the kids, she and John had agonised over the whole Santa thing. Her parents had been truthful with her explaining that he was a myth, the presents were from them not from Santa. It hadn't upset her, she had been happy enough as a child, even to feeling a little superior when one by one, her friends came to the conclusion that he didn't exist. John's upbringing had been completely different to hers. Martha and Peter had been at the other end of the spectrum and had kept Christmas better than the enlightened Scrooge. After much discussion it was finally decided in the Maddox household that they would follow the example of Scrooge and John's parents. So, they had made a rod for their own backs and now she had to try and conjure up some Christmas spirit.

"Mum."

She heard Peggy call from her bedroom. The little minx was supposed to be asleep, it was almost eight o'clock. Evie slipped on her dressing gown. She didn't put on her wig, Seth had been told the truth but Peggy was too young to understand so they had told her that the doctor said having no hair would help her get better quicker as it gave her head more air. Although it had caused a few problems after they had first told her – she and Peggy had been out walking Darwin when they passed a male couple. Both men were arm in arm and as bald as badgers. Peggy had stopped and openly stared at them. Evie had pulled her hand not realising why she had stopped. Then Peggy had said in a very loud voice, "Wasn't it a shame that both men were ill but maybe their wives were at home making chicken soup." Evie had been mortified. The men had smiled, not offended by any of her daughter's assumptions. She had felt so grateful to them that she had moved her wig back to show them her bald head. They had understood immediately and had blown her a kiss in solidarity. It had occurred to her then that the world was a better place when there were no misunderstandings. Peggy always seemed to make a difference, Evie hoped she would never lose that gift.

She walked into her daughter's very pink bedroom. Seth had once remarked that it looked as though someone had eaten too much candy floss and then thrown up over her bedroom.

"Hi baby, why aren't you sleeping?"

Evie walked up to Peggy's bed. She was sitting up with the pillows propped behind her with a serious look on her face. Evie knew that she wasn't upset about anything but when she was mulling anything over she liked to adopt the appropriate facial expression.

"Mummy, I think you need to get one of these."

Evie looked at the picture book that her daughter was holding. It was one of her many princess books, crammed full of happy ever afters. She had seen them all before.

"Lovely Peg, now lights off and go to sleep."

"Mummy, you are looking with your ears instead of your eyes."

It never failed to amaze Evie the things that came out of her daughter's mouth.

"Miss said that we need to use the right tools for the job. So, if we need to look at something then it is no good using our ears, because our ears are for hearing. You weren't looking with your eyes Mummy."

Evie smiled at her rosy-cheeked daughter and looked down at the page she was pointing to. On the beautifully illustrated page was a snowy scene of a castle perched high on an ice-capped mountain. On the opposite page was a room inside the castle where a princess sat at a dressing table. On the table was a mannequin's head not dissimilar to the one Evie had in her own room. In the princesses' hand was an elaborate wig. It was pure white with cascading curls which were decorated with pearls and diamonds. To complete the wig there was a twinkly tiara which looked as though it had been carved from the ice covering the mountain. Even for a story book the effect was spectacular.

"I think you should ask Father Christmas for one of these, Mummy. I know that the rules say he can only bring presents to children but as Seth says, 'rules are made to be broken'. Because you've been poorly I'm sure he won't mind but we have to be quick, we need to send the letter tonight as the North Pole post office closes two weeks before Christmas to make sure Santa has the time to read every letter and make sure the elves are up to speed on the presents."

Evie hugged her daughter for so many reasons that she couldn't even begin to unravel.

"Do you know what Peg, I will write the letter tonight."

"Will you ask him for one for me, Seth and Daddy as well?"

Evie tucked the quilt around Peggy.

"And Darwin, how could I forget Darwin? We must ask for one for him as well."

"OK Peg, sleep now please. I'm sure Darwin would rather have a new bed but we'll just have to see. Now go to sleep."

Evie switched off the light and closed the door behind her. She wondered if Seth's tolerance towards his baby sister would stretch to wearing a wig. She could get him a pirate one – he would possibly wear one of those. John would do anything to make this Christmas easier and the poor dog, well she supposed it may be less humiliating for him than reindeer antlers, although she wasn't too sure.

She felt lighter and happier, as though Peggy had armoured her in readiness to face Christmas. She was going to make this a good Christmas even if it killed her. Things were queuing up to kill her, cancer and Christmas; she would be damned if she let either of them win. She may just break her cardinal rule and make it the best Christmas ever. Anyway, who said that there was anything wrong with that?

Tom
December 2014, Wales

Seek the truth or hide your head in the sand.
Both require digging.

Andrew Nolan

Tom was still struggling with the pervading tiredness. One problem was that more and more people were beginning to notice. Most of his work colleagues knew of his relationship with Alice and teased him relentlessly about the dark rings under his eyes. What was she doing that was keeping him up all night? He wished that was the reason. Both Alice and his mother were constantly nagging him to go and see his GP. He knew he should go.

After that first meeting a few weeks ago his mother had not stopped talking about Alice, he was delighted if not a little embarrassed by her over exuberance. Alice had practically curtseyed when she had been introduced. Susan did have that effect on people, she described it as breeding. Within half an hour of them meeting, Tom had joked that he may as well go home seeing as he felt surplus to requirements; he was only half joking. There was one slightly awkward moment when his mother had brought up the subject of Fiona. It was never a good idea to talk about exes in front of the new girlfriend. Worse than that, Susan had declared that Alice was better in every way, well, except for the obvious one and she couldn't comment on that. The woman was going mad.

There was, however, a small seemingly inconsequential fly in the ointment. Alice refused to talk about her past in any detail. When they had left Susan, he had broached the subject of her parents once more. The first time he had tried, she had merely directed the conversation onto a different subject with such ease that he hadn't really noticed. However, now that she had met Susan, he wanted to know more about her upbringing; he didn't even know if she had any brothers or sisters. It had occurred to him then that she was very deft at avoiding any talk of her private life. So, he had been a little more insistent about her family. She said her parents lived their own lives and that at the present time she wasn't in contact with them, which suited them all. When she was talking, it was as if there was another version of Alice before he got to know her, one he didn't know. There was a hard edge to her tone which he had never heard her use before and found it a little unsettling. He had asked if they had fallen out but she said they hadn't and it was just better for all concerned if they had little contact. Alice didn't strike him as someone who wouldn't be involved with family. He knew though that families were often complicated; even the most outwardly normal families could harbour deep secrets. Was this the case with Alice? His gut instinct told him that there was a lot she wasn't being honest about but for once he wasn't listening. When he asked her whether there were any other family members that she was in contact with she merely said there was no-one, both her parents were only children. But she hadn't added that she was too. He couldn't put his finger on why, but it didn't sound right. It was the first time she had paused, as if the monologue that had gone before was well rehearsed and had been used many times. He had asked her then if she had any siblings. She had said no, she didn't have anyone.

He had told her that she would always have him. He meant it, but she had looked at him with something akin to pity and had told him that "always" never lasted as long as it should but sometimes it lasted far too long.

It had unsettled him more than he liked to admit. He felt she was in an imposed exile from those who she should be close to. He had first-hand experience of her detachment. It was akin to a reversal of karma as though when she experienced something good she had to pull away from it. When he had been taken out of private school and sent to the local comprehensive, Susan had decided that he needed some sort of support. Ever the one to go to the head of an organisation, she decided that they needed help from a greater being so she introduced God into their lives. She was as far away from a religious person as he had ever met or was likely to meet. He had felt it was more like a way of hedging their bets. Susan knew about karma and felt that due to their dramatic fall from grace they would be granted some sort of pass from now on. And because of this fact – as she felt it had become – she wanted to make sure that they would be positioned correctly for all that God was about to bestow on them. But she had quickly tired of this viewpoint since she was, and always had been, an inpatient woman. God was simply on a different timescale to hers. She kept their options open and the local churches benefited from this "options open" policy. During that time though he had been a shy impressionable teenager and although in retrospect the move from one school to another had been beneficial, the transition had been difficult. Mostly, he had to admit this was because of others' perceptions of him rather than the other way around. So, during this time when Susan had dabbled with Buddhism, he had been sent to a local group. He had learnt so much from them and even though he no longer actively practised the religion it had formed part of his own way of living.

Did it go anyway to explain Alice's behaviour? She was a good person; in his line of work you quickly needed to assess people and more often than not he had the measure of his clients. He needed to get to the bottom of her evasiveness. The sister practice in Cardiff had sent over an application form, it was a strong indicator as to their interest in him. It had been on the cards for a while – now though it seemed to be an imminent possibility. He would need to talk to Alice, he knew that she wasn't happy where she was working but again she was vague as to the reasons. He would talk to her about it and by discussing their future he hoped she would open up about her past. It brought to mind one of the sayings of Buddha that had helped him all those years ago.

There are only two mistakes one can make along the road to truth;
Not going all the way, and not starting.

He would help her to open up to him – a thought occurred to him then. There was no doubt in his mind how he felt about her or how she felt about him. To him, the solution was staring him in the face.

Martha
January 2015, England

Consider the hour glass;
There is nothing to be accomplished by rattling or shaking:
You have to wait patiently until the sand, grain by grain,
Has run from one funnel into the other.

Christian Morgenstern

In the end, it had been quite by chance that Martha had solved the mystery of the photograph. Initially, she couldn't make head nor tail of the picture. She had gone upstairs to her bedroom and pulled out the black and white dog-eared photo from her bedside table – the only photo she possessed of her father. She laid the two photos side by side on the kitchen table and stared at them. The likeness was not as dramatic as she had first thought but she couldn't deny that they looked like brothers. The only problem was that the photo she had of her dad had been taken in their back garden over fifty years ago but the other one had been taken only a few months ago. In the black and white photo, her father was leaning on a garden fork, his trousers rolled to the knees and shirt sleeves rolled up to the elbows. The two men had the same shaped nose, slim – aquiline almost – their eyes large and almond-shaped, even the mouths had the same symmetrical smile. There was no getting away from it, they looked an awful lot alike.

She often wondered why she had kept the photograph, why had she stuffed it into her rucksack the day she had walked out on her parents. It had always been her favourite one of him taken before all their lives had spiralled out of control. She had kept it stuck to her dressing table mirror and had grabbed it at the last minute covering it with sweatshirts and shoes.

She wondered afterwards why she hadn't realised what it could mean, but it had taken an old work colleague to point out the obvious during a coffee morning a few weeks ago. Emily, the old work colleague, had invited Martha and several others whom she had worked with for coffee, cakes and a chat. Emily had a huge family consisting of eight children, fourteen grandchildren and a whisper of a great-grandchild on the way. In the vast living room was a large walnut sideboard on which stood the smiling gallery of grandchildren. Their beaming faces looked up from a variety of silver and wooden picture frames, scenes of beaches, parks and formal occasions mapping out their history. She picked up a wedding photograph from the large display. The bride looked radiant and even though the picture was in black and white, Martha was sure she could see the blush on her face.

"Don't they make a beautiful couple?"

Martha turned around to see her host holding out a cup of coffee. She took the drink, after putting the photograph back on the sideboard.

"Yes, they do." Seeing another photo of the man in a smaller silver frame, she asked, "Is he your grandson?"

"Yes and no," she said laughing.

Seeing the confusion on Martha's face Emily explained.

"Do you know, if I had a pound for every time someone had asked me that, I wouldn't have to have a part-time job to pay for all my grandchildren's Christmas presents. This photo is of my dad." She picked up the smaller photo of the man on his own. "Taken when he was young before he met my mother. The wedding photo though was only taken a couple of years ago. In fact, they have just announced they are expecting a baby. He is my grandson and this is my father, his great grandfather. The apple doesn't fall far from the tree does it?"

Martha felt her head spinning, the room was hot, too hot and she suddenly felt unsteady on her feet. She almost dropped the coffee cup and saucer on the pale beige carpet.

"Martha, are you OK, you've gone as white as a sheet?"

She nodded, but they both knew that she was far from all right.

"I'll get Bill to drive you home, do you want me to come with you? Cathy can hold the fort, I would rather you didn't go home alone. I'll phone John if you want?"

Martha knew that Emily wasn't paying lip service and that she would leave her guests and take Martha home such was her concern. She was touched.

"I'm fine Emily, honestly. I don't know what came over me. If you don't mind I will go home – maybe I have a migraine coming on."

So, it was settled, Bill took Martha home. She waved her thanks from her front door and felt bad about not asking him in but Bill could talk extensively on any subject especially when he had a captive audience. She guessed he didn't get much airtime at home with all the family constantly in and out. The first thing she did, before even taking her coat off, was to rush into the kitchen. She pulled open the kitchen drawer where she kept bills and letters that needed dealing with. On the top of the pile were the two photos. With a shaking hand, she once again placed them side by side. Trying her best to be objective, she compared the features of both men. It didn't matter that she was now invested in the outcome, there was no denying that they could have been brothers, or grandfather and grandson as she now suspected, which meant that there was the possibility she was now looking at the son she had given up for adoption over thirty years ago.

Evie
January 2013, England

You were searching for a grain of sand
Along an endless beach
As I was building you a castle that you just refused to see.

Ron Pope

Evie shivered, the wind was bitterly cold. She pulled the thick woollen scarf tighter around her neck and plunged her hands deep inside her coat pockets. The day had begun with a hazy sun which had appeared at dawn and was then traded in leaving a distinctly grey sky. She walked alone into the small church acknowledging some of Theresa's friends. She found an empty pew to the far right of the church and sat down not wanting to make small talk with anyone. Dorothy had died a little over a week ago. Evie hoped she was dancing in her red dress with Harold. She hoped it more than she cared to admit.

The church filled up quickly. She couldn't help looking towards the back to see if John had changed his mind and taken time off work to be with her. She couldn't really blame him, she knew he was busy.

Theresa had fretted about the funeral so much, would it be well attended, what coffin was suitable etc., etc. Evie had tried to be patient with her, after all – she knew how fussy she was ever since they had first met. The problem was it was all too close for comfort.

A few days after she had first met Theresa, she had received a letter from Mr Nathan Devore. She had opened it with shaking hands unsure as to what it would contain. On paper, he was charming and understood her reasons for contacting him. He would be only too happy to meet with her. At the bottom of the letter he had printed his mobile number. Without hesitation, she had dialled the number with shaking hands and then felt slightly sick as she heard the ring tone. That was several weeks ago and they had met up a few days later. She had been really nervous, partly because it was the first time she had ever lied to John – well, a big lie anyway. She had carefully chosen a plain yellow knitted dress with black tights and loafers but had been undecided as to whether to wear her wig or to match her outfit to one of her many scarves. She settled on the wig. She had been so young when she had fallen for John that she had never really dated much before. She knew it was so wrong, but it felt as though it was a date. She knew that it was the wrong way to think about meeting the man who could possibly change all their lives, but she did nevertheless, and it gave her a little of her old spark back. She had wanted to be early, she hated tardiness in other people. However, as it seemed to be doing with a tiring persistence, fate appeared to have other ideas.

She had told John that she was taking a half-day from work and meeting up with an old friend in Cambridge. He had hardly made a comment. She guessed it meant he believed he could stay at work for as long as he wanted with no-one to moan about him working late. She had arranged for Martha to pick up the children from school. It had been easy to lie to all the people that she loved. Up to that point it had been so easy but then fate had intervened. She had arrived at the train station in plenty of time and had sat in one of the "quiet" compartments content to close her eyes and retreat from the world. Then they had cancelled the train, the porter had come onto each carriage to make sure they left the train. The next train rumbled along twenty minutes later but consisted of only three carriages which were already fairly full. She quickly realised there would now be no quiet contemplation on the journey. It was also stopping at more stations, which added an extra half an hour so that by the time she arrived in Cambridge she was very hot and bothered. She had had to stand for the whole of the journey which hadn't helped particularly as she wasn't having one of her better days. She appreciated that she didn't appear to look particularly unwell but even so, she had to remain standing for the entire journey. Not a single so-called "gentleman" had even considered the idea that she may have liked to sit down just for a few minutes. At one point, she had felt a little faint and had contemplated whipping her wig off and declaring to the previously disinterested travellers that she had cancer and would somebody mind giving her their seat for just a few minutes. Sense prevailed and she simply glared at the passengers.

He was in Cambridge for business which had been why he was able to meet up with her at such short notice. Now that she was actually here, she worried that he may be trying to trap her. But then since she was the one to contact him in the first place, perhaps he was concerned that it was her who was some sort of "crank". Because she had given herself plenty of time, it was still possible that she would get to the hotel on time – but that was before the car accident.

By the time everything had been sorted out, she was twenty minutes late. She was annoyed and flustered and for a few seconds had thought about getting on the next train home since she had enough going on in her life without complicating it even further. However, she had come all this way and if she went home now there would be more questions. She took a deep breath and walked up the steps of the hotel and walked in to the foyer.

In their phone call they had agreed to meet in the bar. They would both wear something yellow so that they could easily recognise one another. On the train, she had been surprised at how many business men were sporting yellow ties. She had hoped there wasn't some sort of a conference for yellow tie-wearing men at the hotel she was heading for. She walked through the dark foyer and located the bar. It was busy, but thankfully it wasn't full of people wearing yellow. She walked towards the bar without looking around the room and ordered herself a coffee while she surreptitiously scanned the room for a man she had never met before.

"Genevieve?"

"Yes."

He was standing in front of her, resplendent with the loudest yellow tie she had ever seen.

"Nathan," he said.

They shook hands.

"I'm glad we decided against the whole red carnation thing," he said. "There's a florist convention on today and would you believe it, they are all sporting carnations!"

"I would believe it. My first train broke down, the second train stopped at every single stop imaginable and then when I came out of the station, I was nearly knocked over by a car which then careered into the building opposite. I had to give a statement to the police."

"Oh no, you poor thing, please come and sit down, I have a table near the back."

He took her coffee cup. She followed him obediently to the far side of the room.

"Are you OK?" he asked.

"I'm fine now thanks although it was a bit of a shock – the car missed me by inches. Someone phoned the police and they were there before the driver had a chance to get out of the car. It looks as though he had either been drinking or was high on drugs – either way he could barely speak. Anyway, I had to give all my details to the policeman. So much for being incognito!"

"Look Genevieve, if this is a problem for you, maybe we can do this at a slower pace. It's just that after I spoke to you – well I couldn't wait to meet you."

She looked at the stranger sitting opposite and promptly burst into tears.

As she sat in the church waiting for the service to begin she remembered the way she had felt when he had taken her hands in his. They were warm and smooth, his nails neat and short, his grip had been reassuring and she had felt like a child again being comforted. She had told him everything – it seemed to be her default, telling complete strangers her fears about her illness. She felt guilty, but then John hadn't wanted to listen to the details right from the very start. He had been like a child who puts their hands over their ears and sings so they can't hear anything bad. Didn't he understand she needed him to listen to her? Nathan had understood immediately. He had ordered her a brandy; she sipped it, the liquid burning her throat as she swallowed it. He had talked to her about how his father had died suddenly and how it had affected his three sisters. He told her it was important for everybody in her life to be prepared for every possibility. It had made her feel that she had some hope, maybe because she wasn't fighting so hard to try and persuade him the opposite may be true. It was certainly the most dramatic ice-breaker she had ever experienced. After that, they had talked about everything – they had so much in common, they even worked out that they had both been at a Royal Philharmonic concert at the same time. They ordered more coffee. She had spent several hours

71

with a strange man in an unfamiliar town trying to hide the effects of her cancer and had enjoyed it more than she should have.

She was jolted out of her reverie as the music began, a predictable old-fashioned hymn that she was surprised she knew all the words to. She sang with little enthusiasm and then felt guilty as Dorothy deserved the best send-off not some half-soaked version. She sang loudly relishing the feeling of pushing the air out of her lungs. She felt a presence at her side, looked up expecting to see John, but in his place joining the singing was Nathan. The strange thing was she wasn't really that surprised to see him. They had spoken every day on the phone since that first meeting. She had met him for a coffee in her university where he apparently had some sort of appointment. It hadn't seemed like the truth to her but in a strange way it had actually made her happier to see him. She had told him then that Dorothy had died and went on to explain the connection. He had understood her grief, unlike John who hadn't wanted her to go to the funeral since he claimed that she wasn't a close friend. How did he know who or what was close to her anymore?

He stood at her side in the pew. She sang the words to a hymn she hadn't thought she knew beside a man she didn't know but who understood what she needed when no-one else did. It was so surreal that she thought that maybe she had already died and this was her new altered state.

The service was beautiful, Dorothy would have been tickled pink. It was just a shame that she couldn't appreciate it. Evie had the fleeting idea to have her own in a few weeks so that she could attend. That would have been out of John's comfort zone for sure, he had never liked going to funerals. He had said he found them false but had yet to meet someone horrible who had then died – apparently only wonderful people died if the service was anything to go by. She had laughed at him. He wasn't that keen on any sort of formal celebration if she was honest, *it was one of the things she had initially liked about him; she liked it less now. Maybe that was why he seemed so cross with her.*

She remembered when she and John were first trying for a baby. They had been at it like the proverbial rabbits but nothing had seemed to work. Attending christenings had been particularly hard especially when the older contingency "blessed" with a total lack of sensitivity kept insisting that they would be next. She had remembered coming home in tears wondering why it was so easy for everyone else. A rather acerbic friend had told her to get her own back, the next time she went to a funeral she should tell them, "It'll be you next"; she knew she would never have done it but it had made her smile. Within a few weeks of that conversation she had fallen pregnant with Seth.

The funeral service was over and she watched as heads bowed, Theresa and her family solemnly walked back up the aisle. The music started. It was so fitting but she wasn't sure whether to laugh or cry, either way she felt that if she had started, one way or another both sentiments would have met somewhere in the middle. The sound of Israel Kamakawiwo'ole singing "Over the Rainbow" filled the church. Of course, it was perfect for Dorothy, she was home in her very own Kansas. She felt dizzy all of a sudden and for a second thought she would pass out, horrified the thought of causing a scene as the coffin was carried out of the church. Without thinking she grabbed Nathan's arm. She must have looked awful because he put his arms around her and held onto her. For the first time since her diagnosis she felt the burden had been lifted from her shoulders; it was as if it had passed through her body into his.

The church was empty as they stood together in the cold space. She needed to get to the wake otherwise Theresa would be worried and by God, did Theresa worry. She turned to look up at him not wanting to break the spell. He started to speak but she knew that whatever he had

73

to say she couldn't hear. She would never be able to un-hear it. She was more grateful to him for coming to the funeral than she would ever be able to tell him. It was better for the both of them if she never did tell him, so she kept quiet. She moved forward and gently kissed him on the cheek. He smelt both familiar and unfamiliar at the same time, she supposed it was to be expected. It would have been so easy to have left the church with him, to follow him out of the grounds and go home with him, but she couldn't. That was the thing he understood, he seemed to be tuned into her. She felt John and Nathan were two different radio stations on separate wavelengths; she knew which one she should be listening to but it wasn't the one that felt right.

"Evie, can we meet up this week? I can come to you if it's easier, we can meet at the university."

She could tell he felt her hesitate.

"We need to discuss the paperwork."

"Yes, OK you're right. Of course, we need to meet up to sort through it."

They both knew that wasn't what he had meant. They arranged to meet in two days at the university. Her friend and colleague, Celine, was away in Texas on a field trip, one that she should have gone on but wasn't well enough. It had made her feel so low at the time but then she had met Nathan and he had told her that unless she liked Herman Marshall whiskey then she wasn't missing much.

She sat by his side on a small bench outside the church not quite ready to leave him. They watched as their breath left a mark on the day. She was cold, needed to be in the warmth and she needed to be at the wake otherwise Theresa would be sending out a search party.

"This is just the type of funeral I don't like," he said.

"I'm not really keen on them myself at the minute."

"No, it's just these early ones. I'm not really a mourning person!"

She smiled at him, then realising what he had said she laughed out loud.

"Nathan!"

"I just wanted to see a smile on your face again. Did you hear about the man who was accidentally buried alive? It was a grave mistake," he said.

He had got it so right, she couldn't avoid talking about death, it was all around her, maybe it was what was waiting around the corner for her. What John didn't get was that joking about it made her feel better as though she was beating death because she was refusing to take it seriously.

"My aunt's star sign is Cancer" she said, "pretty ironic considering how she died – she was eaten by a giant crab."

Nathan burst out laughing. He grabbed her hands rubbing them between his own to keep her warm. He looked in horror as he saw tears welling up in her eyes.

"Oh God Evie, I'm so sorry, I shouldn't have been so flippant about it."

He hugged her to him, his arms encircled her as though he could protect her from the world. For the first time since they had met he had read her completely wrong. She wasn't crying because he had got it wrong, she was crying because he had got it so right.

She had started another course of chemo, the ravages of which took chinks out of her carefully constructed armour. She felt exposed, revealed in a way she hadn't felt before, she felt vulnerable, a feeling that didn't sit very well with her. She had a career, a husband, children, she had been so blessed to have it all, but now it was all going to be taken from her.

It was only a few weeks until Seth's birthday. She was tired all the time but she still stayed up late into the night planning with meticulous detail the party of a lifetime. It wasn't his sixteenth, his eighteenth or twenty-first. It was his seventh.

Seth adored pirates particularly since they had, as a family, taken a short break in Cornwall the previous year. They had visited Pirates' Quest which Seth and Peggy had loved. He had run around with his treasure map unravelling the secret code and locating his hidden treasure. It was all he could talk about for months afterwards so she had invited all his class and a few of Peggy's friends to attend his swashbuckling party a week on Saturday. At the moment though, she had her head balanced on the toilet bowl as she waited for the spasms coming from her stomach to subside. She wiped her mouth thinking that she had finished when another wave of nausea gripped her and squeezed her stomach until she felt that the lining was coming away with the contents.

That was another thing that she and John had disagreed about – the party, but if she was honest, she couldn't blame him as she wasn't being entirely honest with him. If she thought about it, she wasn't being very honest with him about a lot of things. In this case he had been against the party from the outset. And she had to admit that she couldn't argue with his reasoning. She shouldn't come into contact with anyone with an infection because her immune system was severely compromised due to the chemotherapy. Young children were veritable bug factories apparently. He had been furious that she was even contemplating the party. What he didn't know was that she had met with the consultant on her own. He had been reluctant to commit to any sort of long-term prognosis but she had pressed him and, in the end, she had asked what the likelihood was of her being alive for next year's birthday. He had capitulated and agreed that she should have the party. She had felt like a boxer taking an unexpected left hook from an opponent; she should have known it was coming but, when it did, it took the wind out of her.

She wiped her mouth once more and carefully stood up holding onto the wall; she felt a little dizzy but she was OK. She needed a glass of water and she needed to phone work to see how the meeting had gone with the Saudi government. The phone rang. She walked from the en-suite to her room, picked up the phone from the dressing table and perched on the stool facing away from the mirror. She knew she must look awful and didn't need the mirror to confirm it.

"Hi Martha, how are you?"

"I'm good thanks love, how are the party plans going?"

It was a tacit agreement between Evie and her mother-in-law that her illness wouldn't be mentioned unless she wanted to talk about it.

"Good, thanks. Did you manage to get the day off?"

"Yes, all sorted. I've also booked the following day off to give you a hand clearing up."

They both knew that Martha would do most of the cleaning while Evie rested.

"Thank you… for everything."

"Don't be daft, I'm looking forward to spending some time with the kids, and you of course. Has Peggy decided if she's going to be Elizabeth Swann or Molly the Pirate? Either way I bet Seth isn't impressed; she's either going to be his love interest or his rival and my pieces of silver would be on Peggy!"

"I know she is going to be such a madam when she grows…"

The unfinished sentence sat heavily on both women. Evie was glad that Martha hadn't marched out a cliché. She regained her composure as Martha gently took up the thread of the conversation.

"Yes, she is and thank God for that! She told me the day before yesterday that she thinks Seth likes a girl. Apparently, Peggy spoke to her at break-time to see if she would make a suitable step-sister. I asked her if she meant sister-in-law. She looked at me as if I was the five-

year-old and said, "Of course not, that would mean Seth would have to marry her and he's only seven for Pete's sake."

The two women laughed as if it was the most natural sound in the world, and maybe for those few seconds it was.

Martha
January 2015, England

I saw the long line of the vacant shore,
The sea-weed and the shells upon the sand,
And the brown rocks left bare on every hand,
As if the ebbing tide would flow no more.

Henry Longfellow

She thought back to the hardest day of her life, when the lady came and took her screaming baby from her arms, only a few hours after she had given birth. He had been the most perfect thing she had ever seen, pink and soft with a sprinkling of black hair; she could still recall the smell of him. The nurse had placed him in her arms even though she had been advised not to hold him and after all this time she was still so grateful to that young nurse. He had settled quickly once they had placed him in the cradle of her arms. Over the years when the pain had got too much, she had closed her eyes, opened her arms and remembered the feel of him. It hadn't dissipated with time; she could still feel him as he had fallen asleep. She had felt afterwards as though she would never recover, and for a while she didn't think that she would. She had eventually left home without a backward glance, found a job and rented a poky little flat, she worked, she ate and she tried to sleep. Other than that, she did little else because she had created a self-imposed exile from life.

Then she had met Peter and like the colouring books that she had loved as a child – black outlines showing form, coloured pencils to flesh them out and bring them back to life – Peter took the blackness of her past life and replaced it. She had found a measure of happiness and was content, until she became pregnant unexpectedly for the second time in her life. She had been desperate for the baby to be a girl. It was hard enough being pregnant again in such a short time, to have another boy she felt would have been unbearable. After another gruelling labour, she had a second baby boy weighing 8 lbs 2oz. The baby didn't cry, but she had, great sobs that had racked her exhausted body; she had cried in fear that they were going to take this one away too. Then they placed him in her arms and she swore to him that she would never let him go. She had lost a lot of blood and there had been talk of surgery to repair something but she couldn't take it all in. At that precise moment she had made Peter promise her this would be their only child, she couldn't go through it again. He had been so shocked and upset at her reaction to the birth, he had readily agreed.

From that day on he referred to her as little China, mainly, because of her one child policy. Although she often suspected it was because he thought that she was so fragile, breakable; she didn't ever try to change his mind, she preferred his version of her story.

In all their married years he kept his promise and had never brought up the subject again. She had been sorry after he passed away; she knew he would have understood, but he had always held her up on a pedestal unlike her parents and maybe she just wanted to stay there, the view was always better the higher up you were.

She understood now holding the photo of a man who could possibly be her son. He was her first born and somewhere inside her she felt he deserved to know what had happened before John did. She knew that it was a strange ideal but it was how she felt. She had loved John every day of his life. When he had fallen, she had picked him up, when he was happy she had smiled with him, when he had graduated, she had cried tears of joy. Then, he had married his childhood sweetheart and she had let him go. The only gift she could give her first born was to tell him first why she hadn't been able to do the same for him.

It made her take a look at the past and see the errors she had made. She knew that her mother had been sick, even at the time the gradual deterioration of her mind had been glaringly obvious but both she and her father had tried to ignore it, block it out because things like that didn't happen to them. She had blamed everyone and everything apart from herself. She needed to make amends and she knew the first place she had to go to.

She figured it was the best place to start, at the beginning. She had been doing a little shopping on the high street and then popped into the chemist for a nit pack, as Peggy had come home from school with more friends than she had gone in with. John had rung her to see if she could pick up the shampoo etc. She would help him do it tonight. She didn't think he realised that it was probably best if they were all treated. Seth would not be impressed, it would be a nightmare with his long hair. She picked up the combs and shampoo from the chemist and after a quick look of sympathy from the assistant about what she would be doing that evening she left the shop. As she walked back up the high street, she had to struggle against the strong breeze that was blowing in the opposite direction.

She passed it almost every day, either on her way to Pam's Papers, the library or the café, but she ignored it as if the magnificent stone structure didn't exist. For the first time in decades she paused outside. She took a deep breath and walked up the front steps. She hesitated for a few seconds, took another deep breath and then pushed the large oak door inwards. For the first time in three decades she entered a church other than to attend a funeral, wedding or a christening.

The interior of the church was surprisingly warm. She ran her hand across one of the ancient radiators, it was scorching hot. It was a good start, she couldn't really explain why she felt that the warmth was welcoming. She moved towards the front of the church. The aisle replayed her footsteps as she walked towards the altar. She had expected to feel uncomfortable after such a long absence, but all she felt was a sense of belonging, of coming home. The old habits returned, she hadn't forgotten. She genuflected then sat on the hard, wooden pew. It was like being transported back to her childhood and she realised that it hadn't all been bad. Before her mother had become seriously ill they had been a happy little family, at least for some of the time. She had enjoyed going to church then, had liked the ritual of it. The smell was the same – old, faintly musty, but with a muskiness that added an air of mystery. She opened her bag and after a few seconds her hand found the small plastic box at the bottom. She pulled it out and removed the lid, tipped the string of beads into the palm of her hand and finding the first, she began the prayers she had learnt by heart.

When she had finished she returned the beads to the box and slipped it back into her handbag. She had come to a decision and it didn't matter what anyone else thought about it when she eventually came around to telling them about her decision. Sometimes you have a need to do the most foolish thing because the alternative is to live with the regret of not making a fool of yourself and surely nothing could be worse than that.

So, several weeks later, she was sitting in the local café and for once she was not tackling the crossword but checking e-mails. She preferred using her laptop in public because she heard so much about trolls; she wanted to be in company in case anything horrible happened. She didn't understand this new cyber world and most of the time it scared her. The only troll she had known was in the stories she had learnt as a child – the one that hid under the bridge. It was quite strange, she hadn't realised until recently how many tales, fables and fairy stories her father had entertained her with and how well she remembered most of them. The problem was for their family there had been no "happy ever after".

The screen displayed twelve replies to her enquiries regarding short stay accommodation. She was amazed they had all replied to her request for two nights stay starting on February 19th. She stirred the camomile tea bag in the cup of hot water and, as always, left the bag in for as long as she could. John joked it was so she could get the maximum relaxing effects from the tea. Maybe he was more in tune with her than he realised. She clicked on the first reply – yes, they would be more than happy to let her stay at their establishment for two nights and in fact they would be absolutely delighted to have her. When she scrolled down looking at the finer details, she decided that it wasn't for her. It was what she both loved and hated about the small independent guest houses, but in this case her decision was a firm rejection, she didn't want to stay where they had a large vivarium. Each to their own, but she remembered a work colleague once telling her that he had named his pet snake Harry after Harry Houdini because it was so good at escaping. She shuddered and moved onto the next reply. This one turned out to be a strong possibility so she noted it and moved on. After about an hour, she had decided on a small bed and breakfast on the town's beachfront about half an hour's bus journey from Oxwich beach. It sounded almost perfect.

Evie
February 2013, England

Time is like a handful of sand –
The tighter you grasp it,
The faster it runs through your fingers.

Henry David Thoreau

It was the day of the party and she had never felt so ill in her life, she had stopped vomiting but her mouth felt sore. At least the ulcers that had plagued her over the last few weeks had begun to improve. Wasn't she a lucky girl! It was a Saturday morning and John was already up and about, he had risen early to start decorating the house. She knew she should feel grateful given how poorly she was but all she felt was the all too familiar sting of disappointment. He was trying to help but she felt he missed the point, he seemed to be busy doing things to help her, rather than spend any time with her. She pulled the blinds apart and looked out onto their back garden. Even though it was winter the sun was shining and everything looked starkly beautiful, stripped back to its bare beauty. It took her breath away, as though it was the first time she had really looked at it – maybe it was. She was living her life in high definition now the possibility of losing it all sharpened her senses. When she had been little, her mother had tried to show her how important each of her senses were. She had isolated each one in turn starting with sight, putting her hands over her ears and telling her to breathe through her mouth. She then did it with her ears, making her close her eyes, then with the rest of the senses. She had loved doing it as a child but only as an adult did she realise the full value of it. It made her stop and think. It occurred to her that she hadn't done the same to Peg and Seth – something she would rectify tomorrow. For the first time, she didn't allow herself to become maudlin by how much she wouldn't be able to teach them, instead she looked forward to the prospect of the fun they would have. With that in mind she got dressed in the pirate's outfit complete with the wig of titian curls, the red cumberband and the striped trousers. Her make-up took a little longer, the false eyelashes were so difficult to stick on. She looked in the mirror – an imposter returned her stare. However, the imposter was an improvement on the real thing so she went with it. She slipped the absurdly large silver hoop earrings in her ears and went to see how John was getting on.

She watched as he balanced the skull and crossbones bunting in one hand and the sellotape in the other. Interior design was definitely not his strong point. He had somehow managed to stick several triangles of the black and white bunting together and was furiously trying to untangle them whilst simultaneously attempting not to fall off the kitchen chair. How many times had she told him to use the ladder? For some reason he seemed to think that using the correct items for a job made him less of a man. He turned, saw her and promptly fell off the chair pulling all the bunting he thought he had already secured down onto the floor with him.

"John, are you OK?"

"Only a bruised ego and bunting that may never be the same again. Apart from that I think I got off lightly. Evie, you look amazing."

She smiled, it had been worth the effort.

"No, really, you are the prettiest pirate I've ever seen."

"It must be the false eyelashes that took me fifteen minutes to stick on. It was a bit like you with the bunting. I stuck my eyes together the first time!"

"You should have put the patch over one eye, it would have taken you half the time and then you would have been able to save me from my serious fall."

"The only thing that was injured was the bunting and I think that may have been fatal!"

"I have a battered ego and a bruised bum."

They laughed and the sound reminded her of how they used to be before fate interfered in their lives. John stopped laughing. He took her hands and led her upstairs to their bedroom. They made love like they had before she had become ill and he felt he might break her.

She had a loving husband, two beautiful, healthy children and had experienced a career that she loved. Only a few hours before, it had seemed like an illusion – her own house of cards, but they were still standing, maybe not for ever, but in truth what in the world lasted forever? If she could barter with fate, would she take away any one of her gifts and exchange them for a different ending to her story? No, she wouldn't, because she had loved the story; it was just the ending that sucked.

Life was all an illusion she thought, like grains of sand it could fall through your fingers. Most people thought that sand grains started out as shells or rocks that had been eroded over time, so in essence the grains would eventually get smaller and smaller. However, there were also ooid grains of sand which actually increase in size. So, instead of nature stripping them down and making them smaller, they were built up layer by layer, consisting of rings similar to the age-rings found in trees. When she had learnt this fact early on in her studies she had loved it because it had surprised her. These ooid-based sands occurred in warm, wave-agitated waters and it had made her think that were they a person, the sea would be bestowing armour on them, wave by wave, layer by layer. She wished now more than ever that she could be like the ooid sands and become stronger not weaker from all the buffeting that life was giving her. She tried not to think of the biogenic sands, the ones once described as the cemetery of sea creatures, a sand made up of the tiny skeletons of plants and sea creatures. She too would soon be a part of that aspect of nature that she had studied all her life. As a scientist, she had always been aware of the endgame. She had been well equipped for life and known how to live it but she had always believed that its conclusion would have been when she was ready for it – but it would appear that science can never replace a person's humanity.

Maybe she should have put the eye patch on as John had suggested, because sometimes not seeing everything that was in front of you was a much kinder thing.

The party was in full swing, the music blaring from Seth's iPod. She had taken the prudent step of inviting their neighbours Craig and Jane to the party, it meant there would be no complaints about the noise. Maybe they never did mind the noise she thought, as she watched Craig chatting to Martha and Jane telling Peggy and her friends a story; maybe they just didn't want to hear what they were missing out on. She wished she had had this much clarity about things when she had been well. She heard a knock at the door and watched as John left to open it. She wondered who it could be – there were only two kids who couldn't make it and both mothers had phoned. She heard a bit of a commotion and went out to see if everything was OK.

Later on, when she was getting ready for bed, she realised that part of her had been afraid that it was Nathan. He was a man of his word though and he had promised that he would never do anything that would cause a problem for her or her family. Yet, she had worried for those few seconds before she had reached the hallway. Would he do anything though even if he had promised her he never would? His feelings ran very deep – did she really know what he would do, did she even know him as well as she thought she did? They had got on so well from the very first meeting and that had never changed. They talked as though they had known each other all their lives, and in some ways, they had. Still, there was enough drama in her life, more than enough.

So, when she had seen John embracing Celine, it had been a relief. Celine was her number two at work, her Girl Friday or recently given her ill-health her Girl Monday through to Friday. The fact that she was even here was a surprise. Even though she was a good friend and had always been invited to the kids' parties, she usually cried off because she was either working or dating. So, it came as a shock to see her standing there bright as a button and with a new man in tow, and the man appeared to be carrying what looked suspiciously like an enormous bag of sand.

"He's a sand artist, Evie, and if I may say so, a bloody amazing one," said Celine.

"Why, thank you, Mam!"

He was obviously American, possibly Texan from the long lazy drawl. So that was the little bit of Texas she had brought back with her after last month's field trip. It was typical of Celine – no bottle of Jack Daniels for her!

"Where can I set up? Celine has the tarpaulin in the car so don't you go worrying about me making a mess of the old homestead."

Evie wondered for a second if he was putting it on – did Americans actually talk like that, even the ones from Texas? John had turned into a mute and just kept looking alternatively at Celine and her new beau.

"I'm sorry Evie, this is Travis – Travis, John and Evie."

They all smiled at each other, handshaking was out of the question as Travis was still holding onto the very heavy bag of sand.

"Here Travis, why don't you set up in the kitchen, there should be enough space for you," said John.

"Thanks man, this bag is getting mighty heavy."

Evie watched as her tall, slim husband showed the man-mountain the way to the kitchen.

"Celine?" said Evie.

"What can I say, you were talking about doing something a little different – to make the party special. I know my turning up would be a good start and well, I didn't want to leave Travis at home with the girls so I brought him along and it just so happens he is a very talented sand sculptor."

Evie laughed. Celine shared her house with three other girls from the university, two were quiet, but the third was even more outrageous than Celine. She could appreciate why Celine didn't want to leave him at home.

The girls followed the men into the kitchen and set about clearing a large space on the floor for the tarpaulin that Travis had retrieved from the car. Evie watched in amazement as the huge man with hands the size of buckets created a pirate ship complete with main sail, foresail and flying jib. He even added a few pirates, one of which looked suspiciously like Celine.

"Mum, this is awesome!" shouted Seth.

The other kids had gathered in the kitchen to watch Travis put the finishing touches to the ship. Shouts rang out as they noticed small details that the well-informed Travis had added to the boat. On the side was the name "King Seth's Revenge" with Seth's date of birth. Seth shouted with delight as his friends read the inscription. Travis added a few final details and the ship was finished complete with a pirate at the side together with Peggy's name.

"Thank you so much, Travis," said Evie, touched by the small, thoughtful details on the ship as much as the effort that had gone into making the whole thing.

"You're welcome, Mam."

"This is the best freaking party ever," exclaimed Seth.

And much to his delight, his friends all agreed.

Evie watched her family and friends, especially Celine – who could be in bed with her new beau but was here enjoying the party. She felt a sense of calm wash over her. She was tired, but for the first time since her diagnosis – the second diagnosis – she knew her family would be OK without her.

"You OK, love?" asked John as he careered past her with renegade pirates in tow.

"I'm fine," and for the first time in a long while she meant it. She had suddenly felt exhausted, overcome by emotion and fatigue. The ever-watchful Martha had noticed, pulled a chair across and promptly sat her down. The dog, glad for a respite from the legions of adoring children, sat by his mistress and encouraged her to stroke his throbbing head. As she stroked Darwin, she felt as though she was watching a home movie about her and her family. She could see they were all having a great time and even though she had been the one to set up the day – at that moment she wasn't an active part of it. That would be John, behaving like an idiot with his black beard and swashbuckling ways, chasing the kids around the house. That would be Martha checking the food was hot and plentiful and that would be dear Celine being at her house, playing the adoring aunty.

Sand: Porosity

(a measure of the empty void, for example, empty spaces in a material)

Evie had done a short course in Latin when she had been in university, it had helped her get a handle on all the scientific terms that had been overwhelming her. It had been as though someone had switched on a light, her lightbulb moment.

The one that had resonated with her the most was the Greek for porous, it comes from "Pore" which means Passage, the action or process of moving through or past somewhere on the way from one place to another. The other meaning was a narrow way allowing access between buildings or rooms.

Either way it got to her; it seemed to encapsulate that whether it was in human life or in nature there was always a shift forward, a move towards somewhere. You couldn't stand still, nature always showed the way.

As Albert Einstein had said "look deep into nature, and then you will understand everything better".

So, she had subsequently tried to move forward to learn and to change. Now though all she felt was empty and so instead of being the energy moving between the spaces she felt like the void itself.

Martha
February 2015, England

You can't leave footprints in the sands of time
While sitting down.

Nelson Rockefeller

Martha looked out of the front door but the street was empty, the taxi was now almost ten minutes late. She still had plenty of time to get to the train station but she was now worrying that maybe the taxi had either forgotten about her completely or had been involved in a fatal crash. She had been carried along on a mission since realising the man in the photo could be her son, without pausing to wonder if it was nothing more than a wild goose chase. She made a decision that if the taxi didn't turn up it would be a message from God advising her not to be foolish. However, if she didn't go now, John and Pam would wonder why she suddenly wasn't going to visit her "sick friend" and there would have to be explanations. She didn't want to kill off her friend by saying she didn't have to go and visit now because the friend had died, even if she was imaginary. Pam had been suspicious from the minute Martha had told her she would be away for a few days visiting the sick friend. Why had Martha never mentioned her before? She realised that when the daily news was your livelihood – you were always on the lookout for breaking news!

She looked at her watch, the taxi was now almost fifteen minutes late; her anxiety increased and she could do with a camomile tea. She wouldn't have time to have one at the station since she would literally have to get straight on the train – if it was still there. She was getting too hot bundled up in her coat, hat and scarf. She loosened the scarf and pulled off her hat, stuffing it in the pocket of her woollen coat. The sun was streaming through the stained glass of her front door heating up the tiny hall, sprinkling a kaleidoscope of colours on the grey hall tiles. She heard an impatient beep outside; she didn't have time to feel any relief but grabbed her small suitcase and pulled the front door behind her.

The taxi driver was utterly disinterested in his fare; he neither apologised for his tardiness nor made any attempt to help her with her luggage. She didn't care, she could manage perfectly well without any assistance from him. As she sat on the cold leather seat behind him, she wondered uncharitably how he had managed to wedge his considerable girth into his seat. As she told him her destination and he pulled away from the curb, she looked at his fat hands changing gear. The nails on his fingers bulged as if the fat had filled up every other part of his body and was looking for an escape route. She instantly felt guilty, wondering if he had some sort of medical condition that made him eat until his body needed to explode. He didn't utter a single word as they travelled the short journey together and, for a second or so, she was transported back to that same silent journey with her father all those years ago. She was suddenly grateful to the silent chauffeur. It felt like some sort of synergy – the first time she had lost her son – on this journey, she was trying to find him.

The train journey, however, was pleasant and she engaged in conversation with a lovely young couple who were headed out on a gap year. She had wondered what they would have thought of the thirty years or so gap she had in her studies. She lay back in the seat and closed her eyes, exhausted from all the planning. The good thing was Swansea was a terminal station so even if she fell into a deep sleep, she wouldn't miss her stop.

She looked around the guest room. It was pretty if a little twee, she thought that chintz wasn't the look most hotels were going for although she had to admit it was like being transported back to better times – like visiting with a favourite aunt. She was tired and felt grubby after the journey and wondered why that happened following prolonged travelling. She had been on long car journeys with John and the kids and by the time they had arrived at their destination she had felt as though she hadn't bathed for a week. She located the hostess tray in a small cupboard to the left of the dressing table, filled the tiny kettle that looked as though it had come from a doll's house and pressed the button. She looked through the offerings of tea, coffee and hot chocolate and was pleasantly surprised to find a selection of fruit, camomile and peppermint teas; still she decided on her usual camomile. Even though she was tired, she had a feeling she would find it hard to fall asleep. She texted John and Pam to tell them she had arrived safely then kicked off her shoes and lay down on the bed. The button popped and steam curled out of the little kettle in such a delicate little puff it was like the breath of a baby dragon. She smiled, she had only been in Wales a few hours and she was already conjuring up dragons. Her phone pinged in response to a message from Pam, she had asked Martha to send a "selfie" of her and her "friend". Martha laughed out loud, she would find someone later and make up some excuse to have a photo with them. She poured the hot water over the tea and let it steep in the cup, carried it over to a small silver floral dressing chair, removed the silver and pink cushion and sat down. There was a small rectangular window adjacent to the chair. She looked out and found to her delight that she had an almost perfect view of the sea. She had been slightly disorientated as she had made her way up the winding staircase unsure as to which direction her room faced. The view was spectacular; she watched the fading light of the day as it kissed the sea goodnight, the hues of pink and crimson making the sea appear to blush.

There was a knock at the door. She hesitated, she knew no-one in the town. She opened the door and there in front of her stood the receptionist. In her hand was a wooden tray laden with a plate of sandwiches, a pastry of some sort and a large piece of cake, a magnificent chocolate creation which she couldn't conjure up a name to describe!

"I ransacked the kitchen; if you are not hungry just leave the tray outside the door and one of us will pick it up. You looked so exhausted, I assumed you wouldn't be going out for something to eat and well, it's a long time till breakfast."

"Oh, that is so kind, I am a bit peckish actually. Thank you so much, that is very thoughtful. Do you want me to pay now or will you put it on my bill?"

"No charge, compliments of the house."

"Oh really, that's so kind. Thank you so much."

Martha took the tray and the girl left. She was dumbfounded, she had never known such thoughtfulness. It really was like visiting with an aunt she thought, smiling. She hadn't realised how hungry she was until she had seen the food spread out on the tray. She ate the ham and pickle sandwiches and the warm beef pasty, leaving the cake because she was too full. She carefully unpacked, laying out the clothes she wanted to wear the following day. The day she would spend on the beach where John, Seth and Peggy had been and where she hoped to find some trail of the other member of her small family, one that she had missed more than he would ever know.

The morning after Martha arrived in Swansea, the city experienced a force of nature that took all its inhabitants by surprise. The calm night was swallowed up by a ferocious first light. Winds of seventy to eighty miles an hour howled across the city, as if a pack of wolves had emerged from the darkness. Rain emptied from the black, angry sky as if from a celestial bucket. Above the cry of the wind, thunder roared and bony fingers of lightning lit up the deep, slate-grey of the morning light with the capacity of a thousand power stations.

Martha peered out of the window where less than twelve hours before she had witnessed a sea so calm it could have been mistaken for an old master's seascape of "The Doldrums". But no artist could have painted a bleaker picture than the one before her framed in the small rectangular window. The day was almost as black as the night before, it was as if the night was reluctant to takes its leave. She looked at the clothes she had laid out. Although she had expected and planned for some inclement weather, she just hadn't expected it to be this bad. This was a time when you feared for the welfare of reporters standing too close to the violent sea as they shouted unnecessary words to explain how bad the weather was. She did wonder when she watched these news items whether the producers had ever lost one of their reporters to the sea. She couldn't do anything about the weather and if she had to wait until tomorrow to go, then so be it – she had waited all this time so one more day wouldn't kill her. She was a pragmatist at heart which had helped her through many a dark hour so she decided she would shower, get dressed and have some breakfast. She walked across the soft silky carpet to the tiny bathroom, although bath-cupboard would have been a more fitting description. Refreshed following a nice, hot shower, she dried quickly and dressed in the clothes she had selected the previous night. She laced up her walking boots and with a quick glance in the mirror she left the room. As she descended the windy staircase that had disorientated her so much the previous evening she was greeted by a smart woman of a similar age. The woman seemed to glide as though she wasn't making contact with the tread beneath her feet. She was reminded for a second of Peggy's shoes where wheels came out of the soles. If she had to describe the woman there and then in one word it would have been graceful. Martha felt scruffy beside the glamorous woman who nodded in acknowledgement as they passed.

"Good morning," she said.

"Morning," returned Martha.

The woman's make-up was flawless even at seven in the morning. Martha felt that make-up was a bit like a gin and tonic. It made you feel great but was recommended for after 6pm.

The woman didn't have a single hair out of place. Martha involuntarily smoothed her own wayward curls. The hair was really something to behold; in this day and age of social media, Martha thought it should have its own Facebook page. It was swept back in a chignon, dark chocolate brown and glossy, with what she imagined was an awful lot of hairspray. She feared for the woman near any naked flame. As the two women made their way down the stairs into the breakfast room in companionable silence, Martha was relieved to see a no smoking sign on the wall.

The woman was a bit of an enigma. Martha watched as she gracefully moved around the room, speaking to each of the guests present. It was fairly busy for a cold wet February but Martha got the feeling that many of the guests had been before. She was glad she had chosen this B and B, she had felt welcome from the minute she had stepped inside. Martha picked up the menu and looked over the morning's offerings. She was used to having muesli and fruit for breakfast but today she wanted a change. There was a full cooked breakfast, a selection of breads and cold meats and porridge.

"Are you ready to order?"

Martha was surprised to see the same lady standing in front of her. She definitely seemed to glide about the place. Martha hadn't heard her approach, which given that the floor was slate was quite an achievement.

"Well yes, no. What I mean is… I quite fancy a nice cooked breakfast, but there are one or two things I'm not sure of."

"The laver bread?"

"Yes, what is it?"

The woman laughed, a delicate tinkling sound. It reminded

Martha of the sound made when a spoon was gently tapped against a crystal glass to get the attention of the diners at a function. She had accompanied her late husband to many and the sound felt warm and comforting.

"If I had a pound for every time I was asked that question I would be living it up in Barbados instead of having to go out in this awful weather. It's actually not bread at all but – and don't be put off by this, it is seaweed. Locally sourced like our bacon and sausages. We fry it in the bacon fat to cook it, unless you are a vegetarian?"

Martha shook her head.

"It really is very tasty, you should give it a try."

Martha had the feeling that even if the woman had actually received a pound for every time she was asked, she still would have been right where she was.

"Yes, OK, I will give it a go."

"Good for you. My daughter says that we should do one thing every day that is out of our comfort zone. Her theory is that if we keep expanding our comfort zone, very soon we will be comfortable with almost everything and well, that has to be a good thing doesn't it."

Martha wasn't sure if the woman was asking her a question or if it was rhetorical. She plumped for the latter and remained silent. She wondered if that was why the woman seemed so serene. Was she simply very comfortable with her life? It made Martha feel suddenly more positive and as she looked out of the window she noticed that the rain had stopped.

"Good, I will put it in a separate dish for you and then if you don't like it, the rest of your meal won't be spoiled."

Martha thanked her and watched as she went into the

kitchen to give her breakfast order. Something had resonated with her – it was the action of putting the laver bread in a separate dish so the rest of the meal wouldn't be spoiled. Of course, it made sense, but she felt more that it was a lesson for her. She was doing something way out of her comfort zone and that was a good thing, but whatever the outcome, she needed to separate it from the rest of her life or the consequences could be devastating for her.

She also hoped the woman didn't go too close to any naked flames in the kitchen with her hair saturated with hairspray or her own consequences too would be devastating.

A couple of hours later, Martha was sitting on Bob, which would definitely have raised a few perfectly plucked eyebrows back home. Bob, however, was a bright orange bus. And Bob took his name very seriously – there was no argument to the fact he was a bus and also very orange! She found the Welsh to be very friendly, almost everyone at the bus stop had exchanged pleasantries with her. At first, she had ignored them, assuming they were talking to someone else but she quickly caught on. By the time the bus arrived she had even initiated a few conversations herself.

The scenery was breathtaking. She had loved the train journey the day before as she crossed the border from England into Wales. The majestic mountains and vibrant valleys decorated her window. She watched the sheep grazing along the vertical sides of the mountains, like little land clouds. Today, the views were of the sea as the bus followed the coastal road. The first stop was the local university, she felt the familiar pang of disappointment settle within her – the wasted years – but she quickly dismissed it. It was an emotion that had been recycled too many times. The bus exchanged its passengers, some on, some off. Then they were on their way again. The tide was flooding again making its way back to the upper shore. The road was dusted with sand that had been washed across the sea wall by the morning's violent storms and there were several small branches that had become orphaned in the high winds. Darwin would have loved a few of them to play "fetch" with. But what did she hope the outcome would be? She deliberately kept her expectations low. It had become her life's mantra. Expect the worst and you will always fare a little better, hardly the stuff of inspirational quotes. But she was expecting something or she wouldn't have travelled across the country lying to her family and friends. She thought of Evie, her beloved daughter-in-law. It was Evie who had spurred her on because she knew that if she had seen the two photos together she would have marched Martha to Wales herself to see if she could find anything about him. She had tried not to let the anticipation build but it was like climbing a mountain; the further up you went, the longer the drop. Still she needed to do it, it was long overdue.

The bus filled up considerably over the next few stops, which meant that the empty seat next to her was soon filled. Martha smiled as the woman took the seat next to her and wondered if she should start up a conversation; it did appear to be the way to do things in Wales. The woman gave a stiff smile and all thoughts of conversation were wiped from Martha's mind. She could feel her legs getting wet and looked up at the roof of the bus to see if it had sprung a leak. The roof was orange and it was bone dry.

"Oh, my dear, I am so sorry. Look what I've done to your…"

The woman spoke in what Martha considered was an old-fashioned BBC accent. When Martha was a child, she thought people who spoke with such an accent were closely related to the Queen. The well-spoken woman seemed at a loss as to what to call Martha's walking trousers.

"It's OK, they dry really quickly, don't worry," Martha replied.

The woman's long, waxed coat was living up to its lofty reputation for being completely waterproof. This was wonderful for the woman but not so great for Martha. It didn't really bother her though since she knew her trousers would dry quickly.

The woman had an air of aristocracy about her even without the cut-glass accent. She was clutching what looked like a vintage Louis Vuitton handbag. She had short, silvery hair bullied into a precise bob. Martha almost burst out laughing – she was inundated with Bobs. Now that the ice had been broken, they fell into an easy conversation initially about the awful weather and then onto other things. It was no time at all before the woman had to get off at her stop; she was shopping in a small village called Mumbles. She had told Martha that she often went to the beach where she was headed to meet her son for lunch or coffee. The son apparently had a new girlfriend and it was getting quite serious, the woman had seemed pleased about it. The two women waved to each other as the bus pulled away. Martha looked at the name of the village, "Mumbles", she liked the name, it made her think of mysteries and softly spoken secrets, she felt she would fit right in, in the little village of Mumbles.

She arrived back at the B and B in low spirits. She had been determined to just be at the beach, just sit in the café and just think about the day he had been taken from her. At best, she would have found some connection to him, a feeling, some clue or other as to whether he lived in the area or whether, like John and the kids, he had just been a visitor. She had shown the photo to the waitress who informed her that she was a student in the university, not a local; she hadn't recognised him. The waitress told her that the owner would be in that evening, if she wanted to come back. At worst, she had hoped to feel a little better; just being in the same place as he had been, walking along the same sands and perhaps drinking from the same cup that had been washed a thousand times since. It had been a foolish venture all along.

She needed a tea but didn't want to sit up in her room all alone. She popped her head around the breakfast-room door to see the owner sitting at the table in the bay window doing what looked like some admin.

"Hello Martha, how was your day?" she asked.

"It was good, thank you," she replied, lying to both herself and the owner.

"I do that," she said. "I tell people everything is fine. Shall I order us some nice tea?"

Martha was taken aback by the offer. She had never thought of herself as someone who wore their heart on their sleeve. After all, it was a lot safer if your heart was protected beneath layers of skin and tissue and false pretences.

"Would you like English Breakfast, Darjeeling, peppermint or camomile?"

"Camomile please."

This time Martha was taken aback by her own actions. She would usually have said that everything was fine and retreated to a safe distance. Maybe she had simply run out of steam. She took the chair opposite and sat down. The view from the window was dramatic, an angry sea pushed its armies towards the retreating sands.

"Can I do anything to help? You don't have to tell me anything you don't want to, but if I can help, I will."

"I'm looking for someone."

"Go on."

"I'm not sure if he is from around here or whether he was here on holiday last year. I have a photograph."

"Let me see, I know most locals through my charity work."

Martha picked up the bag she had carried with her all day. She had put the picture back in the small zip compartment on the front of the bag after she had taken it out a few times to show a few people. Her hand felt the zip, it was already open. She felt her heart rate quicken, the flap was hanging down, the pocket empty. It didn't stop her from putting her hand in the space just in case by some miracle it had stuck to the wall of the pocket. It wasn't there! She couldn't believe it, she had been so careful. It was the only link, the only chance of finding him and now it was lost.

"Martha?"

"It's gone. It was here in my bag, the photo, it was here and now it's gone. I zipped it up, I wouldn't have been so careless. Would I?"

"Martha, take a breath, you are breathing too hard. Do you have another photograph?"

Martha shook her head. However, she did have another photograph, not of him but of her father and the similarities had been strong enough for her to have come all this way. She should have brought it, but she had decided against it, so it was in her bedside cabinet where she had kept it for the last thirty years.

The tea arrived just as Martha realised that she needed to come clean with John about what she was doing since, after all, Seth hopefully still had the photo on his camera. She sipped her tea and for the second time in as many days she told the story of the photograph and also of the circumstances that had led up to it, starting with giving her baby away. She felt the presence of Evie by her side as she laid her life bare in front of this strange but kind woman. And just as Evie hadn't judged her, neither did Roz who sat patiently and quietly as Martha recounted her story. By the time she had finished, a second cup of tea had somehow appeared in front of her without her noticing.

"Go back down tonight, ask around if anyone has seen the photograph. You were planning to go home tomorrow anyway so you could fax me a copy of the photo. I can have a look and if I don't recognise him I will ask around. Now I think you could do with a rest, you look worn out; don't underestimate the emotional impact all this has had on you. Go and have a lie down. I'll get one of the girls to give you a ring in a couple of hours. Then you can go back down to the café for supper and can ask if anyone has seen the photo and even if it comes nothing, you can have a lovely meal. However, it is usually a lot busier in the evening even at this time of the year so your chances would be a lot better because if he is a local, I would presume he would be working during the day. I would have joined you but I have a fundraiser coming up on the weekend and I have some running around to do. I get the feeling though that you are more than happy in your own company. So, do we have a plan?"

Martha nodded, clasping the woman's hands in her own.

She then made her way up the winding staircase, feeling a lot happier than she had an hour ago.

Less than three hours later, Martha was up and showered and dressed in the only decent item of clothing she had brought with her. It was a pretty dress, vintage, green and blues. The greens matched the colour of her eyes. She teamed it with thick tights and flat boots. She even applied a small amount of make-up, after all it was after six-thirty in the evening. She looked at her reflection in the dressing table mirror and deemed herself to be presentable. She still couldn't tame her wild curls and thought of asking to borrow some hairspray but decided against it. She left the room and headed for the same destination as she had attended less than twelve hours previously.

She took a taxi this time, the driver was a pleasant chap and chatted all the way, pointing out landmarks and places of interest along the route. His attitude was totally different to the taxi driver back home who had been indifferent to the point of rudeness. She thanked the driver and gave him a generous tip. It made her think of the film *Pretty Woman* when the shop assistants refused to serve Julia Roberts. It never failed to amaze her, the attitude of some people in the service industry. She wasn't rich but she did at least have some amount of disposable income. She often felt invisible when shopping; although she didn't want the shop assistants fawning over her, she thought some plain courtesy was always a good start.

The wind had picked up again. It wasn't exactly howling – more a significant murmur. She wondered if they would be having a repeat of the morning's storm. She pulled her woollen coat tighter around her. The walk from the car to the café was less than twenty feet but it felt much longer as she battled the elements. As she hurried across the gravel path the wind brushed her lips leaving a kiss laced with saltiness.

She jolted at the sudden memory of sitting on her father's lap and being told the story of the king and the container of salt. She wiped it away with the back of her hand, not willing to remember the man she had loved once upon a time.

She blustered into the café making quite an entrance as the wind howled at her heels. She closed the door of the café and brushed the sand and moisture from her best coat. There was a different atmosphere to the day and Roz was right, it was far busier, nearly every table was taken, but she didn't mind – she could wait until one became available. She had often dined alone, it didn't bother her but she sometimes felt that the restaurant owners felt short-changed by her taking a table meant for two. She made her way to the bar to see how long she would have to wait to be seated. The room was lit by the fairy lights hanging in abundance from the oak beams on the ceiling. The fishermen's rope nets that were hung along the walls had pretty, interwoven flower lights making it look as though the catch of the day was wild blooms. The tables had gently flickering candles. A waitress approached her from behind the small bar and asked Martha's name. Martha explained that she hadn't booked and was more than happy to wait in the bar area. However, she was immediately escorted directly to a lovely table that overlooked the beach and even though it was dark outside, she could make out the sand and sea from the multitude of hurricane lamps on the decking. The waitress explained that Roz had rung through and booked the table for her. Martha was touched and felt a childish delight in her special treatment. She didn't recognise any of the staff from earlier and felt a surge of hope that if the photograph could be located maybe one of them would know him. The waitress who had escorted her to her table returned with a bottle of water and a menu.

"I was here this afternoon. I had a photograph which I think I may have left here. Has anyone handed it in by any chance?"

"I don't know, I only came on an hour ago, let me go and ask and then I'll come back to get your order."

Martha thanked her and held her breath in the hope that the photograph was stuck up somewhere behind the bar. However, there was something that made her think it was almost as if it had been spirited away. She wasn't usually given to such fanciful ideas but there was something about this country that changed her. She had thought she had been so careful putting it back in the front pocket; she could have sworn that she zipped the pocket back up. The waitress returned empty-handed.

"I'm sorry, we've looked everywhere in the lost property, which if I'm honest is a very small cardboard box full of beach toys, we did empty it, but there wasn't a photo. The chef that was on this afternoon has gone on holiday and won't be back for a couple of weeks, but if we take your name and address we could post it on to you if he knows where it is."

"That's very kind. Thank you I would appreciate that."

"No problem. Now what would you like to drink?"

"A glass of white wine, preferably dry please."

The young girl nodded and headed towards the bar

Martha watched as she picked up a large wine glass and pulled a bottle of white wine from the wine cooler opposite; she had a relaxed easy manner, confident in her place in the world. Martha realised that she had never really felt like that. She had been embarrassed by her mother's dominance over her father and it had left her reluctant to let her friends into her home life. Even when she had been in university she hadn't opened herself up to the world around her. She guessed it was why she had fallen for her lecturer; he didn't want to come to her home for obvious reasons, instead he had shown her a world where she was an equal. She now felt robbed that his actions had resulted in her dropping out of university. Even though he had taken an unexpected sabbatical it had been too painful for her to finish her degree. Of course, in the end it was the decree of her parents that had decided her subsequent course of action. Out of the whole mess, the only thing she felt proud of was not bowing down to having the abortion. She was trying make things right by looking for him but was it for his sake or hers?

Who was she doing all this for? She didn't actually know, should she be here now in this city if she couldn't answer that simple question? What right did she have to turn his life upside down, maybe he didn't even know he was adopted. She was looking to re-write history but did she actually have the right? The only thing she could actually do to address the past was to finish her degree; it would hurt no-one and maybe it would give her a sense of closure. Evie had always chastised her for not going back to uni; she had been the only person to know the real reason and she had been true to her word and never breathed it to a soul, even though Martha knew she had desperately wanted to tell John.

"Oh, you were deep in thought then I didn't want to disturb you. This is a medium white I hope that's OK? I can change it if you don't like it, but I think it's the driest wine we have."

"I think you may have a slightly drier wine. Do you have any champagne?"

"Yes, of course we do. I'll change this for you now."

"No don't worry, just bring me a bottle of champagne as well!"

"I like your style!"

The waitress hurried back to the bar. Martha smiled. She was going to enrol in the local university when she got home and finish the course she started all those years ago. She had to admit she quite liked her style as well.

Sand: Cohesion
(the action or fact of forming a united whole)

A young girl had gone missing. No-one had seen her since she had left the house for school that morning. She was seventeen years old. The parents were frantic – she was their only child. Concern as to her whereabouts was growing, word spread through the town carried on the strengthening wind. It permeated homes, hotels and the local clubs and pubs. The police were investigating several leads. Her disappearance was completely out of character. A lot of guesswork was taking place, facts appeared to be irrelevant because people "knew" people and gossip was always much more exciting than the truth. Some decided she had had a row with her boyfriend, this was regardless of the fact that no-one actually knew If she had one. The men's darts team currently beating their rivals from Pontypridd thought that she had simply run away from home after a family row. Her friends were concerned that they had missed something crucial and were relaying every conversation they had had with her during the previous few days. Some of her teachers felt that she had been a little quiet of late. All conjecture with little known facts and no idea where a young girl might have gone to on a cold February night.

Alice
February 2015, Wales

She told the seashell her story,
Whispering every secret her memories held.
Then she laid the shell at the ocean's edge
And watched the tide pick it up and carry it out to sea.

Unknown

Alice sat on the edge of her bed and wiped the tears from her face for the second time. She would have to re-apply her mascara once more, it was just like painting over the cracks. Tom was due in half an hour, in little more than an hour she would have to start explaining that she had to go to London at short notice. She had concocted a story that would allow her some breathing time – time away from Tom so she could let him go. He would thank her in the long run as Harry had done. She had originally intended on staying until the end of the month but now with this meal booked she needed to speed things up; she had a horrible feeling that he was going to ask her to move in with him. She knew that her time with him had run its course. It was why she had decided to leave Wales and find somewhere new to go to. She knew that if she didn't leave, he would find out what she had done; she couldn't bear that and would rather die than see the revulsion on his face. He had sounded so happy and excited, she wondered if he had been promoted again. Her mascara stayed put this time, she guessed she had just run out of tears which was inevitable after all the ones she had shed.

She thought she had known love, but it wasn't what she had experienced before; it was so different with Tom. She knew with Tom it was never going to end unless she did something about it. She needed to take the control back since she had allowed herself to be drawn into the possibility of a normal life, but for her that was never going to happen. The only person she had confided in was Hannah. Super-smart Hannah, who was never one to let sentiment get in the way of her decisions.

She thought back to their conversation the previous night when she had made supper for them both and they had gradually worked their way through two bottles of red wine. It had loosened both their tongues and Alice had found herself opening up to Hannah. She didn't tell Hannah the whole story or anything even close to it but she had alluded to the fact that she had a dark secret she was hiding.

"Do you love him enough?" Hannah asked.

"What do you mean, surely you either love someone or you don't?" she replied.

"Well, obviously not. Otherwise we wouldn't be having this conversation. This is the real world, Alice, not some fairy tale. Life is complicated, so we need to examine the facts of your situation. In order for you to move on from your past mistakes you need your relationship with Tom to be robust. Do you feel you don't trust him to feel the same about you if he knew your past history?"

"I can't tell you or him Hannah; it's something that I find hard to come to terms with myself. I may never feel strong enough to tell anyone."

"Look, I don't care what it is you have supposedly done. Knowing you as I do, I have probably either done 'it' or something worse than 'it'. It is just a matter of perspective, Alice, and I think you are being too sensitive to look at it with enough detachment."

It had shaken her then, even after a bottle of wine dulling her senses. Hannah thought she was the outlandish one, the one who didn't do regrets. She had no idea and Alice hoped she never would. Hannah would never even come close to the awful thing that she had done. It had sobered her into the realisation that she would never be able to walk away from her past. She would have to try and stay a few steps ahead for the foreseeable future. It answered Hannah's question, she did love him enough, more than enough – she loved him too much. However, for her it meant that she would have to leave him behind; she didn't want to see the repulsion on his face when he found out what she had done, it would kill her, it would be too much for her to bear.

For Hannah life was simple, there were no grey areas, her approach to life was like that of a game of chess. It was a battle against numerous opponents, to survive you had to beat your adversary and move on to the next battle. No grey areas, just black and white like the checkerboard on which the battles were fought. Hannah had started an affair with one of her lecturers in the university where she was doing her PhD. It had lasted for more than a year, then she had stopped seeing him. He had decided to go back to his wife. Hannah had been matter of fact about it; for her, the battle was lost the minute his guilt over his wife overtook the feelings he had for her. She had walked away without a second glance. The lecturer, surprised at her detachment, had changed his mind and begged her forgiveness but she had remained steadfast in her decision. As with any good chess player, you had to look not just at the next move but several moves ahead.

So tonight, as she got ready, all this played through her mind. She wanted to be more like Hannah, but she guessed even Hannah would struggle with what she had done. It was one of the main reasons she had never been able to tell her, although she had come close once or twice. Hannah wasn't good at false emotions. In the end it didn't matter what anyone else thought, she had bestowed on herself her own punishment.

Tom wanted to take her out for a nice meal, not unusual in itself, but she had a bad feeling about the evening. The weather was awful, she said she preferred to stay at home and had offered to cook instead. He had been insistent though, he had some good news – they needed to go out and celebrate. She wondered if he had made the decision to move from the law firm where he currently worked to the one in Cardiff which had been trying to poach him for a few months. She opened her wardrobe sifting through her clothes for something suitable to wear. What was the dress of choice for the last meal with your lover before you left him without a backward glance or any sort of explanation as to why? She knew she had little choice, she knew how deep Tom's feelings ran for her and realised that she could never have the strength to tell him that she didn't love him – it was as far from the truth as the Arctic is from the Antarctic. She pulled out a short woollen dress in a soft grey, it suited her sombre mood. She pulled on a pair of thick grey tights. The only concession she made to colour in her palate of grey was a bright green scarf which she looped around her neck. She had lied to Hannah and had told her she obviously didn't love him enough. So, they had devised a plan. She would tell him that she had to go back to London at short notice to help out a friend. He would offer to help, so they discussed how she could initially appear keen about him coming to London and then, once she was there, she would make excuses until he finally got the message. As Hannah had said, once she was out of Wales it would be easier. She didn't know how wrong she was. Alice pulled on her long black boots, brushed her curls until they shone and then waited to see the man she loved for the last time.

She didn't look at the calendar that was hanging on a magnet on the fridge door. She had been far too preoccupied to notice the changes he had made. They would circle dates in red that they planned spending together, adding a little emoji with a knife and fork if they were going out for dinner or a snorkel if they were going to the pool. It was silly and childish which made them love it all the more. If she had not been so preoccupied with leaving Tom, she would have noticed two things. Firstly it was exactly four months to the date that they had met and there was a little red circle with an emoji holding the number four. Secondly, underneath was another emoji holding one word – "Ever".

She walked out the door knowing that tonight would change her life for ever. She felt weighed down by the enormity of her secrets and wished not for the first time that she had the courage to tell someone, to unburden herself. As a child she had loved playing the game Buckaroo. She thought of that poor plastic horse standing stock still as the players loaded him up with saddle bag, pick-axe and other items. When it all got too much, he would buck and the load would be thrown off. Now, as an adult, she understood it from a different perspective, when the load got too much, the results were always a mess.

Tom
February 2015, Wales

Just as the sand dunes heaped one upon another, hide each the first,
So in life the former deeds are quickly hidden by those that follow after.

Marcus Aurelius

Tom felt a little less sure of the situation now as he sat opposite
Alice. At six that morning he had woken up excited at the day
ahead. At ten, he had been at his Mum's, showing her the ring.
At midday when he knew Alice was in work, he had laid a few
clues in her house; he hadn't minded if she saw them or not,
he had just enjoyed the process. Hannah had been a little odd,
but then he had always found her a little strange. She had been
taking the dogs for a walk and had come back just as he was
leaving Alice's house. She seemed to feel the need to remind him
that Alice was at work. He had just said that he knew and they
had both left it at that. By the early afternoon, he was decorating
his house with bunting, which he knew she loved, and had put
two bottles of champagne in the fridge. He had tried to make
one of those towel-sculpture things they made in hotels but his

just kept looking like a skinny chicken so he decided to fold it neatly and laid four red roses on the top. A photo-book was on the kitchen table with an account of the happiest times of his life, all of them with Alice in the last four months. Febus had had an extra-long walk to tire him out. He would make a fuss of Alice as he always did, but he would soon settle.

As a starter, he had the rainbow terrine, venison, beetroot, spinach and sweet potato. It reminded him of the colours of the sands on the Isle of Wight. Alice had mini Moussaka's – baby aubergines stuffed with wafer-thin slices of potatoes, lamb shavings, tomatoes and spices topped with a creamy soufflé sauce.

"I've wanted to bring you here for ages," he said.

"It's a lovely place and the food is amazing. Tom, I wanted to talk to you about Kathryn."

He felt the mood tilt just slightly away from his expectation. What was wrong – they seemed tense with each other as though they had been given different scripts in a play but Broadway was expecting them to produce a smash hit. He needed to regain the momentum. Originally, he had intended on asking her after their main meals but he felt that if he left it any longer he would lose the opportunity. She had already missed the calendar and the CD in the car playing the song that had become their own. She hadn't even noticed. He knew it was now or never, too much doubt was forming for him to leave it till the end of the meal.

"Alice."

He stood up and was reaching into the pocket of his suit jacket, the blue lining shimmering in the subdued lighting. Alice was looking at him, not moving her eyes away from his hand that was reaching into his jacket pocket. The restaurant was suddenly quiet; the other customers had noticed. The quiet was immediately shattered as two policemen burst in. Tom remained in the same position with his hand around the pale-blue velvet box in his pocket, doing what looked like an impression of Lord Nelson.

The police asked for quiet. Tom sat down, removed his hand and placed it in his lap, empty. Tom recognised the older of the two policemen and knew his name was Phil. He was a nice man due to retire at the end of the year but the younger one he had never seen before. Phil spoke to the customers and the staff who had gathered at the back of the restaurant. It reminded Tom of his school assemblies.

"A young local girl has gone missing. She left the house as usual to go to school but she never got there. We are concerned as to her whereabouts. Several searches are being organised. We would like anyone with suitable outdoor attire and who are physically able to join in. Sam here has copies of a photo of her which he will hand out. The weather forecasters have posted a weather warning for adverse conditions similar to this morning so please only join in if you are fit as we don't want to spend valuable time looking for you as well. According to her parents, there is no boyfriend and she is a straight-A student; this is completely out of character for her. She has a passion for being by the sea and loves all the local beaches, so it's where we are concentrating our searches. The CCTV cameras in the area have been reviewed and there has been a possible sighting here at around 2.30pm. It is now almost 8pm."

He didn't say any more but allowed the time-gap between the possible sighting of her and the interval of five hours sink in.

"Do you mind if I go and help?" Tom asked.

"Of course not, I would offer to come too but these boots are too high to go traipsing across beaches. Her poor parents must be beside themselves."

As she spoke, the pictures of the young girl were circulating in the restaurant. The chatter had resumed but now was focused on the drama. Tom was handed a picture by the stout man at the table opposite. He looked at the young girl and recognised her instantly. It was Lilly, the daughter of one of his partners at the firm. Dear God, Bill and Pauline must be out of their minds with worry.

"I know her Alice; she is the daughter of Bill, one of my bosses. I can't imagine what they must be going through."

"Oh God, that's awful Tom, you go and see what you can do. I'll wait here and help where I can."

"OK thanks. I wanted to…"

He stopped suddenly unsure of what to say next. His own concerns seemed trivial compared to the situation unfolding in front of him.

"I love you."

"I love you too, Tom."

As he walked away from her to join the group mustering by the park, he remembered the look on her face as he had stood up to propose to her. It was fear. Why was she afraid of him? It was the last emotion he had expected to see. Had he read all the signs incorrectly; she did have moments when he felt she was distant, but he had believed her when she told him she loved him. He couldn't work it out, had he just been saved from making a fool of himself? He zipped up his coat and walked out into the cold night leaving his own worries behind in the warmth of the restaurant and concentrated on the instructions the search co-ordinator was giving. He joined a group of men who were to take the south side of the beach. The pale-blue velvet box was still tucked safely in his pocket.

Martha
February 2015, Wales

What makes the desert beautiful
Is that somewhere it hides a well.

Antoine de Saint-Exupéry

Word of the missing girl had also reached the café on the beach. Martha sighed as she looked out of the window; the multitude of hurricane lamps flickered, giving her a snapshot of the inclement weather outside. Not the best night to go missing.

The worry about trying to find her first-born son suddenly seemed less pressing. She would try to help, offer her services either in the search or here at the café where they seemed to be setting up an impromptu headquarters. She got up to pay for the meal, leaving the coffee she had ordered untouched on the table. When she had first arrived, the café had been almost full. There had been a table of seven women who constantly seemed to be laughing at something or other but they were now deep in conference with the manager. Their faces all serious – the mirth of a moment ago all forgotten. There had

124

been several tables consisting of couples, some young and some old; some had already left before the announcement, but the ones who remained had split into two groups – those braving the weather and the others helping inside. There had been just one other table where there was a solitary diner like herself; a distinctive looking man who, like her, seemed comfortable in his own company. She watched as a young, tanned couple approached the solitary man and after a quick chat moved on to the muster point.

She decided to approach the man herself who she assumed was a local.

"Excuse me, were you thinking of joining the search?" she asked.

Up close, he was more handsome than she had first thought. It threw her; if she had realised how handsome he was, she would have simply made her way to the group of women who were now giving orders to anyone who would listen. He was muscular in an athletic sort of way, taller than her but a little shy of 6ft. He had short, silver-grey hair that had receded slightly at the edges. He was tanned in that outdoors sort of way which was characteristic of gardeners and builders. His eyes, although small, were a deep blue and sparkled with mischief.

"I have been designated head tea and coffee maker. I can see that you are disappointed that I am not going to be outside battling against the elements in some macho-heroic way."

Martha started to protest.

"It's quite all right, it's just that I am actually not as young as you might believe. I belong to the local choir where the combined age is almost a thousand. I'll leave you to work out how many of us there are."

"I'm no Carol Vorderman. English was always my strong subject at school."

"Well, 'not Carol Vorderman', there are more than ten and less than twenty. So now that we've sorted that out, are you leaving us in our hour of need or can I count on you to keep an eye on me in the laborious task of kettle boiling?"

"Yes, that was what I was trying to ask."

"In your reserved English manner."

"Exactly."

"OK then. I'm Edward and I have the pleasure of meeting…?"

"Martha."

"Very well, Martha. Shall we make our way to the kitchen to hunt down those kettles to keep our young men and women refreshed during their search?"

Nodding, she followed Edward into the kitchen.

They worked for the next couple of hours barely having time to talk as the search parties returned for a quick warm up and a cup of something hot. The weather was re-enacting its scene-stealing show of that morning. Everyone was windswept and exhausted. The co-ordinator of the search was asking for it to be called off until the weather conditions improved. He was shouted down by everyone declaring they wouldn't give up until she was found. So they carried on.

"Martha, a few of my friends have come down from Langland and are going to take over the teas and coffees for a while. Come and sit down, you need a rest."

He picked up two mugs of steaming white coffee and guided her to the back of the café. She suddenly felt like a schoolgirl out on her first date but tried not to think about where that had got her.

"So," he said, "What brings you to Swansea on a cold February night? You really are not seeing us at our best."

"You mean it doesn't rain like this all the time?"

"Of course not."

"Well that's a relief."

"No, it doesn't rain like this all the time. We have many different types of rain. We have spring rain, summer rain followed by autumn rain and then of course you are now experiencing our winter rain."

She laughed.

"Which is your favourite?" she asked.

"That's a very good question. It used to be the spring rain; it always seemed full of new beginnings. But now the winter rain appears to be full of new beginnings."

She blushed.

"So, Martha, at the risk of causing you to blush once more, what is a beautiful woman doing far away from home in the middle of our rainy season?"

This time she didn't blush. They had both talked a little about being widowed. He didn't have any children, she noticed the regret that had laced the statement; it obviously hadn't been a conscious choice. She had told him about John and then she had paused trying to make up the reason she was in Wales on a cold February night. When she thought about it afterwards, she didn't honestly know whether it was because she couldn't come up with a story or whether she was just too tired to hide it anymore. In any event, she told him the truth – told him everything from the very beginning.

She felt it was like having an old jumper; you were familiar with it, comfortable with it, you felt safe in it. Then it began to unravel, until the piece of clothing that it had once been was gone and all that was left was a large ball of wool. She had always worried what would be left for her once it was undone but had never thought that it could be made into something else.

They sat together, knees almost touching under the table, the coffee now cold.

It took me a year to leave. It would have been his first birthday, there should have been other children and other parents, cake and balloons. We should have been singing happy birthday but instead there was silence punctuated only by the ticking of that damned kitchen clock. My mother loved that clock, reminding us all of each joyless second in that miserable house. Years later, I wanted to have piano lessons but the teacher had one of those metronomes. As soon as he started it ticking it brought back those awful memories of that soulless house. Needless to say, I can still only play chopsticks.

"But you went on to marry and have your son."

"Yes, my second son."

"I'm sorry Martha, that was insensitive of me."

"No, it wasn't Edward. It's just that in a way he has been a secret for so long and that was my fault, and I need to make up for it."

"So how did you end up here?"

She told him about John and her grandchildren and the loss of Evie. Then she told him about the photograph.

"You probably think I'm really stupid embarking on this wild goose chase."

"Actually, I think that you're very brave."

As no-one else had known of her actions, she had, until now, made her own evaluation of her trip and hadn't canvassed anybody else for their views.

"Do you really think so? I feel rather foolish sitting here telling you in the cold light of day."

"It's actually kind of dark and in the middle of the night."

They both laughed.

"So, you have searched and I would guess that you have had no luck. What is your next move?"

"I didn't make a plan B."

"Can I make a suggestion then?"

She nodded.

"Stay on here a little longer and I'll see what I can do to help you. We can try and find out if he is a local or was just visiting. Do you have the photograph on you?"

"No, I was so careful with it but I seem to have lost it. I can get a copy but it means me having to tell John the real reason for me being away. I was due to book out tomorrow but I suppose I could stay on. I'll have to tell John something though. I can't tell him on the phone that he has a half-brother."

"OK, but you could tell him that it is something to do with family, maybe an aunt or cousin? Where are you staying?"

"At the Sea Breeze, a few miles from here."

"Does the proprietor have magnificently crafted hair that wouldn't move even in a force nine hurricane?"

"You know her?"

"The delectable Roz; yes she's actually a very good friend of mine. A meddling, nosey one which is just the type you need."

"Are you sure that you have the time. I don't want to impose?"

"Time is something I have plenty of. I retired eighteen months ago and to be honest I'm bored already. I always did have a low boredom threshold, it's why I got into so much trouble in school and university." He winked at her. "After Olivia died, work suddenly didn't seem so important. I finished the projects I had been working on and left without any regrets, so I've been working through a sort of alphabet of hobbies. I started with art – spending hours here on the beach."

"Were you any good?"

"Absolutely not! So I moved onto the 'Bs', but baton twirling and boxing didn't work out very well either."

Martha laughed, she liked the fact that he didn't take himself too seriously. She could learn a few lessons from him.

So she told him what had been running through her mind.

"As I said, I was in uni studying English when I fell pregnant. Whatever happens in relation to my search for my son, I have decided to finish my degree. It feels the right thing to do – sort of tying up all the loose ends."

"That's a fantastic idea."

"I'm sure I've still got my notes on parchment somewhere!"

"You've made me think about something that I have always wanted to do."

"Which is?"

"Sailing around the world, not having a specific destination in mind but just pointing the boat to the horizon and seeing where it takes me. I would have done it years ago but Olivia suffered from the most awful seasickness. Her mother used to joke that when she was a baby she would cry when she rocked the crib, not the other way around. Do you get seasick, Martha?"

Had she imagined the twinkle in his eye? It was this magical country that seemed to expand the boundaries of her reality.

"No, Edward I don't."

"That's good. I think we have a plan. You can stay on for as long as it takes to find out what we can about the boy in the photograph. During that time, I can wine and dine you and try and persuade you to postpone your degree while you sail the seven seas with me. Now, however, I'd better go and see if there is any news. Don't go anywhere."

"I'll be here."

"I'm so glad that we met Martha. I think our paths were meant to cross. Of course, the circumstances are so very sad."

And with that he left, leaving her wondering whether he meant the young girl going missing or the loss of her son.

Alice
February 2015, Wales

On these sands and in the clefts of the rocks,
In the depths of the sea,
In the creaking of the pines,
You'll spy secret footprints and catch far-off voices
from the homecoming celebration.
This land still longs for Odysseus.

Homer

Alice was still at Genaro's. It was almost two hours since the search had begun and intermittently groups of search parties were coming back for the free refreshments kindly provided by Genaro himself. She had been glad of the distraction. She neatly lined up the polystyrene cups as if their regimental order would help with the turmoil inside her. He was going to propose, how on earth had she got it so wrong; she knew he had strong feelings for her, for God's sake, she mirrored them, but a proposal – she hadn't seen that coming! She had been right to leave and this made it crystal clear that she needed to go. Once tonight was over, hopefully with the young girl safely home, she would leave, even if it was during the early hours of the morning. She had little choice now the game had changed. She looked out the back window of the restaurant kitchen. The weather was getting worse, the rain pounding the streets and pavements with the drum of a marching army. She looked at her line of polystyrene soldiers and with a swipe of her hand knocked them to the floor.

There was a loud howl and she jumped as the kitchen door was flung open. A group of men stood in the mouth of the doorway, the wind howling at their heels. The rain had stopped as abruptly as it had started but it had been replaced by winds verging on hurricane force.

"Tea or coffee?" she asked.

"Two coffees and three teas please, love," answered one of the men.

She poured out the teas from a large metal teapot and spooned coffee into two cups.

"There you go. The milk and sugar are on the table behind you."

All the men thanked her one by one as they picked up the steaming cups. They all looked tired.

She lined up more of her cups and watched as the men gulped down their hot drinks. She wondered not for the first time how Tom was doing and was briefly tempted to ask the group if they had seen him but something stopped her. As the last man exited, she heard him talk to a woman near the back door.

"We are beginning to think the worst. There haven't been any sightings of her for over seven hours. We should have found something. Her friends are adamant that she is not hiding out in one of their houses and by all accounts there seems to be no reason at all for her to run away. Good grades, no boyfriend and she does volunteer work at the local homeless shelter. So, where is she?"

"A row with her parents maybe?"

"Possibly, but the word seems to be they all have a great relationship. The perfect family or so it would seem. We both know that's bollocks, Mary. There is no such thing."

"Well, whatever it was, you still need to find her and soon."

"I agree, but to be honest, the weather is against us. It if it deteriorates any further they may call the search off. There was talk earlier of calling out the lifeguard as the last sighting was by the beach."

There was little more to be said. Alice watched as the man caught up with the rest of the group.

Tom

As I walk towards the north
On these lone and level sands,
I realise, while going forth:
There's no one to hold my hands.

All I want is something to eat,
I need nothing much.
Something to quench my thirst with,
No company or such.

Amandeep Bage

Tom was cold to his bones. The wind seemed to push right through his skin, as though it was no barrier. He moved his arms up and down then in a circular motion to try and create some warmth. He knew that if he didn't warm up soon he would have to go back; exposure was a threat he shouldn't ignore. He promised himself a reprieve in ten minutes – that should give him enough time to search this portion of the beach. His lips were sore, salty from the wind's persistence. It wasn't the physical aspects that tired him, he felt unsettled. He couldn't shake off the look on Alice's face when he had stood up to propose. She had looked terrified. He could recall the look so well it was as if he had a photograph in front of him.

He had expected surprise to a certain extent, maybe even some nervousness, but he had never expected fear.

She could be a little aloof at times, but he hadn't dwelt on it. He realised too late now that he should have tackled her about her past. He had long suspected there was so much she wasn't telling him but he had glossed over it, packed it away like one of his files. The problem was he knew at the time that he should have addressed it. He above all should know that we are all products of what has gone before; it can change us, define us or break us. What it doesn't do is to go away without leaving some sort of mark. She wanted a blank sheet on which to create a new life; what she hadn't realised was that the pages were still there from the old one.

The rain, reluctant to leave the beach, had saturated the sand underfoot. The cold air hung around him like an unwanted friend. His search group had scoured the eastern portion of the beach and were now slowly working their way back to the promenade. A few had returned to Genaro's for a rest and a hot drink. Tom promised himself the same but kept putting it off. A part of him knew that he was nervous of seeing Alice. He didn't have the stomach to see that same look on her face once more. It was easier to blank it out and keep on searching. He was cross with himself – shouldn't he have read the clues more carefully, after all he was in the business of evidence gathering.

The portion of the beach he was now on was perilous in the dark. It was littered with rock pools, dressed up for the occasion in wigs of slippery seaweed. Limpets clung on to the surface of the rocks like a destruction of tiny daleks. He moved slowly across the sand, lighting the way with the large torch as he went. He used a stick to feel his way beyond the arc of light.

The plan for the groups on this part of the beach was to move in a circuitous route so that they would eventually return to the starting point after having examined that particular portion of the beach. As he moved forward, he was glad the wind had at last changed its mind and was now behind him, helping to push him forward. Tom felt completely isolated as the group of six men were now far apart from each other. The rain had stopped as though the wind had won the competition for supremacy and it howled in celebration. In all the noise the silence was acute; he couldn't stop thinking about Alice. The terrain was becoming trickier, there were now mostly rock pools, with black shimmering bodies. The surface was slippery and uneven. Alice pushed through his concentration at every opportunity.

It took only a split second, a momentary lapse of concentration, for it all to go horribly wrong. The pain was acute. It shot up his leg quicker than a greyhound out of a trap. He cursed, then dropped the torch as the pain increased. The beam shone away from him. He couldn't see the damage to his foot but he knew that it wasn't good; he realised he was in real trouble. He crouched down to try and see if he could grab the torch; it was just out of reach and he only managed to touch the very end of it. He tried again, but leant too far forward and in the process, he lost his balance and fell forwards. He was soaking wet. The salty water permeated every layer of his clothing. As he put his hands out to try and pull himself up, he felt the silky fronds of the seaweed pass through his fingers. In the darkness, he tried to process the information. The seaweed felt too silky. He felt it again. It was hair – long hair. He grabbed for the torch and this time managed to keep hold of it. He shone it across the surface and there, like Ophelia, lying in a shallow pool of water with her hair spread out beyond her was a young girl. There was no movement at all from her. He couldn't see any rhythmic rise and fall of her chest. He was terrified that he was too late and that she was already dead.

Evie
February 2013, England

Are we etched in stone or just scratched in the sand
Waiting for the waves to come and reclaim the land.

'Tightrope', Stone Roses
John Squire

The party had been a resounding success and had gone on much later
than she had anticipated. Travis had become an old friend overnight; she
had watched as he and John had worked their way through a bottle of
Jameson's whiskey. Today though, John was paying the price for trying
to keep up with his new friend and she was paying the price for all her
efforts. She lay on the sofa, the cushions squashed up beside her, a mug
of steaming sweet, milky coffee in her hands. She held the mug in both
hands, not so much for any other reason than it gave her comfort; she
couldn't face drinking it. Her breakfast lay untouched on the coffee table
in front of her. A soft poached egg on lightly buttered wholemeal toast,
her favourite breakfast. It had been the first meal that John had made
for her on their honeymoon, but now she couldn't look at it without
feeling nauseous. She was just overtired that was all, it would pass. She
put her head on one of the pillows whilst still holding on to the mug,
unwilling to lose the comfort of it. She felt a hot, fat tear roll down her

cheek. Why was she crying, today when everything had gone so well? Maybe it was because it had gone so well. She looked at her mother-in-law's back as she cleared up the mess from the party. Martha had arrived like the force of nature that she was, rubber gloves on, ready to do battle on the debris from the party. Evie loved her mother-in-law but sometimes she wished that she wasn't quite so capable. In her current state, it made her feel that she wasn't making the grade.

She pulled the letter from behind the cushion where she had hidden it when Martha had marched in. She smoothed out the creases. She had read it several times already and knew the contents by heart but that didn't deter from the pleasure of reading it once more. She should feel guilty, particularly since Martha was hovering in the next room. She was too tired and overwrought to feel guilty; she already had a multitude of emotions, there was no room for any more. As soon as Martha left, she would reply; she was desperate to meet with him again but her course of treatment made it difficult. She knew part of the reason was that she wanted to look her best, it was funny how her vanity had only become evident as she was losing her looks. Or did she just want everyone to remember her at her best? She felt her head; the hair was growing back, it felt soft and velvety. The dryness of her skin had improved as well, it was such a shame that her prognosis hadn't been so encouraging.

"Not hungry, love?" asked Martha.

Evie had been so lost in her thoughts that she hadn't heard the hoover being switched off and Martha coming in. She quickly pushed the letter between the cushions.

"No, sorry, I can't face it this morning. You shouldn't have taken the day off, Martha. I could have sorted it all out."

They both knew that she didn't have the energy to undertake the task.

"It's no trouble. I had a bit of a lie-in myself which was good. Dear God, Evie, that man can drink. I don't know where he put it and he didn't even seem a bit tipsy. I bet John is feeling under the weather today."

"Yes, I think he was feeling even worse than me when he left for work this morning. He's struggling, Martha."

They both knew that she wasn't referring to his hangover any more. Martha sat down by her side.

"Have you managed to talk?"

"No. He refuses to discuss the possibility of me not being here next year. It's as if he believes that not talking about it means that it isn't happening. I need his support. There are so many things he needs to know, the children, my funeral, everything needs discussing, but every time I try, he shuts me down."

"Do you think it's also because he doesn't want you to have to worry about it, what I mean is – he wants to protect you, Evie, he always has. I know he doesn't want to face the situation, but he doesn't want you to face it either."

"Neither of us has a choice. I can't pretend it's not happening, Martha; every time I look in the mirror there is less of me both physically and mentally. But at the moment, I can deal with it. Soon enough the time will come when I can't."

"I will talk to him."

Evie knew that she had finally made her point and felt that maybe now she and John would be able to have a frank conversation about her wishes. She remembered something.

"Martha, when you talk to him tell him I want to have a Fred conversation; he'll know what I mean."

When they had first married and had had the inevitable arguments, she was always the peacemaker. She would leave him a little note saying that they needed to have an open and frank discussion about the disagreement. A few years on after Seth was born, she had been exhausted with the new baby and had not had the energy to be the peace envoy after a rather heated argument. That night, after she had put Seth to bed, she found a note at the side of the crib. It asked her if they could have "an open Fred conversation as Frank was otherwise engaged". She had laughed out loud.

Martha didn't ask for an explanation, but just agreed.

Feeling unburdened and less nauseous than she had all morning, Evie wanted to talk about the success of the party the day before.

"What do you think of the hunky Texan?"

"I know – where on earth did she find him?"

"On one of her field trips. I was supposed to go but I don't think John would have been very pleased if I'd have brought him back."

Both women laughed. Evie blushed as she thought about Nathan, but that was different and she wouldn't allow herself to feel guilty, there was simply no room.

"How kind of him to bring a ton of sand with him," Martha said.

They giggled at the memory of the sand being sculpted by him on the kitchen floor.

"He was well prepared though, with the tarpaulin down first and that funny little hoover thing he had."

"Oh so many things have popped into my head!"

"Martha!!"

"I know, I think it's the American accent. There is something very alluring about an accent!"

"I'll have to ask if he has an older brother."

"Or father more like."

"Or uncle, if the father is taken."

"Uncle, cousin or even grandfather, I'm not fussy!"

They both laughed knowing that Martha was actually incredibly fussy and had turned down any male interest in her for years.

Evie often thought her illness was just like being a drug addict; there were some incredible highs and lows. Any hope would see her shooting to great heights only for them to be dashed with a bad scan or blood results. It was the same if she was enjoying herself – the illness would nip at her ankles like an annoying dog pulling her back down into a low mood.

"Did I spend too much time working, should I have stayed at home more with the children?"

"Where did that come from, love?"

"I did love my job and it did take me away for a lot of the time. I tried to juggle everything and I don't know if I tipped the scales in the wrong direction."

Martha took Evie's hand.

"Pam had been nagging me to go and see this American evangelist. She knows my stance on the church and I suppose she was looking for another way to get me back into some sort of religion. I was dead against it. You know Pam though, she wouldn't let it go, so we tossed a coin! It's ridiculous really. Anyway, she won. I did ask to see the coin to make sure it wasn't a trick though. Anyway, he was your stereotypical American evangelist. He was quite tall with a deep tan and piercing blue eyes. He had an annoying habit of punctuating the end of every sentence with a "Hallelujah" which was echoed by the crowd. I was desperate to leave, it was way out of my comfort zone. Pam was in her element however, waving her arms in the air and praising the Lord with the best of them. Then he settled the crowd and began to tell a story. I was just glad of the quiet to be honest. The room was totally silent. When he wasn't shouting he had a rather nice voice and I closed my eyes as I listened to the story.

"Close your eyes Evie and relax."

Martha watched as Evie lay back on the sofa, hands still clasped around the coffee mug.

"A professor of philosophy was taking one of his classes. As the students filed in they saw a large empty glass jar on the desk in front of the professor. He waited for them to settle and then without saying a word, proceeded to fill the empty jar with rocks from a large rucksack. He stopped when he couldn't fit any more rocks in. He then turned to the class and asked them if they thought that the jar was full. They said yes, the jar was full. Again, not saying a word, he took out from the rucksack a bag of small pebbles, he dropped them into the jar and they fell easily into the spaces between the large rocks. He stopped when he couldn't fit any more pebbles in the jar. Again, he asked the students whether they thought the jar was full. This time there was a slight hesitation, but once more the class agreed that the jar was full. Then the professor pulled from the rucksack a bag of sand. He poured it into the jar filling up the tiny spaces left by the pebbles. This time the jar was full. The professor explained, "The jar symbolises your life. The rocks are the important things – family and friends, health and relationships. The pebbles signify smaller things like work. The sand is unimportant stuff like material possessions. If you put the sand in first there will be no room for the rocks or the pebbles."

Martha held onto Evie's hand.

"Even though you spent a lifetime working with your beloved sand, you always put the rocks in first."

Tom
February 2015, Wales

Come live with me and be my love,
And we will some new pleasures prove,
Of golden sands, and crystal brooks
With silken lines and silver hooks.

John Donne

Tom felt sick. The pain in his leg was beginning to cloud his judgment. He needed to try chest compressions on her; she might not be dead. He should try at least, then when they took her body away, he could say he had tried. His hands were so cold he wasn't sure if he was able to get them to listen to the instructions from his brain. He likened them to some frozen pipes in a house. He felt vomit rise into his mouth but swallowed it back. That would be great, vomiting on the still warm, dead body of a young girl. He leant over her and began to push down on her chest as he counted. Nothing – there was no response at all. She did still feel warm though, which, given the conditions gave him hope that she had only just stopped breathing. He continued pushing and counting.

He did consider shouting to see if anyone was near but he concentrated all his energy on her. Then to his amazement he heard her make a sound. He carried on in case it was some physiological response to his actions. He heard it again, clearer this time; he could now see the rise and fall of her chest, she was breathing on her own. He felt like crying both from relief and the fear of what could have been. The immediate problem was to get her back to safety. He fumbled around in his jacket pocket for his mobile but it had gone – probably lost in one of the rock pools. He didn't waste time on recriminations because he didn't have the time or capability to look for his mobile. Time was critical, he didn't know how long she hadn't been breathing for but she needed swift medical intervention. He pulled her to a sitting position, she was a dead weight and he struggled. Then he tried to stand, but the pain in his leg wouldn't allow him to put any weight on his right side. He manoeuvred her to his left, gently hauling her up. He was then able to slip his left arm under her arms holding her across the chest. Luckily, she was a small girl, less than 5ft 2in with a slender frame. She was, however, soaking wet. Her head flopped to the side as he moved her, so he re-positioned her, trying to put less strain on her neck. He needed some light, they were now both upright but it was pitch black and he had become so disorientated that he had no idea which direction led to the promenade. He couldn't just stand there holding her, he had to make a decision about which direction to go, even if it was the wrong one, because standing there in indecision was just as bad; they would both freeze to death.

He heard a faint hum. At first, he thought it was some sort of insect but it was a gentler, calmer sound. He turned to the direction from which the sound had seemed to come. He heard it again; it was definitely a humming sound, not exactly musical but there was a sweet resonance to it. This time there was no break in the sound, it continued gently dissolving the silence around it. He followed its direction, drawn to the haunting hum. He forgot about the pain in his leg and the weight of the girl he carried. He merely concentrated on the sound, hypnotised by it. As he moved forward inch by inch, the wind quieted as if it too listened to the melody. The darkness was lifting and he could see light up ahead; he was getting nearer to the promenade, he was going in the right direction. He was now on flat, hard sand, the rock pools behind him. The darkness had now abated and he could see the halos from the promenade lights. He waved his free arm hoping to alert one of the helpers lining the pavement. Someone had seen him. It wasn't until he was back on the sea front that he realised the sound had stopped.

Once they had been spotted, the rescue was swift. Within minutes, she had been checked over by a doctor and was on her way to the hospital. Only then did Tom relax; he had been concerned and anxious that he had possibly done more harm than good, it had been too dark and the conditions too raw for any sort of assessment of her condition. He sat on one of the benches that lined the promenade, clutching a hot cup of sweet tea. He wondered if Alice was still around or if she had gone home. One of the ambulance crew had wrapped him in a foil blanket; he was glad of it, he felt so cold. His hands were burning and painful. It was a lifelong problem which had necessitated his mother taking him back to the doctor time and time again but the cause of the problem had never really been explained. He rubbed his hands; the pain was worse than usual. He wanted to find Alice and go home for a rest but the paramedic asked him to wait so that they could have a look at his ankle. He knew the paramedic was right; the pain was worse and it was making him feel a little nauseous again. A few of the men in the search parties had come up and congratulated him for finding the girl. He thanked them, wondering what would have happened if he had missed her, he could easily have – in the dark and with the injury to his ankle. What would they have said to him then? The weight of it all settled on him. She would have been found on his patch of the beach the next morning by the ubiquitous dog walker and he would have forever felt he had let her down and also let himself down. He was more than likely just suffering from shock. It had been an eventful, stressful night – he still hadn't processed the failed proposal. He felt tired and so very cold, his head ached, his hands and feet burned as though they were on fire. He took a sip of the hot, sweet tea which scorched his cold lips. The wind had picked up again; he was cold and needed to get indoors. He looked around for some help but people seemed to be busy doing very little; there was a celebratory mood. He waved to a St John ambulance volunteer; he just needed someone to lean on and then he would be all right.

The mug slipped through his fingers and smashed into tiny pieces on the ground. Tom lay unconscious on the cold hard pavement, the remnants of the mug underneath him.

Sand: Accretion

(growth or increase by the gradual accumulation of additional layers or matter)

The response to Tom's collapse was immediate. He was examined and then taken to hospital within fifteen minutes. During the journey, he stopped breathing twice and had to be resuscitated. He was blue-lighted the rest of the way. They managed to stabilise him on arrival at the hospital and he was taken immediately to ITU where he was hooked up to a myriad of machines which bleeped like a binary orchestra.

Word spread across the town once more but this time it was good news; the young girl had been found and according to most accounts she would be fine. It depended on who you were talking to, as to whether she was desperately ill or on her way back home; either way there was a palpable sense of relief in the town. There was now a sense of celebration verging on the manic, most people having consumed more coffee in one night than they would have had in a week.

The news of Tom's collapse was slower and trickled through the town, like treacle from a sponge cake. It didn't reach Alice though. She waited for him for an hour or so after the girl was found, then went looking for the co-ordinator of the search to see if he could help. Tom's mother was about to find out where he was. The local police chief knew where he was but only because he had accompanied the young girl's parents to see her. She needed to be interviewed; why had she run and how had she ended up on the beach with a large gash on her forehead? As her bed was being moved from A&E to Ward 5, Tom was being taken to ITU. They had passed within a hair's breadth of each other. The rescued and the rescuer; it was as if they had swapped places.

Martha
February 2015, Wales

If you want to leave your footprints on the sands of time
Do not drag your feet.

A.P.J. Abdul Kalam

In the little café on the beach, the mood was euphoric as word reached them that the girl had been found safe and, if not well at this precise moment, she would be in a few days. A loud cheer rang out from the exhausted search teams and helpers alike; the relief was palpable.

"Well, Martha, are you going to stay for a few days? It would be good to spend some time together," said Edward.

"Yes."

And just like that, she felt all the hopes that life could hold laid out before her. She felt like one of Seth's pirates having come across a treasure chest laden with gold and jewels.

They left each other after arranging to meet up later that day. Both were tired and needed to catch up on the lost night's sleep. He booked a taxi for her and stood waving until she was out of sight. She settled back in the seat, replaying the night's events over and over in the privacy of her own mind. Each time the story had a happy ending just like the stories her father had told her as a child. She had been thinking more and more about him since she'd seen the photograph. She had made her peace with God and she was trying to make her peace with her lost baby. Maybe it was time she made her peace with him. She knew that until she did, she would always pick at the wound. In no time at all they were back at the bed and breakfast. The taxi driver refused to take any money because, after all, she had helped out with the search.

"But I didn't actually help look for her; I just made the teas and coffees."

"I drive for a living, love. It's me that knows where to go, but if I don't put fuel in my car, it doesn't go anywhere. Do you get what I'm saying?"

Martha nodded, she did.

"Then there is no charge."

She thanked him and got out of the car. The weather had improved considerably. The sun had arrived pushing the moon into submission, the pale disc replaced with a golden coin. She slammed the door, waving to the taxi driver as he left, and made her way up the narrow path; there were bits of debris scattered across the gravel. She felt grubby. She would have a long soak in the shower followed by a mug of hot chocolate and then some much needed sleep. As she entered the hall she saw Roz talking with one of the guests. Making her excuses, she came straight over to her slightly dishevelled guest.

"What an extraordinary night! I had a text last night from a very good friend of mine. Does the name Edward mean anything to you?"

"He said he was going to text you so you wouldn't worry about me. He's a lovely man, Roz."

"That he is. I'm glad that fate pushed you two together."

"Do you believe in fate?"

"Of course, don't you then?"

"I haven't thought about it for a long time. I guess I didn't want to think that the things that happened to me weren't by design – that would be too painful."

Roz took her hand and squeezed it.

"Look around you; the storm was awful. It had been building up for a few days and we all saw the brunt of it yesterday. Today though, did you see the beautiful sunrise? Life is a balance."

"I know, but sometimes the storms leave too much of a scar on the landscape."

"The scars are there to remind us. Are you seeing each other again?"

Martha felt herself blush like a teenager.

"Yes, but we both need to catch up on our sleep."

"Ooh, in different circumstances that would have a very different meaning!"

Martha blushed like a whole load of teenagers.

"I'm a respectable middle-aged woman," said Martha.

"Not for much longer if Edward has anything to do with it, he sounded quite smitten when I spoke to him half an hour ago. Go and get some rest, we'll have a proper chat later."

Martha hugged her and left. She was blushing so intensely, she felt she might spontaneously combust; the heat she was giving off would power the whole town should they have a power cut.

Sand: Flocculation

(the result of a chemical reaction between the clay particles and another substance, usually salt water)

The young girl was doing well. It was the same old story; bullying and jealousy that almost ended up with the death of another young person. The police chief was sick of seeing it too many times. He was now seeing the children of the town suffering from the same mindless bullying that their parents had experienced. He had been one of those kids, small and wimpy, but he had turned it around. However, it hadn't worked out like that for everyone; the young girl was almost another tragic casualty. He was sick of the same things happening with each generation, why couldn't people learn lessons from history? He sighed. Only another few years and then he could retire, he was ready for it. The only mystery that remained was how the girl had come to cut her head. He would have to make sure she hadn't been attacked. The CCTV was being checked in the hope that it would help clear things up.

Tom, the heroic saviour, was a different story. He was stable but the medics were confused by his symptoms. They felt that they were missing something. The mother had arrived, looking like a visiting dignitary rather than a distraught mother with a seriously ill son. She was composed and listened intently as the team explained the situation. They asked her if she could give them a list of his childhood illnesses and a description of his general health over the last few months. She had calmly considered the question and then sat at his bedside. As requested she was given a pen and some paper. Initially she had felt like a schoolgirl ill-prepared for an exam. Then the memories flooded in and the sheets of paper were soon filled with information. She handed them back to the nurse hoping more than ever before that this would be a test that she wouldn't fail.

Alice was on her way to the hospital. Susan, Tom's mother, had telephoned to explain what had happened. So many scenarios ran through her mind that she felt like one of those multiplex cinemas. All thoughts of leaving him had dissipated. He might now leave her and again it would somehow be her fault. She hurriedly drove on towards the hospital and Cubicle 4 in the Intensive Therapy Unit

Sand: Texture
(the feel, the appearance or consistency of a surface or
substance)

The doctor scanned the medical history of the man in Cubicle 4.
It took him the best part of an hour as there was a minor setback
with the elderly gent in Cubicle 1. When everything was calm
once more he returned to the notes. He put them back down
on the desk in front of him and looked at all of his patients. The
bleeps indicating the active breathing of the patients rang out
in the otherwise quiet room. He often felt like a conductor of
a small orchestra. As long as that same tune played out, beep
by beep, they would all reach the end of the score. He ran his
finger over the front of the notebook. The mother had done as
asked and had listed every ailment her son had ever had. There
was nothing obvious but, being a medic, he knew that it was
up to him to establish a diagnosis. He closed his eyes and sat
back in the chair. He thought about his wife and that she had
told him the night before they were going to be parents. It had
taken them both by surprise which, given that he was a doctor
and she was a research assistant in reproductive medicine,
was even more surprising. He felt the warm glow of prospective
parenthood wash over him followed by a minor panic attack;
their lives were about to change dramatically.

He checked his patients and wrote up some additional medication for the gent in Cubicle 1. There was a steady improvement; hopefully he could be moved to HDU the following day and then to a general ward by the end of the week. For several of the nurses their shift was over. They handed over the care of their patients to their colleagues and then gathered by the sink to wash their hands.

"Jeez, Maria, this water is boiling," said Penny, adjusting the mixer taps, "you must have asbestos hands."

And there it was, in that second, the answer he had been looking for. It had just taken one of the nurses to nearly burn her hands for him to see it. He picked up the telephone pushing the notes to one side and ordered some urgent tests for the man in Cubicle 4.

Martha
February 2015, Wales

Knowledge without wisdom is like water in the sand.
Guinean proverb

Martha was packing. She did it with a lot less care than she had at the outset of her trip when her case had been full of promise, mirrored in the careful folding of her clothes. She now filled up the case with crumpled jumpers and trousers. She actually felt more angry than upset, angry for the folly of coming all this way just because of a photograph, but she mainly felt angry that she had allowed Edward to get under her skin. Edward had opened her up to the possibility of a second chance; now she had a gaping hole where that chance had been.

She had been on such a high when she had returned from the beach, her mood so euphoric that she could practically reach out and touch the high ceiling in her room. She had showered, then crawled into a clean, warm bed and fallen into a deep sleep. She had woken up refreshed and in good spirits, with half an hour to get ready.

Four hours after he was due to pick her up, she had phoned him but his telephone was turned off. Two hours after that, she had decided to leave. Obviously the excitement of the night had been intoxicating, but in the cold light of day he had changed his mind. She picked up her phone; it was almost nine and she had decided to get the overnight bus. She just wanted to be home to see John and the children. She was glad now that she hadn't told him everything when she had phoned him last night but had been deliberately vague, saying she would explain everything when she got home. She needed to tell him about his brother. After careful consideration, she realised she was never going to find the son she had given up and couldn't leave it any longer. John had a right to know. No more secrets or lies.

She finished her packing and lifted the case off the bed and carried it to the door, picked up her coat and handbag and left the room. She had looked for Roz a few times since she had woken up but had failed to find her. She rang the small, old-fashioned bell on the reception desk. A young girl who she hadn't seen before came out from the back room.

"Hi, can I help you?"

"I'd like to check out please. I had asked Roz to book me in for a few more days but…" she paused, horrified that she was going to cry, "I need to return home as something has come up."

"That's not a problem, it's easily sorted."

And with the tap of a few keys, the path of Martha's life was changed once more.

She handed over her credit card and waited as the payment was taken. The reception desk was chipped, a small piece of wood that had somehow been dislodged leaving a noticeable scar. She hadn't noticed it before but now it seemed glaringly obvious.

"Thank you, that's all gone through, I hope you enjoyed your stay?"

"Yes, I did very much. Is Roz here?"

"No, she's been at the hospital most of the evening. A friend's son is very poorly."

"Oh no, it's fine."

"Do you want to leave a message?"

"No, don't worry. Just tell her I said thanks."

"Of course, I will. Have a good journey home."

And with that, she walked up the gravel path and turned left towards the bus station and back to the life she had left behind.

She opened her front door and dragged the suitcase into the hall where she abandoned it. The taxi driver had been the same one who had driven her to the station and had been just as surly on her journey home. This time however, she had been glad, almost reassured that some things stay the same. Maybe he couldn't tell if his passengers wanted to talk or not, unable to gauge their feelings, so he kept silent; it was easier not to try. It made her feel sad. The house was quiet, there was no-one to greet her, no-one to ask how her trip had been. No excited tail-wagging dog or mewing cat. The tears came then, slow and steady, even in her distress she did it quietly and with constraint. Rightly or wrongly it was the way she did things.

She had once had a friend who owned a goldfish. It had been her only companion, but she had loved that fish dearly. She had said that it loved her right back. Martha had thought her a bit silly. She realised as she sat in her empty kitchen with her tears dropping to the cold tile floor that she had been very wrong. Because you only had to feel that you were loved to make it true.

The house had a faintly stale smell. She could see that John had called in since there was a small pile of mail by the kettle, but the house wasn't used to her not being there. Even though it was the early hours of the morning and freezing outside she reached across the sink and opened the window. After the initial blast of cold that almost took her breath away the first thing that she noticed was the lack of seasoning in the air. She missed the saltiness of Swansea. She moved the mail and picked up the kettle, filled it and laid it back on the stand. As she waited for it to boil she opened the cupboard and reached for a camomile tea bag and held it in her hand for a short while since she associated it with calm and order. Maybe it was about time she had a bit of chaos in her life again. She put it back and pulled out one of "John's" tea bags loaded with caffeine and chaos. It wasn't a huge step but it was still a step forward.

The breeze from the window touched her gently as it passed by. She took a sip of the caffeine-laden tea. It was nice. She looked around for a biscuit, in the tin there was a new packet. Bless John, he was fully aware of his mother's sweet tooth. It was a packet of salted caramel chocolate digestives. She smiled; everything was salted caramel at the moment, she wondered if there was any food item left that hadn't had salted caramel added to it. She was hungry and took a bite; it was delicious, the culinary oxymoron. Sweet and salty, salt seemed to be featuring so much in her life.

She finished her tea and biscuits and looked at the time; it was past midnight, too late to do it tonight. She opened the bottom drawer of the dresser and took out the old address book, ran her finger down the index alphabet until she came to the letter "P", opened the book and then turned the page to Parker.

There, in Evie's neat writing, were the details of the nursing home where Martha's father had lived for the last few years. Underneath was a little note "in case you ever need it" with a heart next to it. It almost felt like a physical blow, the pain of the loss she felt for Evie at that precise moment. She took the book up to her bedroom and placed it on the cabinet at the side of her bed.

The next morning, she woke and for a split second she forgot all that had gone on in the last few days. Then it all came flooding back. Edward, Evie and her father all jostled for position in her consciousness. She organised them in her mind and then looked at the time; it was almost eight. If she hurried she could shower and be out of the house by half past. She could make it – even though that hadn't been her initial intention.

She opened the heavy door. She was early and the church was empty although she felt an expectancy, the candles were lit and books were heaped on a shelf at the back of the church. She genuflected and then sat down in the front pew. A few parishioners came in, helping to make up the numbers. Then, the old priest walked slowly onto the altar and the mass began. She didn't go up for communion as she hadn't been to confession yet. That would be a confession and a half; she hoped the old priest was stronger than he looked. She recited the words in her head: "Forgive me father for I have sinned. It has been thirty-four years since my last confession. Are you sitting comfortably?" Of course, the last sentence wasn't usually in the script, but she had an awful lot to unload. Maybe she should take a flask of tea and some sandwiches for them to share. They would definitely need a break halfway through.

She stayed on after the service, one or two others did the same. A lady in front of her sat with her hands clasped together as she prayed. An old couple across the aisle knelt, heads bent heavy with prayer. She didn't kneel; she just sat in the hard, wooden pew and reflected on her life. She remembered a quote from George Eliot. "It is never too late to be what you might have been". Seeing that George Eliot was actually the pen name of Mary Anne Evans and that her life was anything but normal by the standards of her time, Martha felt emboldened to take the next step. A couple of hours later, she was home with another cup of caffeine-laden tea. She opened the address book and after looking up the number proceeded to dial. The number rang in a small, independently run nursing home in the coastal town of Hove, where the air was as salty as it was in Swansea.

Evie
March 2013, England

Every time a strong wind blows,
Every sand and dust yearns for being a solid rock
And every solid rock longs for flying with the wind!

Mehmet Murat Ildan

Evie fussed with her appearance in the mirror. She found it took her increasingly longer to get a reflection that she was satisfied with. Her head now had a good covering of hair although not quite enough for her to venture out without a scarf or a wig. She wished she was brave enough to leave the house without either but when she had tried, she had only reached the end of the street before running back in tears. She felt almost naked, like she was in the dreams she had as a child when she imagined being in school in just her underwear. She had always felt a bit awkward when she had breast fed the children, she wasn't the type to do it in a crowd. Either way she felt she should be stronger – felt she was being tested and was continually failing.

She applied lipstick, a subtle peach tone; the brighter reds and pinks she had previously favoured didn't suit her any more. She noticed lines at the corner of her eyes, her skin was dry despite all the moisturisers that she used. There were also deeper lines around her mouth, laughter lines apparently. The irony was not lost on her. It seemed so long ago since she had had anything to laugh about. Maybe that was why they formed, to remind you that once you had laughed so much it left an indelible reminder.

Tonight, was John's attempt at normality, but avoidance therapy she felt was a truer description of his complete inability to face the fact that she was dying. The strange thing was the more he avoided it, the more she faced the facts. So maybe it was a good thing – was he trying to double bluff; she doubted it, she knew him too well. They had been together for what seemed forever. It was going to kill her, she just hoped that it wouldn't kill him as well. He had been trying to talk to her about looking for alternative treatments but she hated the desperation in his voice,. It made her feel guilty as though this whole mess was her fault and supposed that in some way, it was. She worried more about Seth than anyone else. Peggy was more resilient by nature, dramatic – yes, but still she had a core of strength that Seth lacked. He was a kind, thoughtful boy which was good, but he was sensitive in a way Peggy was not. She would miss Martha and of course Nathan, she knew she would miss him – more than she should. Her body had conspired against her "happy ever after", it had re-written the narrative of her life. It would miss out such important occasions; the children's school proms, graduation days and weddings. All taken off her, a slight of the hand of fate.

She finished applying her make-up and looked at her reflection. She toyed with the idea of not wearing the wig that sat on her dressing table since she looked OK; her features larger now that her eyelashes had grown back, more defined, without the distraction of her hair. She knew though that if she did not wear her wig, it would mess with John's game of playing "normal lives". He would look at her and see the disease, not her, and for once she agreed with him. For tonight she wanted him to see her, not the illness, not the prognosis, not the outcome. She wanted to play the game of "normal". She wanted to be a fellow conspirator because at least then she would feel that they were both on the same side.

She placed the wig on her head and gently pulled it down as far as it would go and adjusted it slightly so that it looked as natural as possible. She looked at the stranger staring back at her, the pale complexion, dark rings beneath the eyes, masked, but still faintly visible. The peachy lipstick suited the auburn wig; she looked nice, very nice considering everything, but she didn't look like herself. In a way she was glad, as that would have been too hard to bear. It was easier to be a better alternative of herself rather than a poorer representation of who she had once been. She would play the role that John wanted her to play. She had her alter ego to hide behind. The wig itched but she ignored it. She never felt comfortable any more but this was a minor distraction she could deal with it. She got up from the dressing table with a nod to the bald wig holder and took out a Ted Baker shift dress from her wardrobe. It had a black background with small birds decorating it, some embellished with small crystals so that they caught the light. She teamed it with black opaque tights and ankle boots. It was loose on her but was not as loose as the pale green dress she had tried on earlier in which she had looked like a child dressing up in her mother's clothes. She had liked the Ted Baker shift dresses because they had hidden all her lumps and bumps after having the children. Now they disguised how much weight she had lost. She must email Ted and tell him he was a genius.

The restaurant was out of town and not one either of them had been to before. It was lovely and was a pleasant surprise for them both. The walls were pale cream and totally bare apart from an array of candles in plain silver sconces. The tables were a mix of round, rectangular and square shapes; it made her think of Play School *and choosing which window to look through. Laid on top of each table were crisp, white linen cloths and each had an enamel jug filled to overflowing with woodland flowers. She imagined the staff rising early to go and pick them from the deep dark woods, a bit like Red Riding Hood without the wolf and grandma.*

They were shown to a small snug towards the back of the restaurant and to her relief she noted that it was fairly near the toilets.

"Evie?"

She saw John look at her with that particular look of his, the one that he wore every day when he thought she wasn't looking. The one she had never seen before she had had her diagnosis. He always tried so hard to hide it. Maybe his acting skills just weren't as good as hers.

"I'm fine, shall we order drinks? I'm dying of thirst."

She saw him flinch. Simple everyday sayings messed with their pretence of normal.

"I'll order some water. Do you want still or sparkling?"

Before her illness, they would have laughed at the prospect of going out for a meal and not having wine. The parameters of their lives were shifting. As a child, she had wanted to join an amateur dramatic group but she had been too shy. Now was her chance to act in her very own play, and she was determined to make it the role of a lifetime.

"John, why don't we have a bottle of wine? I quite fancy a red, what about you?"

She had placed her hand on his arm as she spoke as if to reassure him.

"Are you sure?"

"Yes, shall we order a Malbec?"

She had begun her role without needing a script, she smiled from somewhere deep inside her and it reached her eyes.

167

"Red it is then, but let's have something a bit more special than a Malbec."

He called to the hovering waiter and ordered an eye-wateringly expensive bottle of red. She swore she could see tears in the eyes of the waiter as he practically skipped off to the wine cellar. Wasn't she just spreading the happiness!

"Peggy seems to like her new teacher," said John.

"Yes, I know, it's such a relief. She adored Mrs Powell so much I was really concerned that whoever replaced her wouldn't have a chance."

"I know, and Peggy wouldn't have tried to hide her feelings!"

They laughed at their opinionated daughter; it was a safe topic. The delighted waiter, probably already having calculated his tip based on the wine alone, couldn't do enough for them. He poured the wine and with a flourish placed their napkins on their laps. Evie felt like giggling; the wine was helping, she just hoped she wouldn't see it again; she was sure it wouldn't taste so good then. They toasted the new teacher as it was dangerous territory to make any other toast. The talk became easier with each sip of wine and soon Evie was a co-conspirator with John in being "normal". The waiter returned with their starters, he was so full of bonhomie he was practically performing a floor show for them. With a flourish, he placed each plate in front of them. He clicked his heels together and made a gesture that was supposed to alert them to the presence of their plates as if they hadn't just seen him put them there. Giggling, they both started to eat. The waiter returned to ask if everything was OK with the food. They both nodded, trying to stifle their laughter. He returned moments later with a jug of water. Laughing, they toyed with the idea of getting a restraining order on him. But as they both said, he was having so much fun – why spoil his evening?

She was so relaxed that for a little while she even forgot about her illness, but it soon gave her a gentle reminder. She started to feel *a bit queasy, although she had opted for the relatively safe option of soup. She knew that she shouldn't have had the wine but didn't regret it – not one bit. It had been worth it just to meet their new best friend, Georges the waiter. He was now showing her and John photos of his children on his phone!*

Things became a little trickier when the main course arrived. Once again, Georges pulled out all the stops. This time he had an assistant, so that the plates could be put in front of them at the same time. He kissed the air and disappeared into the kitchen with his side-kick. Evie had ordered pan-fried cod with a caper butter, lemon roast potatoes and a medley of green vegetables. It felt like big lumps of card as she tried to digest it. John was tucking into his rare steak with Roquefort sauce; she could see the blood oozing from the steak and mixing with the creamy sauce. She concentrated on her own plate and worked towards her Oscar nomination as she pushed the food around her plate taking small bites to add some realism to the scene.

She managed to control herself almost to the end of the meal; coffee and dessert had been her tipping point. She excused herself and went to the ladies where she brought most of the meal back up. She didn't care, it had been worth it – for John. She re-did her make-up in the mirror, added concealer to the dark circles under her eyes and dabbed a little blusher on her cheeks. She looked a little like a painted doll, not quite real. It would have to do; otherwise her only other option was to escape through the bathroom window and John would definitely notice her absence and then ask Georges to muster a search party for her. On her return, John gave her a quizzical look but she just smiled. She managed to sip a weak tea while John tucked into his dessert. Georges handed John the bill and was rewarded with a twenty percent tip. He hugged them both and invited them to his son's first Holy Communion celebrations the following week. By the time they arrived home, she was mentally and physically exhausted. John had wanted her to stay up and watch a film but her tank was empty – she had nothing left to give. That was the problem with trying to act as though everything was all right; people believed you, even those closest to you, because it was what they wanted to believe. She had given an outstanding performance, as she lay in bed she realised that maybe she should have gone to Am Dram all those years ago.

She sent a quick text to Nathan. They were meeting the following day and she hoped she was up to it after this evening. She needed to be as well as possible under the circumstances since it would be the last time she would see him. She had to be strong because he wasn't aware that it would be their last time.

Today was her last day at work, after more than a decade with the university she had to stand down; the work load was just too much for her. They had been on the brink of the most exciting project of her life. Her assistant and best friend Celine was to take the helm until they found a replacement. She wanted to wear the same clothes that she had worn on her first day at work when she was fresh from completing her Masters. She had wanted to look like a serious scientist so she had worn navy trousers, a white shirt and a navy cardigan. Miraculously, after giving birth to two children she still managed to fit into the trousers, she had bought a new shirt but managed to find the cardigan which still looked presentable. She didn't know why she wanted to dress the same but somewhere in her subconscious it was important to her.

"John, are you coming today?" she asked.

They had argued bitterly for the past week about the "leaving do" her colleagues were holding for her; John felt it was in poor taste. She had disagreed. She wanted it – she had earned it. Then he had said the *words that neither of them had been prepared to voice, that had waited in the wings waiting for one of them to call on to the stage.*

"But you are not leaving work for something else or to take early retirement; you are dying Evie, you are not just leaving work, you are leaving us all."

They had stared at each other, both speechless. It was the very first time either of them had said it out loud; the doctors had made reference to it, the lack of success of the treatment, the stage of the disease, but they hadn't spoken about it. Instead it had festered in each of them, waiting for an opportunity. He had cried then and she had held him until the anger had left them both. He had promised then that he would do whatever she wanted. She had lain awake most of the night, his words returning to her every time she tried to sleep. It wasn't what he had said – that was no surprise to her, she had accepted it as much as anyone could, it was the raw pain she heard in his voice that kept her awake; she was doing this, inflicting this pain.

"Yes, I've organised work so I can take you."

"Are you sure you are OK with it? I'm not sure what they've planned but there will be speeches and probably some sort of presentation?"

"If you can do it, then I'm sure I can too."

If she was honest, a part of her wished he had decided against it. What was that old saying – be careful what you wish for? She had wanted him to come so badly but now, as they made their way, she was worried how he would react to the day. She didn't want to spend it worrying about him. Was it selfish of her to want to have this day and enjoy it as best as she could?

Neither of them spoke on the journey to the university. They had nothing to say to each other; sometimes there just weren't any words. John parked the car opposite the main entrance and they walked hand in hand up the steps. She saw one or two people that she recognised but they didn't acknowledge her; she hoped it was because they didn't recognise her and not because they did. John held onto her hand even more tightly as they walked into her office; she wasn't sure which one of them he was trying to comfort.

"Evie, so good to see you."

Her boss greeted her with a gentle handshake. Was he scared she would break into tiny pieces? He was known for his firm handshakes. She squeezed back with all the strength she could muster.

"Hello John, good to see you too. Please come this way."

He led them along the corridor towards the lecture hall. She knew then that they were doing it the same way they did when anyone retired and, in that moment, she loved them for it. No quiet back door for her, they were giving her the full honour. She hoped John would feel the same; she knew what was coming – he was like a lamb to the slaughter.

They were led to the front of the hall and seated. The room was full of colleagues, some good friends some not so much. She saw Celine, they gave each other a wistful smile. Her boss took the podium and the room quieted, the noisy buzz of chatter gone, like Pavlov's dogs – they were all conditioned.

"I would like to thank you all for coming today to attend the…"

Evie was horrified, her boss, the gruff man who had terrified her in her first few months at work but whom she had come to love and respect, had stopped mid-sentence. His voice had caught with emotion as soon as he had started to speak. She had wondered before they had come whether they would call today a retirement or a leaving do. Either was correct but both wrong. She looked at John, but instead of him looking panicked, she watched with something akin to horror and amazement as he stood up and walked over to her boss. He gently moved Cyril to the side and then started speaking into the microphone.

"I would personally like to thank you all for coming today. Actually, I am being a bit of a fraud as I didn't even want Evie to come today which would have made it a bit easier on Cyril."

There was a bit of nervous laughter.

"All of us here know that this isn't a leaving or a retirement do. This is to celebrate all the wonderful work my wife had done for you, and with you, over the last ten years. When I was arguing with her as to the insensitivity of holding such a function I forgot the most important fact. It doesn't really matter what we call it – which I'm sure is why Cyril found it hard to put into words. This is simply a gathering of all Evie's friends and colleagues celebrating what she has achieved over those ten years."

Evie couldn't breathe. She had never felt so proud of John. Cyril started the applause which was soon followed by a standing ovation for John.

"Well, I bet you are mighty pleased with your man."

It was the Texan, closely followed by Celine.

"I sure am."

Evie and Celine laughed out loud – what was it with that man that made her want to speak with an exaggerated American drawl?

After the initial shaky start the "do" as it was subsequently referred to was a great success. They had presented her with a beautiful vase, a heavy crystal one cut exquisitely to catch the light. A simple silver necklace on which hung a tiny silver vial inside which was a tiny amount of sand. Evie was touched, it was the exact type of sand on which she had spent hundreds of hours researching. She had been looking for the best type of sand to facilitate her research. It was like taking a little of her success with her and not handing all her research to her colleagues. The last thing they presented her with, and she was glad that they still did it for her, was the hourglass. When anyone retired *from the department rather than the ubiquitous carriage clock they were given an hourglass. It was an in-joke to show how fleeting time was. She knew that they must have agonised over this last item given that the time she had left really was fleeting, but she couldn't say how glad she was that they had decided to do it. She had felt John stiffen by her side as she was given a huge bouquet of flowers together with the hourglass but he kept quiet.*

She had laughed and drunk a little and chatted with every single person in the room; she was exhausted. That was when she thought that she had seen him standing by the door talking to one of the admin staff. She had felt faint – they had an agreement; now was not the time to break it. She could feel his eyes on her, watching her, she looked up and he had gone. She then felt disappointment that she hadn't been able to speak to him. How perversely contrary was she becoming. He hadn't taken it well when she had told him she couldn't meet up any more and had begged her to reconsider. He had wanted her to tell John everything and part of her had agreed with him but she didn't have the energy for the fallout that would inevitably come from doing so. She had nearly faltered when he had held her as they parted. Her only concession was that he could still write to her. He held on to it like a drowning man holds onto a tiny piece of wood. She knew that she loved him but she just wasn't sure of the type of love she felt for him – it was all so complicated. Didn't people say when they were having affairs, "it's complicated" but this was different. She guessed they said that as well. She would ring him tonight and apologise for ignoring him, he would understand that he shouldn't have come.

They had been there for several hours when the wave of nausea hit her. She rushed to the toilet and made it just in time. Now was the time to leave; it had been a good day in so many ways. She had dreaded this part, possibly never seeing these people again but as Cyril had pointed

out, she could call in to check on them at any time but he didn't add –
"so this doesn't have to be the last time". They both knew that it was
unlikely, given the way the disease was progressing but the possibility
had made today easier. The tiredness took over and instead of wanting
to linger, all she wanted to do was to be at home with her family, in her
pyjamas and relax by the fire.

She lay on the floor in front of the living room fire with Seth by her side.
She ran her fingers through his blond hair as they lay there watching
cartoons on the TV; his hair was soft and silky but was getting quite
long. He needed it cut, she would book an appointment for him in a
few weeks. When he had been younger, she had always stroked his hair
until he had fallen asleep. Then as he had grown older, he had gone
to bed on his own – not needing her company in order to fall asleep.
Since she had become ill though, he had taken to wanting her to smooth
his hair once more to help him fall asleep. Maybe she wouldn't have
it cut just yet. John had taken Peggy to bed; she had been exhausted
after arranging and rearranging her mother's flowers in the new crystal
vase. She felt Seth slip his hand into hers. She squeezed it gently as she
drifted to sleep.

Martha
March 2015, England

*'Cause sometimes that mountain you've been climbing
is just a grain of sand.*

Carrie Underwood

Martha had been home for less than two weeks when she finally heard from Edward. He had phoned, apologising profusely about missing her that day and for not contacting her until now. He had apparently been at the bedside of the son of a close family friend who had been desperately ill. The son was now home and doing well although he had been diagnosed with some strange condition the name of which she couldn't remember. He asked her if she had another copy of the photograph that she could send him since he was only too happy to help with her search. He still wanted to see her again. She believed him but she wanted more from him because she hadn't waited all this time for some half-hearted attempt to see her again. She simply wanted more, because for the first time in her life she believed that she deserved more. If he couldn't understand that, then he wasn't the man she had thought he was. She had told him that she was no longer actively looking for her son. Edward had sounded disappointed and said that he was sorry she had changed her mind but still asked if she could send the photograph. He had given her his address, she thanked him for getting in touch and then replaced the telephone.

She sat at the kitchen table, her hands still shaking from the shock. She picked up her mobile; she would phone him back and apologise that she didn't mean to be so offhand and that his phone call had been so unexpected. She pressed the button and watched as the little arrow said "dialling" but then pressed the red phone icon and the call was terminated.

She didn't have time for this, she had plans for today and Edward wasn't going to prevent her from seeing them through. She was almost ready to go. She took her warm woollen coat from the hook in the hall and checked the time; it was almost 9.30am and the taxi would be here soon. She had given herself plenty of time to get to the station, had a flask of tea in her bag together with a cheese and mango-chutney roll, an unusual combination found entirely by accident when Peggy had been "making a picnic" and had mistaken it for pickle – it was now a family favourite!

As she sat on the train, she thought about the phone call. He had sounded genuinely hurt that she didn't want to meet him and had suggested meeting halfway but it wasn't enough for her any more; she had made more than enough compromises in her life, she wasn't prepared to make any more. She wanted him to make more of an effort – if he wanted her, then he could come and get her.

She settled herself on the train and sat facing the direction the train was travelling in – not because of any motion sickness, but because she liked to see life as it came towards her, not after it had left.

The carriage was fairly empty; there were one or two businessmen reading broadsheets and listening to something on their phones, earplugs blocking out the monotony of train life. There were a few students instantly recognisable from their unstructured scruffiness. She made a mental note to trawl some of the local charity shops for clothing ready for her return to university in the autumn. She felt a thrill of excitement run through her.

There was one other lady sitting adjacent to her who must have been in her early forties. She was dressed smartly in a black coat which had shiny silver buttons, the cuffs were edged in fur; a black dress, and tights completed the look. She had blonde, wavy hair and she reminded Martha of Evie. The lady smiled at Martha although her general demeanour was one of sadness and then it dawned on Martha that she was possibly dressed for a funeral. She looked at her own navy coat and dress then wondered whether the woman was thinking the same about her. Perhaps the woman too was travelling to re-connect with a father she hadn't seen for thirty years.

She stood on the seafront and took a deep breath; the air was heavy with the saltiness that she had missed so much. It was colder than she had expected, the sun seeming only to light, but not to warm the day. She pulled the thick coat together and fastened the buttons. A gust of wind blew from the north as if testing the robustness of the buttons. So here she was, about to face the man she had hated for most of her adult life. He would be an old man now, less able to hurt her. He had never lifted a finger against her – he left that to her mother – but the hurt was more than he could ever have done to her physically.

She looked up at the home; it was in fairly good condition but the ravages of being perched so close to the sea had scarred it. It appeared to be undergoing a substantial restoration, the splintered wooden windows being replaced by plastic ones – less maintenance and more durable, given its proximity to the sea. She felt that the wooden ones could tell a story that the plastic ones would never hear. She walked up to the impressive front door and hoped it would never be replaced by a plastic one. There was an intercom on the wall to the left of the door. With a trembling hand she pressed the buzzer; she was cold and she was nervous.

"Hello, how can I help?"

The voice that came from the large wooden door was high-pitched but quiet too – almost childlike.

"Hi, I'm Martha Maddox. I spoke to Sally Armstrong yesterday about visiting Mr Parker, my father."

"Yes of course, hello Martha, I'm Sally. Please come in, just pull the handle on the right."

Martha pulled the handle and the door opened into a large, warm reception area. She looked around; there was an air of forced cheerfulness, staff and residents passed by, smiling as though they were auditioning for a walk-on part in a film. Sadness and despondency were unwelcome guests here. There was a large board crammed with pictures of the residents and staff in various costumes to prove this. Pictures of Easter bonnet parades mingled with smiling faces crowned with tinsel. Martha shuddered, she would sooner walk fully dressed into the sea at the back of the home than stay one night here.

She walked towards the reception desk; the carpet was good quality but in what could only be described as a serviceable colour, the walls were papered with a design of tiny flowers. The wall paper looked wipe-able.

From behind the desk walked a very large, well-dressed woman, her hand outstretched towards Martha. She had short, silvery-grey hair, her eyes a deep dark blue. She was striking because of her size and her beauty. They shook hands, the woman's grip surprisingly strong.

"Hello Martha, I'm Sally. It's so lovely to meet you at last; your father talks about you a lot."

Martha found that hard to believe and wondered if it was a stock statement that was rolled out to every relative. The tiny voice was in direct contrast to Sally's physical stature. It was as if an error had been made somewhere and she had been given a skinny little girl's voice.

"Follow me and we'll go and see your father."

Martha followed Sally from the large well-lit reception and along corridors passing numerous rooms as they went. They walked side by side through the vast building. Every now and then the sound of buzzers interrupted the gentle background noise of the residence. They came to a set of large ornate doors with beautiful brass handles and finger plates that were so highly polished that Martha could see a suggestion of herself in them. Sally opened the magnificent doors.

"These doors are the originals from when it was a private dwelling. Imagine all this belonging to one family; sadly a lot of the other doors and fireplaces were ripped out but thankfully, sense prevailed when it came to these. This is also their original position, this is the garden room."

As she said this, she gestured around the room into which they had walked. It took Martha's breath away; it was a very large room interspersed with large pillars. There was an enormous marble fireplace to her left around which were several brown leather chesterfield sofas. However, it was the floor to ceiling windows opposite that really took her breath away. The panorama through the expanse of glass was of windblown grasses and palms that danced to the tune of the sea breezes. As she walked towards the windows, she saw beyond the picturesque gardens the sands of the beach tumbling to the same tune. The sea beyond was the same grey as the brooding sky above it.

Martha was surprised that the room was almost empty, only a few residents being present. Surely the residents would have preferred this to their rooms. As if reading her thoughts, Sally said, "We have a dance class on at the moment in our ballroom; otherwise this room would be a lot busier."

"A dance class?"

"Yes, I know what you're thinking. Surely all the residents are too disabled or poorly to participate in a dance class but you would be surprised. And I like to do things a little differently here. Most of the residents are from the era when dance halls were a big part of their lives. As most of them have regressed back in time, they find the modern world a scary place, so we try to replicate some of the activities they did when they were younger. The dance class is in the form of an old tea dance. We bought lots of old china tea seats from charity shops. We have a young local group who play rock at night in the local pubs and once a week in the day they play songs from the good old days and pretend that the residents are much younger than they are.

Most are in wheelchairs and some are wheeled in whilst still in their beds, but I can tell you this, they all love it."

"That's amazing."

Martha warmed to the large lady at her side. Her love and enthusiasm for her residents was obvious. Suddenly it didn't seem such a bad place to live out your days, although she wasn't thinking of putting her name down anytime soon.

"Sorry, Martha, as usual I'm getting side-tracked. You came here to see your dad not have me give you our mission statement. Your dad didn't go to the dance today; he was afraid he would miss you. We told him that we would fetch him, but he was adamant he wanted to wait for you. And there he is, in his favourite spot over by the window."

Martha looked to where Sally was pointing. She had noticed a few residents by the enormous window but she hadn't taken much notice as they were all in wheelchairs. Sally was pointing to one of the residents who faced the window, an old man with a dusting of white hair. His shoulders were so slumped it was as if actual bones were missing. As the clouds hurried to catch the sun, she saw in the glass the reflection of a frail old man who she recognised as the man she used to call dad.

Steeling herself, she walked towards him. As she neared she understood the need for the wheelchair. One of his trouser legs sat empty and redundant beside its fuller twin. All at once the years fell away and she felt sad for the old man in front of her; the loss of his leg somehow a physical sign that she was no longer his little girl who had sat on his lap as she listened to his stories.

He looked up at her, she felt sick; she wanted to continue to hate him because it was easier to blame it all on him rather than take any responsibility herself. He had made huge mistakes, there was no doubt about that, but he had tried over the years to make amends and she had ignored them. She had thrown out every letter and every card, keeping only the one photo in her bedroom drawer.

"Martha, is it you? Are you really here?"

She nodded.

"Martha are you here?"

This time there was a note of desperation in his voice.

"Martha, your father is almost blind; you will have to go closer so that he can see you."

Hearing Sally address Martha, her father held out his skinny arms towards them. Sally stepped back as Martha took a step forward.

"Martha?"

This time, his voice was slightly stronger, more sure, that she was there in front of him. Her name didn't sound like hers as it left his lips. She looked into his grey eyes; once a vibrant blue, they now looked the same colour as the sea and sky beyond. All the vibrancy had drained away from him.

"Dad?"

It came out as a question, even though she knew that it was him in front of her. Maybe it wasn't his physical presence she was questioning. She moved closer to him; she could smell tobacco on him, so he still smoked. It was familiar though and comforting. She held her hands out in front of her, then snatched them back. She had made a mistake; she shouldn't have come and should have left things as they were. She turned to leave and saw Sally watching her. Martha understood that the welfare of her residents was paramount to her. She stopped, Sally would protect and look after her residents no matter what, because that was her role. It didn't matter to her what kind of life they had once led – all she wanted for them was the best she could provide for them at the end of their lives.

She hesitated, then took his hands in hers; they were dry and papery like parchment. She thought that if she made any sudden movement, then he could well lose the top layer of skin. She felt a sharp stab of sympathy, like a knife-wound which caused her unwanted pain but it seemed to lessen his. Was that what she wanted to do – increase her suffering to make him feel a little better? He felt her stiffen and gripped her hands more tightly.

"I'm so sorry Martha, for everything. She was ill, but back then no-one talked about it or even understood it. I should have been stronger for you and for the baby. He came to see me a few months ago. I'm so glad that you found him. I prayed to God every day that you would. He was so lovely, we talked all about you then he told me I was a great-grandfather. But how could I be when I wasn't even a good father? He admitted that you didn't know he was coming to see me so I made him promise that he would only come again if you knew about it. Is that why you've come today, Martha? Did he ask you to come and see me?"

"No, he didn't. I thought it was time we made our peace."

He smiled and nodded, neither brought up the many wasted years when they could have done something about it.

"I think he thought I was senile when I said I was so glad you'd found him; he smiled and said that I must be a bit confused as you had never lost him. Maybe he was young when you got him back. Anyway, we didn't dwell on it, it wasn't important to either of us. I felt a connection with him Martha and I know he felt the same."

So, John had seen him. She wasn't that surprised and it wasn't her right to have stopped him. She did wish he had talked to her about it though. But then she hadn't told him lots of things, so who was she to criticise? She guessed that her father had confused John with her first child. Had John known what he was talking about or had he put it down to the confusion of an elderly man? She had to speak to John as soon as she got home. No more secrets or lies, she had to tell him everything whatever it cost her.

She found breathing difficult because her chest was so tight. It was as if all that he had just told her filled every space in her body with his pain at being outcast for all those years. So, she started telling the truth. She told him that he had in fact met John, who was her second child. She told him about Peter. She told him he would have loved Peter if only she had given him the chance to know him. They cried as she told him they had lost Evie. That she had never found her first child.

She held his tired and shrunken body in her arms and told him a story about three princesses and their father the king. She told him about the folly of two of the princesses and the wisdom of the third. She felt the tears come once more as she told him about how the king found his lost daughter. Then she told him that she was sorry. She didn't need him to tell her he was sorry; he had lived with it every single day of his life – it was carved in the lines on his face. Now was the time for making peace.

John
April 2015, England

The moon will light the clouds,
Just as the tide shall shape the sand.

Anthony T Hincks

"Do you think she's ill, Pam?" he asked.

"I honestly don't know. She hasn't said anything to me, but then I have to say that she has been a little distant of late."

John and Pam had met in a café near John's office for a quick coffee to discuss Martha. They were both worried about her, particularly since February when she had come back from nursing her mysterious friend. John was worried that she had actually been to see some sort of specialist or doctor. Too much of the situation reminded him of Evie and it terrified him; he wasn't sure he had the strength to go through that again.

"I know what you mean, she has changed since she came back from wherever she actually went to during February."

"Have you tried to talk to her?"

"Yes, several times, but each time she shuts me down and says that everything is fine."

"I don't know what to suggest John. Personally, I don't think that she is ill, she has always been fairly open about most things."

"Not everything."

Seeing the puzzled look on Pam's face, John wondered if he should tell her of his suspicions. He knew that his mother often confided in Pam, but this was different. He had his suspicions, but that was all. He felt as though he was breaking a confidence, even though one had not been made.

"I went to see her dad a few months ago."

"Oh, John, does she know?"

"No, I suppose it's been on my mind a lot. I had a feeling when Evie was alive that she knew more than she told me. I felt there was something Mum had told her, but I couldn't be certain. Anyway, after she died it became unimportant, until now. It made me wonder that if Mum wasn't ill, what else could be upsetting her? I have never bought the whole story that her father was senile; if that was the case, Mum would still have visited him – not abandoned him."

"How did you find him? Martha has always been so cagey about his whereabouts?"

"Evie had obviously done some digging in the months leading up to her death. She had notes in one of her journals, about searching for lost relatives. On the reverse of one of the notes was an address for a nursing home in Hove so I rang them; they confirmed that he was a resident. I went to see him the following week."

"Did he remember her?"

"She was all he talked about. He explained about his wife, Martha's mother. She had been abusive to Martha and to him for many years but he hadn't known how to handle it, so he had tried to cover it up. Then a few years after Martha left the family home she attacked a woman in their church. She was sectioned, then subsequently diagnosed with schizophrenia. As he said, if only he had done something about it sooner maybe all their lives would have turned out differently."

"Poor Martha. She never talks about her upbringing, I guess it was too painful."

"I know. There was something odd though, Pam. After he had asked how she was, he kept saying that he was so glad that she had found me. I said that she had never lost me and he laughed; he grabbed my hands in his and said that I was lost but he was glad that I had no memory of it."

John looked at Pam who had gone as white as the petals of the snowdrops in the grass outside.

"Pam?"

"How old was Martha when she left home?"

"About nineteen or twenty I think. Dad said that by the time he met her, she had been in a deep depression. I guess that's why none of us pushed her too much about her past because we didn't want to remind her and maybe bring about another episode. I have always worried that it would come back one day, more so after Dad and then Evie died."

"So, she was a young girl with a mentally ill mother and a father who didn't know how to handle the situation and she was studying for a degree in the local university. Why didn't she just grin and bear it? Less than eighteen months later she would have graduated and she could have left then. What precipitated her to leave halfway through?"

"Her parents were very religious and the social climate was very different then. I think she was pregnant, Pam, I think that was why she left so abruptly. What I don't know is what happened to the baby, did she have an abortion? Is that why she hasn't been able to go to church all these years because of the guilt?"

"But her father thought that she had 'found you' so he must have known that she didn't have an abortion. Also, he must have known that the baby was a boy not a girl. So, she must have had the baby."

"Then where is my brother?" asked John.

Alice
April 2015, Wales

It's when I write "I love you" in the sand
That the ocean carries your message to all of those who sail upon her.

Anthony T Hincks

Alice pulled into the service station because she needed to get some food and fill up the car. She watched as the numbers turned over at the pump and thought of them as the number of miles she needed to put between her and Tom. She hurried across the tarmac; it was unseasonably cold for April, there seemed to be no sign of the promised spring. She pushed the door to the service station shop just as the teller was changing the sign to "Pay at kiosk". Alice gestured towards the sandwich refrigerator, the woman nodded and allowed her to pass. Quickly, she made a selection and paid for the fuel and the sandwich and a bottle of coke.

It was dark and following a brief respite the rain had returned. She turned on the engine and watched as the car digested the fuel, its full belly registering on the fuel gauge. She carefully pulled up to the exit. She could see headlights in the distance but reckoned she had enough time to safely pull out onto the road, so indicated and started to move out. The lights that had seemed so far away were on top of her and she barely had time to pull back. The driver of the articulated lorry blasted its horn in anger as it passed.

She sat shaking in the same position until she heard a knock on her window.

"You OK?"

The kind woman from the station looked concerned which made Alice feel even more wretched.

"Yes, I thought I had enough time to pull out; sorry I should have been more careful."

"Not your fault, the lorries think they own this stretch of the road. I was watching you – you didn't do anything wrong. Anyway, as long as you're OK, I'd better get back. Brad over there has only just started and well, let's just say that when they were giving out the gifts, he must have been stuck in the toilet."

The woman laughed at her own joke and tapped the driver's door as a goodbye. Alice looked up and down the long road and carefully pulled out. She was reluctant to give the woman a second chance to ask if she was all right, as she may just tell her everything. She may have said that she was running away from the best thing that had ever happened to her and it was for that very reason that she had to leave. It had been a week since she had last seen him, a week since she had walked out the door of his house, a week with no note, no contact and no explanation. She had tried, she had written e-mails, texts and letters but all had been ignored or discarded in either virtual or real bins. In the end, she reasoned that it was better that he hated her for leaving him, rather than hating her for what she had done. Tom had rescued the young girl just in time; how could she expect him to save her as well.

She had stayed for just single nights at various bed and breakfast establishments along the way. She didn't exactly have a route or even a plan but she just knew she had to put down the miles between her and Tom. She was tired now and she needed to decide her next course of action. She had reached the border between Wales and England and it felt symbolic in a way she couldn't really explain. She pulled off the main road taking the B roads down country lanes, passing large hotels and smaller rural hostels. Finally, she came across a fairly large bed and breakfast. It was an impressive house, almost a stately home. It had a good-sized car park at the side of the building which was nearly full. She figured that it was busy which was good. She knew she was being paranoid but she couldn't help it; Tom would be actively looking for her – others would be looking for her too.

The foyer, which was part of the main bar, was almost full of men dressed predominately in casual clothes. She assumed they were here for the golf course that was situated in front of, and beyond the sweeping gardens. She gave her credit card to the man behind the bar; he took it and pre-authorised a tab for her. He was a large man with an impressive beard who reminded her of Brian Blessed. She wasn't particularly concerned about using her credit card since she had very little cash on her and furthermore, she wasn't a fugitive from the law – just from life. He took her details and then unhooked a key from the large panel by the side of the optics. She hadn't had an actual key to a room for years; it was a Yale key with a small plastic fob which bore the number 12. She booked the room for three nights in the hope that it would be enough time for her to collect her thoughts and come up with some sort of a plan. She took the key from Ron – "Ron and Katie if you need anything lass" – thanked him, and then made her way to her room. Ron had said that it was one of the best rooms in the house. Didn't they always say that? It was situated at the rear of the building and she guessed that he may actually have been telling the truth, as she opened the door into a large, modern, room. It had a huge king-size bed on which she dumped her bag; she then walked over to the pretty picture window on the far side of the room. She lifted the blinds and looked out at the view, there was a tiny stream at the back of the rear garden. It was so tiny that it looked like a vein pulsing through the body of the garden. There was a shed to the left which looked like some sort of small woodworking cabin. There was sawdust everywhere, wood snow her father had called it when she had watched him working as a small child. She felt as though it was a good omen, the whole place felt warm and welcoming, and then she saw the sign. Hanging from the entrance, swinging back and forth in the gentle breeze – "Noah's Bark". She knew it was just a play on words, that it was only a coincidence, but she still had to rush to the en-suite bathroom to vomit the cheese sandwich she had bought from the service station.

John
April 2015, England

We built a castle near the rocks
We built it out of sand
Our fortress was an ice-cream box
With turret, tall and grand
Our men were twigs, our guns were straws
From which we'd sipped at lunch
We had the best of wars...
Till someone's foot
Went
Crunch!!

Jack Prelutsky

John watched as his mother fussed over the children. Peggy was the class champion for the week which was proving to be very tiring for all concerned. The title and the accompanying badge were given to one child every week who had done a kind deed the previous week to earn it. It had been a new initiative that had been wheeled out several weeks ago and for the duration, Peggy had come home every Monday afternoon crestfallen that for that week she wasn't the class champion. John quickly realised that Peggy wanted the accolade not because it meant that she had been recognised for her kindness to her fellow pupils, but because she liked the badge – a lot. It was gold, with a royal blue ribbon that was long enough to go around the neck. For the whole week, she had asked Martha to make sure that she had something blue to wear with her badge every day. John had lost count of the number of times that she had made Seth re-enact the ceremony by which she had been presented with the badge. Seth and Peggy were as different as clay and metal. Seth could be moulded to do most things, Peggy was unyielding and, like metal, it would take some heat before she would bend. He wondered as he looked at Martha if she herself considered the differences in personality between the two children and wondered what her first born son was like. It still felt odd to John to think that somewhere in the world he had a brother. He liked the feeling which the word "brother" induced; it made him feel as though he had found an anchor when he hadn't known he was adrift.

He knew that he had to talk to his mum about his discovery and the fact that he had been to visit her father. The opportunity hadn't arisen since last week, but he knew that he was putting it off.

"When is your meeting?" asked Martha.

When she had said meeting she had used her fingers to indicate speech marks. For a second, he had thought that she was referring to his need to talk to her. Then he remembered that she meant his date with one of the mothers from the children's school. Her son Sean was in Peggy's class, John had chatted to her a few times when he had picked the kids up from school. She was divorced and had an older child, a girl in the same class as Seth as well as Sean in Peggy's. She seemed nice and they had arranged to go to see a film the following night. He had forgotten all about it, thank god he had mentioned it to Martha the previous week when he asked if she could babysit.

He needed to start writing things down; it would have been very embarrassing to have stood her up.

"Tomorrow," he said.

"Why did Gran do this with her fingers," asked Peggy, doing an imitation of Martha's speech marks.

"It's nothing for you to be bothered about young lady," said Martha, smiling at her granddaughter.

"Are we getting a rabbit?" said Peggy excitedly filling in the gaps the adults had left.

She started running around the kitchen shouting that they were about to get a rabbit. Seth looked up from his iPad, shook his head and returned to his game.

"We are having a rabbit and I'm going to call him Peter after dead Granddad."

"Peggy, will you stop calling my father, dead Granddad," said John.

"Why? He's dead and he was your dad, which makes him my Granddad, just a dead one,"

"Why don't we just call him granddad Peter instead," suggested Seth.

"OK. We are having a rabbit which we will call Peter after Granddad Peter. Do you think Darwin will mind? I am going to have to give him a good talking to, we don't want any bloodshed. If we are going to have two pets, I want to keep two pets, not have one eaten and the other banged up in jail for eating him."

"Peggy, we are not having a rabbit," said John.

"No, I know Dad, not until I have a stern word with Darwin. Don't worry yourself about it, you just enjoy your date with Sean's mum and I'll sort out the new pet."

Both Martha and John stared at Peggy as she begged Seth to

come off his game and do a search for rabbit houses on his iPad. John wondered if it would just be easier to get a rabbit.

"Where on earth did that girl come from?" said Martha.

John smiled at his mother; now was the time to suggest getting together to talk about his visit to her dad and the subsequent revelations. However, just before he had the chance to broach the subject, Martha pulled him to one side.

"John, I need to talk to you," she nodded in the direction of the kids who were happily looking up rabbit hutches – Peggy had found one that had three storeys. "Can you pop in lunchtime tomorrow?"

"Yes of course. Is everything all right?"

"Yes, nothing to worry about."

He only wished he could believe it.

Evie
March 2013, England

On a day like today
We pass the time away
Writing love letters in the sand

From: Pat Boone, 'It's A Pity To Say Goodnight'
Billy Reid

She lay on the sofa frustrated by her lack of energy. Since the party, she seemed to have lost her spark. She had thrown all her energy into the planning and executing of Seth's birthday party and now she had come to a grinding halt. She knew that it wasn't just the physical aspects of the cancer; she had also been laid low by the emotional weight of it. Peggy's birthday was in August – she neither made a prediction nor a plan.

The previous day, Celine had called over. Evie had seen the shock on her face; she knew she had lost more weight and could see the lost pounds being unwittingly calculated in her friend's scientific brain. Evie had tried to make a joke of it.

"At last, 'Models are us' have accepted me as a size zero model. Although they did add that maybe I could do with losing a few more

pounds since you can still see me when I turn sideways!" Celine had laughed but the laughter hadn't reached her eyes, which glistened as though covered in a fine layer of gossamer. They had chatted about some of the staff in the university – there had been some new members of staff employed. It made Evie feel even more isolated, distanced by the talk of people she didn't know. More and more, she felt as though she was watching what was left of her life whilst sitting in an empty cinema, the screen full of people she knew and loved. She had once been a participant on the screen; now she was sitting alone in a cold empty theatre.

She looked at the items on the floor by the side of the sofa. Celine had kindly brought her the work equipment she had asked her to bring, the Munsell colour chart, the ex-situ x-ray fluorescence gun, and her trowel. She had wanted to feel them in her hands once more, to remind her that she was once a useful member of the human race, but it had had the opposite effect. After Celine left, her battered and bruised heart had burst apart with the pain. She picked up the file with the Munsell colour chart and flipped through the cards; how many times had she used this without giving a second thought that one day she wouldn't be able to any more. The trowel was in her plastic box by the side of the cling-film and foil. When the kids came home from school they had been fascinated by the items. Seth particularly loved the ex-situ x-ray fluorescence gun, he thought that it looked like the ones the Stormtroopers used in Star Wars. She had explained to him how she used it to analyse the metal and element content of the sands and soils she examined. He was even more impressed than if she had actually been a Stormtrooper. Peggy asked why she had gloves, sampling bags and a camera – was she one of those people who look at dead bodies and find evidence to arrest the killer? Evie had wondered how a five-year-old would know about such things, but then Peggy was no ordinary five-year-old.

She looked out of the window; for a change the sun was shining, highlighting the smudges on the large bay window where Darwin had left the reminders of his sentry duty whilst protecting his family. He knew his mistress needed more protecting than before, so the smudges on the window had increased. Poor Darwin, he barked at anything that encroached onto his territory, he wouldn't let anything or anyone harm his beloved family. If the love of the dog was the measurement scale by which her survival was dependant, she would have been immortal. Instead of the Udden-Wentworth Classification Scale for particle size, there would be the Darwin-Maddox Empathetic Scale' she would be in the top percentile, her survival would be guaranteed. Darwin padded over to her and pushed her hand with his nose, she stroked his head, he whined, a gentle, soft sound. He knew what she had been thinking, he just wished he could make it come true.

She suddenly wanted desperately to be outdoors working in the elements one last time. She wanted to take Darwin, her protector, something she had never done when working, but this was her new world full of new rules. For the first time she felt a slight benefit, she was no longer bound by rules and regulations, if she wanted to take her equipment and do one last field trip, no-one could tell her she wasn't allowed to take the dog. She eased herself up into a sitting position, feeling weak but determined. However, she knew that she would need to be accompanied by someone other than the dog since she just didn't have the requisite physical strength. She thought of John and quickly dismissed the thought' he would be too busy – the subtext being that it wasn't a good idea for her to be out in the elements. She appreciated that he would have a point but it was something that she needed to do. She walked towards the kitchen, the dog following behind her. She picked up her phone – he had told her anytime. She could phone anytime and ask anything of him – should she contact Nathan? Her hand hovered *over her contacts. She sat at the kitchen table, somewhat disheartened by all the planning it would take. She scrolled through her recent calls, selected the number she wanted then pressed "Call".*

She sat quietly, the dog at her side as she listened to the ringing tone and was just about to give up when the call was answered. She didn't explain her feelings but simply stated that she wanted to go out in "the field" one more time. He hadn't argued or tried to talk her out of it, in fact he said that he was already on his way home and had felt a sudden need to see her.

She felt the journey had been such a long one, but as she slowly dressed in layers of warm clothes, she felt finally that John was coming back to her – both physically and metaphorically. She rang Martha who happily said she would pick up the children from school and, as the following day was a Saturday, they could stay the night. Evie asked Martha if she would explain to Seth that she had Stormtrooper work to attend to.

John had made her wear so many layers of clothes that she made the Michelin man look like he was on the 5:2 diet. They didn't talk on the hour-long journey, she had little energy so she slept as John drove, Darwin tucked in the foot-well of her seat. John stopped once in order to grab a hot coffee for himself and a weak tea for her; they shared a pack of sandwiches and then continued with their journey.

It was a good day, the dog ran around the beach, barking his delight at not being at the vets – his usual reason for going in the car. Darwin sniffed and dug, then collapsed on the rug that John had spread out on the beach and fell into a satisfied sleep. Evie covered him with a blanket; he may have a fur coat, but it was still cold. She started to dig just as though she was working whilst John watched her, propped up on his elbow at the side of the sleeping dog. It was so therapeutic; she sieved and analysed using the x-ray fluorescence gun to determine the metals present. The beach had a groyne, an old wooden structure stretching from the beach into the rough sea. It was badly worn, the metal screws holding the angled wood rusted and badly corroded. It was such a simple solution to prevent erosion of the beach from longshore drift. When she had been a young girl, her parents had taken her to a beach with a wide, rocky groyne. She had asked her father what it was, he told her it was the rocks that had fallen out of the pockets of Neptune as he raced back to the sea. Her mother had explained the truth and it had started her love of geology, but even now, a part of her preferred her father's version.

She was tired, she had worked tirelessly for over an hour, she knew that a year ago she would have found that pathetic but today she was proud of herself. She shouted to John who gathered her up in his arms and returned her to the car just as the heavens opened. She laughed as she watched John ushering the dog back to the car whilst trying to gather up her rug and equipment. Instead of making a couple of journeys back to the car, he kept trying to gather up everything in one go but as soon as he added another item, yet another would fall from his grasp. He finally managed to pick up everything. The smell of wet dog in the car was overpowering; in fact the only one who wasn't bothered by the smell was the wet dog himself who had once again fallen fast asleep, exhausted from his adventures. John struggled out of his wet coat and threw it onto the back seat. He then put it back on, jumped out of the car but returned a minute later and once again removed the coat which was now even wetter. In his hand, he had a rucksack from which he withdrew a flask and a packet of chocolate digestives. He took out two china cups and proceeded to pour hot, weak tea. They sat in silence drinking the tea and eating the biscuits watching the storm act out in front of them.

Tom
April 2015, Wales

You don't need to be the tide to rise and fall
You don't have to be a wave to touch the shore;
Just be a little sand-grain and feel them all.

Munia Khan

Tom had finished work for the day and it was only just past five; his newly tailored life was reaping benefits. The partners had been very supportive of his new working hours, but he tried not to think that it was just because they were up to speed on the latest disability at work laws. The new drug regime was helping to stabilise his condition. It had taken a little fine tuning, but he felt better than he had for months.

He felt better physically but emotionally he was in a bit of a mess. Alice had gone, she had left without a trace.

He walked up the street towards the side-road where he had parked his car. He had forgotten how busy it could be at this time of the day; usually he would have been working for at least a couple more hours. This was a brave new world for him, one where he had to adapt to what he had been told was a potentially life-limiting condition. For him, life was now even more precious and he wanted to spend it with Alice. He had to see her face to face; only then would he believe her if she told him she didn't love him. He unlocked his car and pulled onto the busy main road. She had definitely been cagey about her past – maybe there was something murky; whatever it was they would deal with it. He had waited around for too long, so now was the time for him to take some action. The great worry that shadowed his every thought, waiting in the wings, desperate to be on centre stage, was that she didn't love him. His failed proposal coupled with his recent diagnosis had sent her running for the hills.

On his way home he thought about doing an internet search. He remembered teasing Alice that he thought she may be in witness protection; maybe he had been closer to the truth than he had realised. He would put her name in Google and see what came up. He didn't truly believe that it would explain anything but he was willing to try anything; it was as if she had vanished, or had been spirited away.

When he arrived home though he found the dog cowering on his bed, whimpering. Tom was worried at first, until he saw the debris scattered all over the kitchen floor. Febus had found a whole pack of butter that must have dropped out of Tom's shopping the previous evening. He knew this, because there were little bits of silvered paper all over the kitchen floor – it was as though a ticker-tape parade had taken place. Even though that was sufficient evidence for Tom to work out what had happened, the dog had been sick, a frothy yellow mess that had taken him a whole kitchen roll to mop up. The dog sat and watched as Tom worked, the silence punctuated by Tom muttering about his useless dog and the useless dog groaning in obvious discomfort. By the time he had finished cleaning up and made his peace with Febus, he was too tired to do anything about Alice.

In fact, he didn't get a chance to do an internet search for a few days. Ever since Alice had vanished, he hadn't seen his mother but he had spoken to her on numerous occasions during which she always vented her anger. It was a dramatic U-turn and apparently she had "known all along that she would be a waste of time!" Tom kept his own counsel; he could easily have pointed out how much she had liked Alice but he neither had the energy nor the inclination to correct her. He merely held the phone away from his ear as he stroked the dog.

Now, however, they were seated opposite each other with him trying not to make eye contact with his mother. It was Easter Sunday and the rest of their party hadn't yet arrived at the restaurant which meant both he and his mother, who had arrived separately, sat in silence with an apparent herd of pachyderms in the room between them. For this very reason, he was glad he had decided not to arrive too early even though it did feel ridiculous for he was, after all, a grown man. He knew his mother too well and knew that she would speak the truth and not dress it up in a dinner suit – he was not ready to hear it from anybody, especially her.

He thought back to the weeks he had spent in hospital after his diagnosis. Anderson-Fabry Disease – it sounded more like the author of fairy tales than a complicated, potentially life-limiting condition. The reason they said that he had collapsed was because he had had a "Fabry crisis." As it turned out, it was fortuitous; otherwise they may not have diagnosed it until it had progressed further. He was on enzyme replacement therapy, and his prognosis was, how did they put it – "encouraging". It was better than none, so he embraced it.

"Tom!"

How long had he been lost in his thoughts? He jerked up his head directly in front of his mother's glare.

"Not now Mum, please."

She had been gathering her thoughts as a storm collects clouds. Both had an inevitable outcome.

"But…"

She was stopped in her tracks by the arrival of the rest of the lunch party: Roz, Frank and their daughter Sophie, Bill and Penny Bell and Pam and Gareth Stewart and, lastly, Edward. For the first time that day he felt like laughing; he had literally been saved by the Bells. On their arrival, the sombre atmosphere was sucked up and regurgitated into something more fitting for the day.

As it was Easter Sunday the restaurant was exceptionally busy. Their starters had taken forty minutes to arrive and over an hour after the starters had been cleared away they were still waiting for their main course. He could feel his mother bristling. Susan didn't tolerate bad service and the thread of annoyance regarding Alice made a tapestry of limited leniency. The young waitress attending to them had looked close to tears after a barbed comment from Susan regarding the starters. As the waitress passed by, red-cheeked and harassed, he distracted his mother.

"Edward, tell Mum about that paper you've read regarding the 'singing sands'."

All eyes turned to Edward, interested to hear about the haunting sounds that Tom had heard when he had rescued the girl from the beach.

As Edward spoke, Tom found himself tuning out of the conversation. If he had been looking at the situation objectively, would he truly hold out much hope for their future? He worked in the legal profession; if he was in a court of law, what would be the decision of the jury? The barrister would probe further than he was prepared to go.

"I put it to you, Tom, that all along you knew there was something wrong with the relationship. That night you were going to propose you saw the fear in her eyes; why do you think that was Tom?"

"I don't know," he imagined answering.

"Remember you are under oath, Tom. I put it to you once more. You knew that she wasn't as committed to the relationship as you were. In fact, I think we both know the reason that she left. Don't we?"

"I don't know what you are talking about," his imaginary voice replied.

"The reason she left was that she didn't love you. Isn't that right Tom?"

"No."

"Then you tell me the reason, Tom."

"I can't, I don't know. I don't understand it."

"I think you do, Tom. You didn't ask her, did you?"

"What do you mean?"

"You didn't ask her what the problem was, because you already knew the answer."

"No."

"The answer, Tom. What was the answer she would have given you if you had asked her what was wrong?"

"She wasn't in love with me."

"Could you repeat that so we can all hear?"

"She wasn't in love with me. It was nothing to do with my illness; it was because she simply didn't love me."

Tom felt sick. It was the first time he had truly allowed his mind to consider this possibility. He had always reasoned that it was because of his illness, but he couldn't get that terrified look of hers from his mind when he was going to propose to her.

"Tom!"

He looked up to see his mother glaring at him from across the table.

"Roz was asking you a question."

He glanced at Roz who was blushing from being caught in the middle of something.

"Sorry Roz; my mind was elsewhere."

"We can all see that!"

Tom was furious and was on the verge of sharing his anger with the rest of the party when Edward intervened. He expanded on the previous conversation.

"So, as I said – Tom, you actually heard the noise that was emitted from the sand. What was it like?"

Tom knew that Edward was attempting to diffuse the situation. They were all tense; it had been a tough few months. He supposed his mother was just hurt for him. He wished she was a little less obvious but he was indeed hurt and more than a little embarrassed. He was grateful for the distraction.

"I can't really explain it. It was like hearing a new type of music for the first time, as if you had only heard jazz music before and then someone played you something classical. It may also have had something to do with the fact that I was out of my mind with pain and on the verge of collapse from a medical condition I didn't even know then that I had. She was only a slight girl, but she was semi-conscious and a dead weight. It's well documented that pain can do strange things to the mind, but even so!"

"I did a little research after I found that paper. As I said to you before, it is a recognised phenomenon, although I think that you may be the first person to use it as a navigational tool!"

"I am still convinced that without it I wouldn't have known which direction to go in. I read the paper you gave me; it was very interesting, especially because it said that it only happened during certain conditions. The strange thing was that, although the rain had stopped by the time I found her, the sand was still wet in parts and according to the paper the sand needed to be bone dry."

"Maybe the fact that it was almost gale force conditions helped to dry the sand?" said Edward.

"Yes, that's a possibility, but the conditions were far from optimum for the sound emitted to be so strong and to go on for so long."

"Do you think that it was something else that you heard?" said Bill.

"No, quite the opposite actually. Alice and I listened to a recording of them on YouTube and it sounded exactly the same as I heard."

"But you still think that the conditions were wrong?"

"Not wrong but certainly not optimum," said Tom.

"I think that maybe you were just very fortunate and to be honest, considering your subsequent collapse, I think you were due a bit of luck. I have read a lot about sand in the last few weeks and its different properties. Do you know that they are doing research now to harness the energy from the sand that is heated up during the day and convert it into usable energy? How amazing would that be? Those Arabian princes will be laughing all the way to the bank again – even if all their oil supplies dried up."

Tom was glad of the distraction as the group began an in-depth discussion about whether they thought it was a valid way of capturing energy. Usually an eager participant in these robust debates, he zoned out once more thinking of Alice.

"How fascinating sand is don't you think, Tom? As Edward said look at all the different qualities it has?" asked Susan.

"Mm," he replied.

He could tell his mother was annoyed at his non-committal answer. He should have known she was going somewhere with it.

"We all know that a tiny grain of sand can become a pearl when it becomes lodged in an oyster, but at the end of the day it was just a grain of sand on a beach full of millions of other grains."

She thought she was so clever, surreptitiously hijacking the theme and having a dig about Alice. He knew she was actually trying in her own twisted way to tell him that there were plenty more fish in the sea. Was she right; had he got it so very wrong? Did the apple not fall very far from the tree? His own father had been a bit of a waster. Was his mother just trying to warn him?

The main courses arrived much to everyone's relief and the subject changed to the food in front of them. Tom had lost his appetite, knowing Susan would continue to score points against an adversary who wasn't even there. He wished he had ordered something light like the pan-fried bass; instead a bloody steak covered with a rich wine sauce was placed in front of him. He moved the pommes soufflé around the plate hoping no-one would notice his lack of appetite. He managed a few mouthfuls of the steak cutting up the rest and hiding some of it under the garnish of rocket. He didn't think he could stomach the whole thing much more; he shouldn't have come, he had spoilt it for everyone else.

The waiters came and cleared away the plates and he was relieved that the young girl didn't ask if there was something wrong with his, but simply scooped up the dish and piled it on top of the empty plates. There was talk of coffee and desserts; he did think about excusing himself saying he didn't feel well, which in some part was true, but he knew everyone would panic because of his newly diagnosed condition.

"Tom, I don't know about you, but I'm absolutely stuffed. Do you fancy taking that big useless dog of yours for a walk?" asked Sophie.

Tom would have hugged her in thanks if it wasn't for the fact that she was sitting at the other side of the table.

"If no-one minds, Soph." He looked around the table and saw them all nodding their consent, even his mother smiled. OK, it was more of a grimace, but it was a start.

As they said their goodbyes and gathered their coats, Tom felt as though a huge weight had been lifted from his shoulders. All day he had wanted to speak to Sophie as she had met Alice several times. He wanted to get her perspective on what had happened.

They left the restaurant and travelled in Tom's car back to his house. Sophie had come with her parents, who would now be taking Susan home instead of their daughter. Tom was supposed to be taking his mother home as she had decided to leave her car at the restaurant so she could have a drink. He hadn't realised quite how much of the champagne she had been quaffing; he had missed the bullet once more. The journey home with a tipsy Susan in battle mode was not to be taken lightly.

They sat in silence during the short journey, each mulling over the subject in both their minds. Sophie waited while Tom went into the house to fetch Febus who bounded towards her with gratitude all over his happy doggy face. Rather than travel back to the beach, they decided to walk through the park. Febus was delighted with the change of venue from his usual walk and set about leaving a trail of his scent to alert all the birds and beasts in the area that he was in town.

"So, do you want to talk about it?" asked Sophie.

"I do, but to be honest Sophie, there isn't a lot to say. I got sick, she was wonderful. I improved, she buggered off."

"It's as simple as that?"

"Well, no I suppose not, but as far as I'm concerned there isn't much more to go on."

"Are you sure? I know I probably shouldn't say this, but Susan said to my mum that you were very serious about her. She didn't say any more, just let Mum fill in the blanks. Were you planning on asking her to move in with you?"

"Worse than that Soph. I was going to ask her to marry me!"

"Ooh, that serious?"

"Well, obviously she didn't think so."

"When I saw the two of you around Christmas, I was surprised when you said that you'd only met her in the October. You both got on so well, I thought that you had known each other a lot longer. I did notice one thing though; she was very nervy when I said that I was a reporter. I know we've had this conversation before; I think everyone has something to hide – always looking out for a story, blah, blah, blah. But to be honest, Tom, I do have a sixth sense for these things and that girl had something to hide."

"Why didn't you say something to me?"

"What would I have said, 'Oh, you two are like a married couple – you are so in tune with each other – but watch out, she's got a dark secret she's hiding from you.'"

Tom gave a sad grimace; she was right – what could she have done? He wouldn't have listened to her anyway. When they were young, she had always had the journalistic bug. Many a time, they had followed kids home from school when she had decided that they were up to no good. It had resulted in them winning a community youth award from the local police when they had discovered a gang of boys stealing from two elderly spinster sisters. One sister would be kept talking at the door of the house whilst the boys crept indoors – the other sister too poorly to know or care that their things were being stolen from under her nose.

Did Sophie have some sort of professional intuition? He had to admit he had felt Alice stiffen when he introduced them. What could that mean anyway? It wasn't as if she was some crazed psychopath. At the time, he had been frustrated that she didn't tell him much about her past. He hadn't pressed her; instead he shared his colourful past, hoping that he would gain her trust and she would open up to him. It hadn't worked and then he had rushed into proposing to her. It felt right at the time though, or had he been subconsciously scared that he was losing her and so had tried to keep her?

"Tom?"

"You've set me thinking about all the things that didn't add up."

"Such as?"

"I don't know anything about her, hardly anything if I really think about it. She never talked about her parents. I asked her once if she had any siblings; she said she didn't so I said that was something else we had in common. She stared at me and said, 'You and I are very different, more than you will ever realise.' I pressed her about it but she wouldn't talk about it. Actually, that was our first argument. She would tell me little things about an aunt or a cousin – always about someone not particularly close. I suppose she felt it was enough to put me off the scent."

"But the scent of what?"

"Exactly."

"OK, I'm going to be devil's advocate so bear with me. She may have just been that type of girl – there are ones like that out there who are fond of the first flush of romance then bugger off once it goes to the next level."

"I've thought of nothing else since she disappeared and to be honest with you, I've asked myself that question so many times."

"And?"

"I keep coming back to the same conclusion."

"Go on."

"OK, when I'm at a low ebb I agree with you that she simply wanted to walk away, but something nags at me that there is more to this. The other thing is, if she had wanted to walk away, wouldn't she have sent me a text to say that she wanted to end the relationship?"

"I don't know, Tom. Some people are just cowards. However, that said she didn't seem like that to me if I'm honest. She…, I don't know quite how to put this…"

"Go on," he urged.

"Well she seemed like someone who was running away."

Martha
April 2015, England

Salt-waves caress sand
Tickling my toes and heart
In their short-spun wake.

Haiku poetry

Martha was preparing supper for John. Her hands shook as she rolled the pastry on the floured board. It was a strange feeling to be afraid of John. She smelt burning; quickly she turned and saw smoke rising from the pan. She grabbed a cloth and dumped the saucepan and its acrid contents into the sink. She turned on the cold water tap and, as the water gushed, the loud hiss eventually stopped like a steam engine coming to rest. The leek and chicken were unrecognisable – a charred coating being the only evidence of its former contents. She sat at the table and like the pan sighed until she was out of steam. He was due any second; he was supposed to have called in during his lunch hour but had been unable to leave work because of some crisis, so now he was calling after work. Thankfully, the children had an after-school club and then were going to a sleepover. This was going to be hard enough without any distractions. Was making his favourite dish of chicken pot-pie with a cheese pastry lid accompanied by mash and gravy going to stop him from being angry with her? She doubted it. Still, she got up from the chair and rummaged in the fridge to see if she had any more chicken and leeks. She found a packet of chicken breast, but no leeks and supposed that maybe it was a good thing – why ruin the taste of his favourite meal? She was certain that once she sat him down and told him what was on her mind, he would never want to see her or the damn chicken pie again.

She sat down again, this time with the packet of raw chicken breast in her hand. She had left the back door open because it was promising to be a beautiful spring day and was glad now because the awful smell that had initially caught at the back of her throat was almost gone. The voile moved as the breeze pushed passed it, shooing clean air into the room. She stood defiantly and once more started making the pie. She left the pastry and began to remake the filling, added butter and oil to a pan then chopped the chicken into small cubes and, as the chicken browned, she added some sherry and stock. She looked around the kitchen for something to flavour the pie and was annoyed that she hadn't bought any extra veg. Instead, she cut some of the herbs from her window box and added them to the pot, finished rolling the pastry then carefully placed it on top of the chicken mix. Finally, she added a wash of beaten egg and a sprinkling of parmesan. The pie was made. She popped it in the oven.

She looked at the time once more, feeling nervous at what she had to do. Peggy had learnt this week the importance of ringing 999 if there was a problem. The teacher was very proactive at informing the children of what they needed to do in an emergency. Peggy had been desperate ever since to be the first in the class who had to put it into practice. Martha was glad she hadn't been here to see the burning pan. She didn't want her to be a witness to the inevitable raised voices. John was mild-mannered but if you pushed him too far he could lose his temper. She had only seen him lose it a few times whilst he was growing up but each time, it had been dreadful. She heard a beeping sound and for a second could not place where it was coming from but then realised it was the pie – she had put the timer on the oven because she was so distracted. She opened the oven and there on the shelf was a mouth-watering golden pie.

She suddenly felt nauseous, ran up to the bathroom and was sick. She heard the front door slam.

"Mum? Mum, where are you?"

She wiped her mouth and made her way back downstairs. John was standing in the hall.

"God Mum, are you OK? You look dreadful!"

She looked at the face of her second born son. She felt as though she had to sacrifice one son for the other. Would the wise King Solomon have known what to do or would he have asked her to cut one in half in order to show the other one that she loved him more? At this, great sobs came from inside her and she watched as John came towards her and hugged her and told her that whatever it was, they would deal with it, because as a family that was what they always did. She was so glad that Peggy was having a sleepover because she would definitely have rung 999.

When she had calmed down he made them both a cup of tea, a normal one for himself and camomile for his mother. She smiled; he didn't know that she was taking a walk on the wild side.

"I've been drinking your tea recently," she said.

"I guess that's not the great secret that you wanted to tell me."

He always made her laugh, even as a small child he had been a joker. She didn't want him to stop making her laugh – would he when he knew the truth? She knew though that she couldn't put it off any longer.

"You may hate me after I tell you this and, if you do, all I can say is that I'm sorry and that I thought it was for the best."

"Look, whatever it is, just tell me. I'm a grown man, Mum; you can tell me anything."

She wasn't frightened to tell him. She had wanted to do so for such a long time. It was the thought that he may think less of her that was terrifying her more than anything.

She looked at him, scared to read the expression on his face. But all she saw was love and concern. She wondered if she would see that same look once she had finished her sorry story or would it be like those masks in the theatre, the comedy and the tragedy. One happy, one sad; she recalled from her school days, Thalia and Melpomene. Who knew she would have her very own Greek tragedy.

"As you know, I was estranged from my parents for most of my adult life. I gather that you also know that my mother has died and my father is in a nursing home."

"I know, Mum. I went to see him." He looked up at her as he spoke. "I'm sorry, I should have told you."

So, her father wasn't confused; he had met John, but he hadn't told her until now. Like mother, like son.

"What I never told you was the reason that I wanted nothing to do with them. I sort of intimated that my mother had serious

219

mental health issues with a late diagnosis of schizophrenia. It wasn't that in itself, although of course it didn't help what came next. It has taken me an awful lot of years to come to the realisation that I can't blame everything that happened on them. They are partly to blame, yes, but I too have to shoulder a lot of the blame."

"Blame for what, Mum? I know you have had your issues with them. When Evie was alive she initially talked about them all the time; how she couldn't understand how you were estranged from them when you were so family-oriented."

"Oh John, how can I tell you something that I should have told you so many years ago?"

Martha felt the icy breath of fear breathing down her back. She wanted to stay in this moment while her son still loved and admired her. She knew better than anyone how hard it is to find out that parents are human and have feet made of clay.

"I think I know what you are trying to tell me. I just wasn't absolutely sure until just now."

Martha felt her legs shake as the fear encased her whole body. She couldn't move or speak. She waited for John to say something.

"I think that somewhere I have an older brother, one who was born when I think you were still in university. I think that you held your parents responsible for making you give him up for adoption and that your father regrets it with every bone that is left in his body."

Neither of them spoke for a minute, digesting the truth that had been served up for them. Martha broke the spell, after having kept the secret for so many years, she couldn't wait any longer to tell him everything.

"I went to see my father a few weeks ago. There were a few things that precipitated it. I felt foolish then that I had left it for so long, all those wasted years. He mentioned you – he was so delighted that you had been to see him. But what I don't understand is how did you know about your brother?"

The word brother sounded strange coming from her and being directed at John. She had put this moment off most of her life and yet, now, all she felt was a huge sense of relief.

"Evie had always gone on and on about your past; she felt strongly that you were hiding something from us. She knew how much you loved the kids, but when she told you she was expecting Seth and then Peggy, she said there was a sadness that you carried within you. She initially thought it was because you had only been able to have one child – "Little China" as Dad had fondly called you. Then Evie thought there was more to it. If I'm honest, I didn't really take much notice; she would witter on about doing something but I was always busy. Then suddenly, she stopped talking about it. I didn't realise at first, it's like that ticking clock that annoys you and you don't realise it has stopped because at first you enjoy the peace, then you start to miss it. It took me a few months and then I became obsessed. I asked her why she had stopped talking about it but she dismissed it saying that she had given up. Initially, I believed her but occasionally when we were all together I saw the two of you exchange a look. Anyway, of course Evie became ill then and everything else just went out of the window. After Christmas I went to see your dad. I suppose it had been in the back of my mind for a while. I was going to tell you I'd met him but then you went on your trip to see your "sick friend". When you came back you were so distant I was worried it may be you that was ill. So I called Pam to see if you had confided in her. We talked about your past and the fact neither of us knew much about your life before you met Dad. I told her about the strange way your dad had referred to you having found me and then it all fell in to place. Am I right Mum, do I have an older brother somewhere?"

Martha nodded unable to speak.

"I understand, Mum. I really do."

She let the tears flow, then the dam burst its banks. The dam which over the years had been carefully reinforced, but even a carefully constructed one can fall apart in a very short time. She sobbed as her second son held her, still loving her even though she had kept so many secrets from him for so long.

She repeated her apologies over and over again, as if the words could rub out the pain little by little as she said the same thing again and again.

"I don't blame you, Mum, and I understand your reasons, but it did take me a while to absorb the fact that I'm not your only child. I realise that Evie must have got you to tell her and that was why she stopped nagging me to talk to you about it all."

"I am so sorry that you had to find out like that; even your dad never knew. I suspect he may have put two and two together but he never said. I had backed myself into a corner because I had never been honest with your dad nor with you. I had opportunities along the way, but chose to ignore them, putting it off until there was a 'better time' but there never was. Evie made it her mission to try and persuade me to firstly tell you and then to make amends with him. I'm not sure if she went to see him or not, but after she found out, she became obsessed about finding the boy. I couldn't entertain it. I felt I didn't deserve to disrupt his life and yours. She asked that if she did all the work and found him, would I agree to sanction her search."

"And did you?"

"Sadly, by the time she had got the reason out of me and had taken a few months to persuade me to allow her, she had started to become unwell. I am so sorry John for everything I have put you through."

"There is nothing to be sorry for. I admire you for having the strength to walk away and find a new life for yourself. "

She made them both a cup of calming camomile tea, which for once John didn't refuse, and then she told him about her trip away to find his brother.

Several months later, life had once more settled back into some sort of normality.

Tonight, she was making pasta. She had made the dough and was attempting to pass it through the shiny new pasta contraption that the kids had bought her. Her grandmother would have said it was like a small version of the mangle she used to pass Martha's clothes through. She had just phoned the nursing home which she now did every day to see how her father was. She had spoken with Sally for a while then replaced the phone, laughing. Her father had apparently developed a nasty eye infection which of course in itself wasn't anything to laugh about. Seth, however, on meeting a great-grandfather with only one leg had developed a theory that he was some sort of a retired pirate. The eye infection had necessitated an eye patch – all he needed now was a parrot on his shoulder to complete the look.

She opened the oven door and slid the large dish onto the shelf. The lasagne would be ready in forty minutes. She looked around her sparkling kitchen which she had spent the entire morning cleaning from top to bottom. She had changed the water in the vase of flowers. Peggy had stayed with her most of the previous evening as John had promised to take Seth for his first golf lesson. Peggy had arrived as though she was the one tasked with looking after Martha and not the other way around. The little minx had bounded in clutching a bunch of freshly picked hyacinths which were allegedly from her back garden. It was the tulips hiding among them that had alarmed Martha – they looked suspiciously like the award-winning ones from her neighbour's garden.

Evie
April 2013, England

Let my toes teach the shore
How to feel a tranquil life
Through the wetness of sands.

Let my heart latch the door
Of blackness, as all my pain
Now blue sky understands.

Munia Khan

Evie could barely stand in the shower any more but she refused to
allow John to fit the small fold-away seat that had arrived a week ago
and leaned threateningly against the bathroom wall. It was a slippery
slope and one she felt she was sliding down too quickly. It would be
the seat to begin with, then it would be John having to bring her bed
downstairs. She knew the drill. Peggy had seen the box and asked if it
was for her bedroom. After some confusion, it had turned out that she
thought it was the longed-for window seat for her bedroom. It had been
complicated trying to explain to her that it wasn't that simple. She said
that Chelsea had one in her bedroom. Chelsea had a sprawling house
which apparently had several window seats. Evie wished that Peggy
would find normal friends.

She let the warm water cascade over her body. She felt shaky
like Bambi, unable to stand for much longer but unwilling to leave

the warmth of the shower so she gently slid down the tiles until she was able to sit on the shower floor. She relaxed, more comfortable in the new position. She washed her body with the mango-scented body wash; anything to try and rid herself of the smell of impending death. Her body no longer felt familiar to her. As she moved her hands over the map of herself she felt she was in a foreign country, unsure of the contours. Once out of the shower, she towelled her body dry and dressed in sweat pants and a long-sleeved t-shirt. She sat on the edge of her bed, exhausted from the effort.

She heard the dog bark downstairs. Poor Darwin – he had managed to develop a very strong bladder since she had become so unwell, but even he sometimes had to admit defeat. She made her way slowly downstairs because she had learned the hard way that it was better to go slowly and get there eventually than rush and hurt herself. Darwin was delighted to see her as she entered the kitchen and greeted her like a long-lost friend and then rushed to the back door. She opened the door and could see that they had had a light frost during the night. The dog hesitated even with his full bladder. Evie reminded him that he was possessed of a fur coat and should get out there and do what he needed to or she would turn the tap on. He bounded out the door once the decision was made. She sat at the kitchen table while she waited for his return. She felt so cold even though she had pulled a long cardigan over her clothes so she got up to make herself a cup of coffee. Once outside, Darwin could be busy for several minutes as he checked the perimeter of his garden for any interlopers.

She filled the kettle, spooned some coffee into a mug and added a splash of milk. As she looked around the kitchen, she saw a pile of cards on the work surface so she picked them up. Get well cards. John must have collected them up from the living room yesterday once they had realised that the likelihood of getting better was less than a big fat zero.

She loved and hated him for trying to second-guess what she would have wanted. Was it insensitive of him to pull them all down or would it have been horrible of him to leave them up, facing her all day with a request that she couldn't fulfil? Either way, she loved and hated him for doing it. She understood that it was difficult – what were visitors supposed to do? Come with a bunch of grapes and say, "Here, enjoy these while you can still eat solids." In today's society, you could get a card for almost every occasion, even one for your cousin's fiancée's cat's birthday, but there still wasn't a suitable one for someone who was dying. It seemed unfair to her somehow. John, the kids and Martha would get an abundance of sympathy cards once she had gone – she was sure of that – but one for her now when she needed it the most – none! Maybe Funky Pig or whatever that card company was where you could design your own cards would be helpful.

"Shit, you've got cancer, no getting well for you but all the best anyway." It might not be the best, most uplifting message but at least there was truth in it.

She heard a scratching at the door and there, shivering from his extended patrols of the garden, was Darwin. He shot past her and headed for the living room which had a roaring fire lit earlier by John. Every morning for the last few weeks he had lit her a fire before he went to work. She loved the smell of the wood as it warmed the house.

She had warmed to her theme of greetings cards for the terminally ill. She picked up her steaming mug of coffee and joined Darwin who wagged his tail in approval as she entered the room.

She tried some verses for her new range of cards unable to come to a decision of what the cover design should look like.

"Cancer has got you and soon you're going to die,
They will pump you full of morphine which will really make you high,

People will avoid you or rush to be by your bed,
And bravely hold your hand until they're sure that you are dead."

OK, so it probably wouldn't go down a storm at Clintons, but it would definitely have brought a smile to her face. Maybe she should suggest it to John. She smiled because although she may have developed a black humour these last few days, John hadn't. As her skin had thickened, his had become so thin she was apprehensive about talking to him about anything at all since even the most benign of conversations appeared to be laced with her tumours. She had seen Nathan again – despite all her protestations she had agreed to see him, weakened by the illness eating her away; she had phoned him and had met him the same day. Unlike John, Nathan was receptive to her black humour. Why couldn't John understand her need to make light of it, to show it that it wasn't in charge of her? It made it so much easier to face if she didn't take it too seriously. Nathan had an innate understanding of this. She called him "demise wise"; he had looked shocked and then burst out laughing. He told her that he was the perfect death companion. Even when they had first met, they had talked about John, but now they didn't. Evie didn't want to make any criticisms of John to Nathan. Nathan understood this, their relationship had changed, so had the rules.

They would swap sick jokes about death and dying. She likened it to aversion therapy; the more she laughed at it, the less she was scared of it. As Nathan had said, "The only thing in life we are sure of is death and taxes," although he did have to admit that Benjamin Franklin had said it first. And as they both agreed nothing was scarier than dealing with HMRC. It was probably easier to get St Peter on the phone at the pearly gates than to get to speak to someone at the tax office.

Nathan made her laugh when there was very little left to laugh about in her life. It was becoming harder to see him though, John had begun to cut his work hours down although the more he was home, the

228

more distant he was from her as though seeing her made him angry. The physical evidence of her demise was incontrovertible; he couldn't pretend anymore that it wasn't happening. She had tried to talk to him. Martha had given him the message about the "Fred" conversation but he appeared to have just ignored it. She was trying to accept their fate – why couldn't he?

That said, she still raged within herself at the injustice of it all. She was in the middle of the Weetabix phenomenon – something which she had never in her wildest dreams or nightmares believed she would ever have developed a fixation on. It had all started innocently enough, before they had been sure quite how bad it was. She was bored, unused to having time on her hands and had decided to tidy the pantry, to put some order if not in her life then at least in her pantry. Domesticity was not John's strong point so in order to take some of the pressure off him, she decided to arrange it in a sort of "meal order". Initially, she had felt invigorated, having a task that she could manage in small parts herself and not to have to defer to John or Martha. Soon though, she tired and so the job had taken much longer than she had anticipated. She had worked through the breakfast cereals through to main course dry ingredients when she noticed that one of the packets of pasta was out of date. She toyed with the idea of leaving it there; she couldn't think of anything horrible that would befall her family if the rigatoni was served a few weeks past its best. She then began checking the other dates just in case. It was then that she saw how long the "use-by date" was for the Weetabix but she didn't give it a lot of thought at the time. This week however had brought it home to her that Peggy and Seth would be eating their Weetabix long after she had died. It hurt her in ways that she couldn't really fathom.

In a fit of pique, she had ripped the box open and consumed three of the biscuits with sugar and warm milk. It had been too much for her stomach to take and she had brought most of it back up again. Still, she felt as though she had won a minor battle. She knew that in the end she would lose the war, but for the moment it had made her feel better.

The problem was that it had planted a seed in her head about other things; things that would be on the earth after her demise. She had had a massive argument with John a few days ago and she knew he was still upset and confused about her sudden rage. The unfortunate thing was that she knew that if she explained it to him, he would have felt worse than he did already. He had brought home a few plants for the garden and said that he wanted her to be able to look out on something pretty. Initially, she had been surprised but pleased at his thoughtfulness, but as he made them a coffee to take out into the garden after he planted them, she read the labels. When he had brought the coffee to her she had been sobbing. No amount of cajoling brought her round; she told him to throw the plants away as she stormed out of the room. She knew he had been bemused and upset but she could never tell him that the plants were perennials and, while he thought they were pretty to look at now, they would come back every year and it had been more than she could bear.

She thought back to the previous Christmas; the future had been less defined, there had been more hope in the air. They had both agreed not to exchange presents, each having their own reasons for doing so. He had double-crossed her though and had bought her a beautiful gold and silver charm bracelet. On the bracelet were four charms. One was of two children hand in hand, the second was a heart, the third a sand-timer and lastly a tiny God-brick. For anyone else it would have been a strange charm to receive unless she was thinking of a career change to become a bricklayer or such, but she knew why it was there. She had felt awful that she hadn't bought him anything apart from helping the kids to select their presents for him.

As she looked out of the window at the drab garden, she knew she had been wrong about the plants; she needed to make amends somehow. She didn't feel that she was a particularly lucky person. She had always worked hard at anything she had put her hand to, but as she sat listening to the local radio station she felt that she had been dealt a bit of luck. The newsreader bleated on about the local economy and the lack of jobs for youngsters. Then she mentioned that an old housing estate was to be demolished to make way for a new development of shops, cafés and bars. She knew precisely the estate they were talking about – she had a few days to organise one of her friends to help her. For once, time wasn't running out for her; she had three days until the whole estate was being razed to the ground.

Alice
2015, The Welsh Border

I stand amid the roar
Of a surf-tormented shore,
And I hold within my hand
Grains of the golden sand –
Taken from a dream within a dream.

Edgar Allan Poe

Alice walked to the top of the mountain; she could feel her lungs burning as she moved in the thinner air. She stumbled over the loose stones as she reached the peak. She was so very tired and it made her clumsy, but even in her low mood she felt a small frisson of pleasure at having reached the summit. It was relatively small as mountains went. For her though it felt like a small triumph, in a physical sense. Hannah had always preached about goal setting each day. The problem was where did she go now? She sat down on a large rock after drying it with the back of her gloved hand. It was surprisingly cold and she was glad she had listened to the tour guide and worn an extra layer of clothes. She looked around taking in the beauty around her. She could see the dramatic velvet valleys and hills, the silver threads of the multitude of rivers and streams producing a rich tapestry, but it left her unmoved. She could appreciate the magnificence of nature in front of her but she didn't feel it inside.

All her life she had strived to do the right thing, not to hurt anyone; she had felt as though her presence on the earth was something to be earned, she had to make her mark without scarring. She had failed dismally.

There were a few positives. Her attention to detail made her good at being a vet but then she had been suspended because of the terrible incident, so maybe not. In the months before the terrible incident she had put her traits into Google not really holding out much hope other than being labelled pathetic. But it hadn't; it had given her a sort of diagnosis something that had surprised her. A fifth of the population were described as being "highly sensitive". There had been a check list and she found that she answered yes to all the questions. Yes, she felt things too keenly both for herself and for those around her.

"Too". She was too sensitive, she was too thin skinned, she was too late. Just three letters, one word was all the difference between what had happened to her and what she could have been.

Those three letters had shaped her whole life.

She felt tired; the wind cut through her unused to anything hampering its route this high on the mountain. She couldn't change what had gone. She was like the butterfly effect; she had gently flapped her wings and the effect had been felt by so many people. And that was the worst thing for her as an Highly Sensitive Person. She could only have a good effect on others; anything else was just too much for her to bear.

She didn't have any more energy; her fuel tank was empty. Her bottom was getting cold; the cold hard rock unforgiving, and even though she had wrapped up warm the cold was seeping through her clothes intent on getting to her very bones. The problem was that too thin skin of hers didn't prevent things from penetrating her, either physically or emotionally. She closed her eyes returning to the blackness that had enveloped her for so long.

She went back to that day, the one she had replayed over and over again but each time the ending was the same.

Tom

But everyone who hears these words of mine
And does not put them into practice is like a foolish man
Who built his house on sand.

Matthew 7:26

Tom picked up the fat files from his desk and took them to the central office. Shirley thanked him and reminded him that he had a meeting with Mrs Pritchard at 11am. He had an hour to spare so he went back to his office and made a strong black coffee. He was glad he had made the decision to stay on in Swansea and not move to Cardiff. Both offices had left the final decision to him but, in the end, he knew he had to consider his health. He felt the proximity of the sea and the stunning walks afforded by the sweeping Gower coast would benefit him far more than the hustle and bustle of a large city. He tried for the third time that day to ring Alice; once more it rang and rang and then went to voicemail. He didn't leave a message this time; he had said it all before. He knew that he couldn't leave it alone though. If nothing else he had to be sure she was OK.

He pulled out his iPad from the drawer and typed in Alice's name in the search engine; he wasn't convinced that there would be any information about her but it was worth a try. He typed Alice Summers. Several came through. He ignored the actresses, the lawyers and the owner of a small café. Then under the heading of one of the national papers there was an article about a court case. He would have ignored that too but there was a photo, and there was no mistaking that the girl in the picture was her. Shaking, he read the article; it was dated almost four years previously.

Alice Summers formerly of 10 Waverly Crescent was found not guilty of manslaughter.

He took in an audible breath of air.

The jury took less than thirty minutes to come to the unanimous decision. Her solicitor released this statement

"Alice and her family would like to thank everyone for their unwavering support during this very difficult time. She feels no victory just sadness that it had come to this for the truth to be told."

Tom could feel his heart racing as he read on:

Alice Summers was charged initially with the murder of her former boyfriend Noah Watts. The CPS subsequently reduced the charge to manslaughter. She was alleged to have attacked him with a metal lamp after a bitter row; he died instantly. Alice had sustained severe bruising to the neck consistent with attempted strangulation. The prosecution vigorously denied this and attempted to suggest that it had been self-

inflicted to deflect blame. He was described as a gentle boy but this was swiftly disproved after an array of ex-girlfriends took to the stand. The picture was soon painted of his violent controlling behaviour. One ex-girlfriend had an injunction to prevent him from coming within a mile radius of her. Family and friends had witnessed first-hand his increasingly bizarre behaviour. They described him as being obsessed with her and using a variety of "disguises" to follow her to work and on the rare occasions he allowed her to go out with friends. She had tried to end the relationship previously but on the day in question she had ended it in the morning but for reasons still unclear she had returned to his flat in the evening.

He flew into a rage and attempted to strangle her. She managed to grab a metal lamp and brought it down on his head causing catastrophic injuries. Summers is thought to have moved away from the area after a short stay in a psychiatric unit.

Tom couldn't take it all in. How could he have not seen the signs; it was his job to dig deep to evaluate. He had just been too close to see what was under his nose. It explained so many things, more than he could marry up in such a short time. His overall feeling was that he needed to find her and it was crucial that he find her quick. If he had had to explain the sudden time constraint he wouldn't have been able to but he knew that it was a fact. And the clock had started ticking.

Alice
The Time Before

Everything was black. She knew that she was losing consciousness, she didn't have much time. She hadn't realised how very dark black could be. She could feel the life draining out of her as if some celestial being had an eraser and was rubbing her life away bit by bit. She was now watching a pretty display of shooting stars. She knew that it probably wasn't a good thing but it was better than the absolute blackness. She thought back to her childhood; she was so glad she hadn't known what was to come. She thought about her parents; they had no-one else. They would be hauled out in front of the cameras to plead for the killer of their daughter. They would be distraught. Her mother hated being in the limelight for any reason; this would be her worst nightmare. Her father would exhibit his stoicism. Her mother would then fold in on herself and maybe never be able to straighten out the creases.

She felt the pressure on her throat ease. It still hurt like hell but she managed to take a small breath. So, she wasn't dead yet. She kept very still and took a few gasping breaths. She couldn't feel Noah's presence near her; maybe he had gone into the small garden to dig a hole to bury her in. She remembered playing musical statues as a child, she kept still until she was sure it was as safe as it could be to open her eyes. She must have passed out for a few minutes as she dreamt she was on a golden beach; the sun was shining and she could feel the warmth on her face. She was wearing something long and floaty that billowed in the wind. Her hair was coated with a fine spray of salty dew. She was like something out of the movies. Why was she on a beach? Her mind was like a spider's web; some thoughts stayed while others fell through the gossamer. She remembered now that she was far from the idyll she had just imagined. She also remembered that she had to stay very still.

She opened one eye. Her heart was beating so loudly that she was sure it was betraying her to Noah. The room appeared empty so she opened the other eye. The room was dark, lit only by the large metal floor lamp. Noah was nowhere to be seen. The room was a mess; the chair in the corner was on its side and there was broken glass on the wooden coffee table. She remembered it all now and wished that she hadn't. She started to cry.

All her girlfriends had been envious at first. He had been the epitome of charming; the only thing missing it had seemed was a coat of armour and a white horse. She had tried not to feel too smug and had more or less achieved a sort of detached wonder at the life she was leading. He had given her confidence and because of her new-found belief in herself she had secured a job as a vet in one of the most prestigious practices in the area. She had for the first time in her life felt the uncertainty and worry about most things slide away like slowly removing a heavy coat. She had even been shouted at by a particularly prickly cat owner who had threatened to sue her for malpractice but it had been like water off a duck's back; for her this was nothing sort of a miracle. Not a biblical miracle but still for her it was a turning point. She felt she had developed the elusive thicker skin that everyone else seemed to possess.

She had met him by chance in the most innocuous of places, or so it had appeared at the time; it was only later it transpired that it had been by design. She had been out walking the family dog; it had been a beautiful autumn day. Dry and crisp, the air tinged with the chill of the winter to come. The path she often took led her to pass by a small shop which sold a little bit of everything. He had come out laden with bags and had literally fallen over the dog, all the produce spilling to the floor. When she looked back afterwards she could she how contrived it had been. He had ample room to walk, the bag was filled with items she herself would have chosen – the same sort of food stuffs: stinky cheese and plain crackers. Her favourite wine and a book that she had started reading a few weeks before had tumbled to the ground in front of her.

Only much later she had found out that he had brought a pet into the practice for a consultation. One of the other vets had seen to him; the animal was old and diseased, and the vet had recommended that the kindest thing was to have it euthanised. They offered a service whereby they would counsel the owners about the best way to dispose of the remains. They had joined forces with a local funeral director and because they had a small parcel of land at the rear of the practice some owners liked the idea of having somewhere to visit their old friends. As she had helped get this initiative off the ground she was put in charge of the day to day management of it. The kindly vet had explained all this to him and pointed her out. But Noah had never taken them up on the service and much to the surprise of the vet he never returned. Later the poor vet had thought he may have told Noah too much about Alice: her single status, her soft caring nature. It was innocuous enough but in the wrong hands? Noah had become obsessed with her after that and had followed her home on several occasions. He had also followed her family and friends. In this way he came to know her likes and dislikes, what she liked to eat and drink, how she liked to spend her leisure time. He learned how to swim so that after the meeting at the shop he "bumped" into her at the local pool – not the one he had been learning in twenty miles away. He had targeted her from before the beginning. As they had said in court, she didn't stand a chance. He had seen in her what she had tried to very hard to cover and he had exposed it to everyone.

Initially when they had started to go out he had been everything she had wished for (he had done his homework thoroughly) but as the relationship progressed he couldn't help but show his less caring side. He became jealous of her having any interactions with men regardless of age. He alienated her from her friends, either arguing with them or preventing her from socialising with them. By this time, she had begun to realise she had made an awful mistake and so she ended the relationship. She didn't hear from him for over a week then he turned up at the practice with a puppy demanding to be seen by only her. Once more he charmed her. She hated to admit it but she had felt lost without him; such had been his hold on her that she was scared to function without him. It turned out to be the biggest mistake of her life.

They carried on in some sort of normality for a few months but it wasn't the same. She had thought once more of ending the relationship; she knew that her friends and parents would be delighted. It wasn't that easy: she had tried once and she knew that he would be much worse the second time round She was caught and she didn't know the way out.

Then his father was killed in a car accident and her world fell apart.

He must have thought he had killed her, so she lay there completely still. She heard humming; he had returned. She kept perfectly still. The humming continued but she couldn't hear it as well. She chanced a look. He was standing with his back to her but she could see only too well what he was doing. She took her chance. She jumped up and, grabbing the heavy metal lamp, wacked him across the side of the head. He went down instantly. She hit him with such force the bulb shattered from the shock, reverberating through the metal column, and a flurry of glistening shards rained down on them both. She had thought it looked so pretty as she slunk to her knees. She was just glad that he had stopped that awful annoying humming.

Tom

Circle in the sand
Round and round
Never ending love is what we've found.

'Circle in the Sand', Belinda Carlisle
Richard W Nowels / Ellen Shipley

Tom was on the phone to Sophie; he needed another head to help him figure it all out. She was in work but the beauty of being a journalist was that she had the freedom to go and chase up a story at any given time. She had filed her work for the day and, with a nod to her boss that she had a lead on a story, grabbed her coat and bag and left the premises. She waited for Tom in front of the building holding two steaming cups of coffee. He pulled up less than three minutes later.

"OK, so what's the plan?" she asked.

"I haven't any idea. I thought you could do some research on your phone while I drive; wherever she is or has been it will be away from here. I know she lived in London but she was always vague about the exact place. The article in the paper gives details of Noah's family but again no address. However, they both have relatively uncommon names so I thought the electoral register maybe?"

"So, what is Noah's family name?"

"Watts, Noah Watts. The only other relative as far as the article said was a sister, Lauren – same surname."

"OK that's a good start. I'll start looking, you head up the M4. I think we will only find any answers if we start at the beginning."

"I agree."

Tom indicated and pulled the car onto the motorway.

"I've found something. I did an address search and there are eight entries for Lauren Watts in the London area. Hold on, I can discount two as they are too old and one is a child. That leaves us with five possibilities."

"Good work Sophie. Can we rule out any of the others? I still feel that we need to hurry."

"Give me a second. OK, according to the tabloid article she was in her early thirties when the case was being heard so that would make her about thirty-five. If we widen the parameters slightly to allow for any errors then we need to only look for a Lauren Watts between the ages of thirty-two to thirty-eight. The age brackets are thirty to thirty-four and thirty-five to thirty-nine, but another two are outside of those so we have three left. All three are within those two age groups, one in the first and the other two in the second."

"OK then let's have a look at the addresses and we can work out a route."

Tom drove on as Sophie paid for the search on her credit card and downloaded the addresses of the three "Laurens"; in less than ten minutes they had addresses for all three. They couldn't have been further away from each other if Tom had drawn a

244

triangle and deposited them at each of the corners. They decided on the first one for the sole reason that it was the nearest to them and it seemed prudent to try that first. He looked at the sat nav; they would arrive at the first "Lauren" at 2.30pm.

Sophie dozed as he carried on up the motorway; they were only about an hour away now but the feeling of unease didn't lessen.

"Sophie, we're here."

He gently touched her shoulder to wake her. She had gone from dozing to a deep sleep, snoring so gently and quietly that it had helped soothe him as he had driven.

"OK. Sorry Tom, I was only going to have five minutes."

"Do you want to wait in the car?"

"No, I'll come with you. No offence but it may be a little less threatening if I'm there."

"Yes, you're probably right. Are you ready for this?"

"Absolutely."

He knew that Sophie was enjoying the drama of it but it didn't offend him. She had come at very short notice to help a friend in distress; nothing else was important.

They walked up the quiet street. It wasn't the best of neighbourhoods but Tom had seen worse. Some of the houses had fallen into disrepair, but most, including number 16, were well maintained. Number 16 had a pretty front garden with a brick path. They rang the bell on the shiny black front door. They waited. It was then that Tom realised he had no idea what he was going to say.

The door was opened by a smart woman in her late thirties. She was tall with black shiny hair in a pixie cut. She matched her front door. On her feet were bunny slippers complete with floppy ears. It was an anomaly to say the least.

Tom had lost the power of speech and he didn't think it was just because of the bunny slippers.

"Hello. We're sorry to bother you but we are from the census register. Is this a convenient time to ask you a few questions?"

Tom watched amazed as Sophie flashed her press card at the woman. She held her hand over the bold "press" only showing her picture and name.

"Well, I am a bit busy but if you're quick I can spare a few minutes."

Tom wasn't entirely sure whether Sophie wanted him to speak, so he kept quiet.

"According to the register you live here with two other people; is that correct?"

"Yes, that's right."

"Could you confirm their relationship to you?"

"Of course; my husband and my mum live here. She came to live with us a couple of years ago as she wasn't managing well on her own."

"Good. This is one of the reasons for the census. Were there any other options open for you regarding your mother's care? A care home maybe? Sharing the responsibility with a sibling?"

Tom suddenly understood where Sophie was going with this.

"There were a few options but I wasn't happy with the standard of the care homes around here and I didn't want to move her too far away. In the end this seemed the only option."

"Thank you, you've been very helpful. Our society is changing, we have an ageing population and no long-term plans for how to deal with it."

"Was that it?"

"Yes, thank you."

Sophie turned to walk away.

"Oh, one last thing. You didn't say about any help from your siblings?"

"I'm an only child."

"I see. Well, thank you very much for your time."

Tom was impressed; he had been all set to ask the woman outright if she was the sister of Noah Watts but he could see now that just turning up and asking probing questions about a family tragedy wasn't the best way to achieve their goal. He needed to act like Sophie – that it was work and not anything else.

They jumped back in the car.

"That was impressive. OK on to the next one."

He put the second address in the sat nav. It would take them at least another forty-five minutes to get to the next address. He felt the anxiety building again.

Alice

*If my thoughts of you
Were to suddenly become grains of sand,
I will have made for you, an island.*

Isaac Fowler

She shivered; she was so very cold and tired. She had kept on running away from what had happened to her but, now that she had come to a sudden stop, it was as if it had claimed her, as she knew all along that it would. She was tired of replaying that day over and over again like an old neglected cinema that only has one film to play.

It had plagued her day and night; it was too close to home for her. It was the one thing she couldn't argue with Yes, he was difficult; yes, he was violent and abusive and had done the same to other women. However, Lauren was right. If she had never met him he would have still been alive. She had looked at her parents as Lauren had finished and had seen the pain on their faces. She also thought she saw blame. It had broken her.

So, she carried him everywhere with her, to keep him alive in some sort of penance.

She had had enough; it was getting dark, her whole body felt numb with cold. The weather was worsening. She could see a band of rain headed straight for her. It would be so much easier to let go. She relaxed her taut shoulders and sat back against one of the rocks. She had lost the fight.

Tom

If lighthouse becomes a burning candle,
Flickered upon ocean's insanity.
Your sailing heart there anchors to handle
The obsessed breeze towards sand dune's vanity.

Munia Khan

The drive across the city was excruciatingly slow. It was now peak time so they squeezed between buses, cars and motorcycles to gain some advantage, all of them competing for a slice of the road. Tom looked at the fuel gauge; the nose to tail driving was draining the tank. He would keep an eye out for a petrol station just in case. The sat nav kept recalculating as the traffic became denser. They were still at least twenty minutes from their destination. Sophie had dozed off again and had resumed her melancholy snoring. He was tired and would need his medication soon. He felt sick to his stomach that it was Alice who needed looking after and, as she had always told him, the timing was crucial. He was lucky over the next few miles. A few gaps opened up in the traffic which he filled as though his car was made out of mercury. They were almost at the second Lauren's house.

He gently roused Sophie once more, who woke up faintly embarrassed that she appeared to have developed narcolepsy. The street was in a much smarter area than the previous one. All the houses were well maintained and most looked as though they had a substantial amount of money spent on them. There were the fashionable lollipop trees – flavoured in bay, olive and cherry – standing to attention at doorways, manicured front lawns and immaculate pathways. Tom doubted that any of the inhabitants tended to their own gardens. He looked at Sophie as they walked up the path to number 26; she smiled in encouragement. He found himself bizarrely wishing that the previous Lauren had been the right one. This time the front door had an ornate wrought iron overlay. A large iron knocker protruded in the middle. He knocked the door and they both waited. Nothing. Tom knocked again.

"It's very quiet," said Sophie

"The whole street is quiet; it's unnerving. They are probably all at work slaving away to pay for all this," he said

"I'll try once more."

Neither wanted to face the fact they didn't have a plan B at the moment.

Tom reached out to knock the door once more. There was no need; the door was opened to reveal the second Lauren Watts of the day.

"Yes?"

She was older than her previous namesake and far less attractive. She looked as if she had the worries of the whole world on her narrow shoulders. She was thin but in an unhealthy looking way; she looked as though a few hot meals would do wonders for her. He couldn't have explained how he knew but he was certain that this time they had come to the right house.

"We are carrying out a census," said Sophie

"No, it's okay Sophie. We are not carrying out a census. We are here to ask you if you know an Alice Summers and if you have seen her recently?"

The woman changed from vaguely hostile to openly hostile.

"No comment. You can both crawl back under the rock you came from you reporters are all the same."

She went to close the door.

"Wait! She was my girlfriend; we aren't reporters." Sophie coughed in protest. "I didn't know what happened to your brother until today."

"Well you are lucky then. My brother wasn't so lucky, was he?"

"If you knew her you wouldn't say that."

"Well I did know her and she ruined my life; she took away my family. Noah was all I had left and she murdered him."

"Did she though?" asked Sophie "I've read about the case and the opinion of everyone apart from you was that he was a dangerous controlling bastard who bullied and abused his various girlfriends until they had to take out restraining orders on him. I understand that he was your brother and family is family but even you have to admit he had it coming. Whatever you feel or felt about Alice, would you want her suicide on your conscience?"

"Why do you think she is suicidal?"

Tom noted the change in her tone when Sophie mentioned Alice possibly taking her own life. The frightening thing was that she wasn't particularly surprised. As though she had long suspected it was a realistic possibility.

"Why do we think she is suicidal?" said Sophie. "Because she has disappeared; we haven't seen or heard from her for over three weeks. She was in a bad place before she left. We found out that she had been making plans for a while leaving work and putting her home on the market."

"Have you reported her as a missing person?"

"I tried but the police weren't that interested," said Tom. "They said unless there was evidence of some foul play they couldn't take it any further. She is an adult and at liberty to leave. I got the feeling that they just saw it as a lover's tiff."

"Come in for a minute."

Tom looked at Sophie who shrugged; they had nothing to lose. They followed Lauren down a well-appointed hallway with what looked like the original black and white checkerboard tiled flooring. He remembered Alice saying once that most people looked at life in colours of black and white, wrong and right, but most of the time it was somewhere in-between – shades of grey. They were led into a large bright living room that flowed into a dining room which in turn led onto a slick kitchen at the end of the room. She gestured for them to take a seat.

They sank into a large grey velvet sofa. Tom removed one of the numerous cushions that had been scattered haphazardly with a great degree of care.

"Can I get you some tea or coffee?"

Her persona had changed once more and Tom caught a glimpse of how Noah had been able to lure Alice. When she wasn't being aggressive and was actively pleasant she looked prettier; it also made her look several years younger than the census age bracket she was in. What worried him was how quick she changed from world weary opening the door, to openly hostile, then becoming passive to the complete genial host. Everything was so much clearer to him and his heart ached for Alice. He would have to be very careful.

"Coffee would be great," said Sophie.

"And for me please," said Tom.

Tom guessed that Sophie was of the same mind as he was. They watched as the slight figure of Lauren made her way to the kitchen area. He looked around the room. It was all greys: the walls pale grey, the sofa a silvery grey and all the cushions and rugs various shades from dark grey to almost white. It reminded him of the architect of the room herself; the same but so many different aspects of her morose personality. Then he realised that there were hardly any personal items – no ornaments, no pictures, and not one photo of any family or friends. The room was completely impersonal.

Lauren returned with a silver tray laden with large grey pottery cups and saucers. The milk was hot and in a large silver jug, the sugar was in cubes in a pretty little bowl. She was now fully in the role of genial hostess.

"Thank you. Look, Lauren, we are very concerned about Alice. Is there anything you can do to help us?"

"I don't know. If you're asking have I seen her recently then the answer is no. I can tell you briefly about the events leading up to Noah's death and the aftermath if you think it may be relevant?"

"To be honest we don't know where to go or who to ask so anything you can think of will help."

There was a pause as if Lauren was weighing up whether she did have any relevant information, but Tom felt it was like changing gears; each time she changed a different persona would surface. He didn't care as long as she could help in some way.

"Noah was what they refer to nowadays as a difficult child. As a brother we had our spats, but on the whole, he was OK with me; maybe we were more alike than I'd like to admit. Anyway, my parents really struggled. He hit me only once and I wacked him straight back so he never did it again. It was different though for my mother; she had no control over him. She was continually being hauled in to see his teachers during his school years. My dad was rarely home especially when we were young; he was building up his empire. Mum would punish Noah but he would just laugh in her face and do the opposite to what she told him. We sort of muddled along, then I had a place in university. I could have also gone locally but I wanted out. It was such a toxic environment to live in. I should have gone locally; it might have changed what happened next. By now Dad had left Mum and moved away which in real terms didn't make that much difference as he was hardly ever home anyway. The timing was bad for Noah though. He felt abandoned by me and Dad, and with only Mum to try and steer him his behaviour escalated for a while. But then he seemed to settle down. Somehow, they muddled along for the next few years. Noah even managed to stay in a job and rent a flat.

Then Mum died. I was working away after having graduated the previous year. Noah was back living with mum as she had become nervous of being on her own so he had reluctantly agreed to move back home. I felt at the time that it was the wrong thing to do; he was so much happier living on his own but for all his erratic behaviour he loved Mum and was worried about her. Her health had been failing for a while. I suppose I should have helped more but I was doing so well at work it wasn't the right time for me. Noah was devastated; he said that the stair carpet had been loose; Mum had been nagging him to fix it but he had forgotten. She had tripped and fallen from the top to the bottom and broken her neck. So, then there was just the two of us. I came back to help organise the funeral and I never went back. Noah was in a bad place so I got a job here. He bought his flat and I bought this. Don't be too impressed. I was doing well at work but most of this was Dad's blood money, a payoff from the guilt he felt after Mum died. Dad didn't even come to the funeral. It upset Noah so much that it took me weeks to persuade him not to go and see him. He did eventually calm down but it simmered under the surface.

Noah had plenty of girlfriends but he couldn't keep any of them for very long. He was always great at the beginning but before long his controlling and abusive behaviour would come out. Then he met Alice. To this day I don't know how their paths crossed. I loved her from the first time Noah brought her to meet me. She was different to all the others; she was smart and funny. The best thing was that Noah was also different; he treated her so much better than any of the other girls I had met. He was almost reverential with her as though she was made of porcelain. It carried on for so long that I even began to believe that he had changed, that she was what he had needed in his life all along. She and I became so close and for the first time in my life I felt as though I had a proper family.

Then of course it began to break down. It was hardly noticeable at first. All couples argue, and they were no different, but he reverted to type. I think he was disappointed in himself but he was powerless to stop. He started following her to work; when she was out with friends he would turn up out of the blue and argue with her. She was like a rabbit caught in the headlights. She didn't understand this new version of Noah. She put up with it for longer than I thought she would but it came to a head when he hit her boss claiming that he and Alice were having an affair. She kept her job but I know it had shaken her up badly. She wanted him to go to some sort of counselling to deal with his issues but he refused. They had only been apart for a few days when he changed his mind and agreed to go. Initially it helped him a great deal and I wondered if I should have made him go years ago. Mum dying had such an affect on him and of course he was always looking for Dad's approval and never got it. Anyway, he was so much calmer. He started phoning Alice initially just to tell her about the counselling then they met a few times for coffee. The problem was the nice Noah was so believable and charming so she got sucked in again. I thought about advising caution but to be honest it was easier for me to have him busy and happy and I loved having Alice around.

It was all going great, then I had to go away for work. Then several things happened all at once. I have wondered since if it hadn't been such a perfect storm if all our lives would have turned out differently.

I went to see Alice at their flat. To be honest I was a little worried about Noah; he had become obsessed about Dad, phoning several times a day. Dad had rung me to say that he was going to have to change his number as it was upsetting his wife. Alice had tried to help but he wouldn't listen. That day though she was different; she was talking positively that maybe they could overcome all his problems together. I wasn't sure but I was relieved that she was planning to stick around. I had gone around to tell her I would be away for several weeks on a course with work. She was fine about it and told me not to worry about him and the 'Dad thing'; she would sort it out.

Anyway, I went and the unthinkable happened less than a day after I had left. Dad was killed in a car crash. I was tied up in a conference and couldn't answer my phone so his wife's brother rang Noah. He was devastated. I think he had always hoped for some sort of a relationship with Dad; of course that would now never happen. He went into meltdown.

At that exact time Alice had come home from work. He had lashed out at her verbally and physically so she left. It was his normal behaviour to lash out when he was hurting. I guess she had put up with it for the last time. And if she had left it there then I think he would have been alive today but that night for some reason Alice went back to the flat. It was at the very least stupid and at the worst provocative. It was one of the reasons she was charged with his manslaughter. What was her motive for going back that night? She never did tell anyone. She went back that evening and less than two hours later he was dead."

Tom and Sophie felt exhausted listening to her. Lauren stared at them with emotionless eyes. She continued,

"Alice had a breakdown a few months later."

"Did you keep in contact at all either during or after the court case?" asked Sophie.

Lauren looked at Tom as she answered.

"You have to remember that she had just killed my brother. The night I returned home Noah was already dead. I had to go straight from the airport to the hospital to identify his body. I couldn't see Alice as she was being questioned by the police. We spoke on the phone and she kept saying sorry over and over again, as if had she used any other words I wouldn't understand

258

how she felt. It was a day or two later when the press sniffed out the story. They found out about my mother's "suspicious" death. No-one had ever said anything other than it had been a freak accident. It got Alice and Noah's neighbours thinking and they told the reporters of his volatile behaviour. I knew better than anyone what Noah was like but some of the "stories" that came out; there wasn't an ounce of truth in them. One of them even said that he had seen Noah digging a small hole in the parcel of land behind the flats. So the police had to excavate; they discovered bones. The bones turned out to be of his dog. Still they managed to use this against him. He couldn't defend himself; every day there was a new accusation. Most of the stories printed were complete fabrication. The bloody press – I hate them.

"So they started printing about my errant father, my doormat of a mother and my violent brother who probably deserved what he got. It was too much for me. I had no-one left, they had all been taken. It wasn't fair for them all to be dragged into the public eye, especially my mother, so I started to blame Alice. The more I blamed her, the easier it became to deal with everything. I had a focus for all my pain."

"You turned on her, even though she was the innocent party and by your own admission you had been very fond of her?" said Tom.

"It's easy for you to look at it in the cold light of day and judge me, but it wasn't that straightforward."

"Yes, it was. OK, the press made it worse for you but as hard as this may sound most of it was the truth. Alice was just caught up in it; she was the innocent party."

"No, she wasn't. I agree that she was defending herself that night but why on earth did she go back. She had no reason

259

to; they had split up. Did she want to start a fight? Maybe she enjoyed the drama of it."

"Do you really think that?"

"I don't know what to think. All I know is that thanks to her I no longer have any family left. She took the last one away from me. And OK they were a messed-up bunch, but they were my messed-up bunch. Look, I loved Alice and in my calmer moments I know what Noah was like but I liked who he could be when he was with her. The press didn't help; they set us against each other. Maybe if I had been stronger or if they hadn't found out about the grave thing."

"What do you mean?" asked Sophie.

Tom and Sophie looked at Lauren expectantly but she seemed reluctant to elaborate.

"Lauren?"

"Look, Tom, I thought you knew; that she would have told you."

"I didn't know Noah even existed till a few hours ago. What grave thing are you talking about?"

"It will sound a bit weird and I know Noah liked to do weird things but after a while it doesn't seem as bad."

"Please just tell us Lauren. Time is getting on; we are going to be losing the light soon and we are still no further as to where to look for her."

"OK, but don't shoot the messenger. I guess Alice hasn't told you much about her family – her mum, dad and brother?"

"All I know is that she is estranged from her parents but I was under the impression that she was an only child. Yes, I'm sure she said she was, or did I just assume it? I'm not sure of anything any more. Go on."

"Alice had a baby brother. He was six years younger than

her but sadly he died when he was three. I don't actually know what he died of, Noah never said; but he said she talked about him all the time. She even took him to see the grave before all the troubles started. The cemetery is a few miles away."

Tom was beginning to get an awful feeling in the pit of his stomach.

"Noah was actually very good regarding Matthew. He regularly took her to the grave often taking her parents as well. Then, when all the bother began, her parents started taking against him and they wanted them to split up. He felt hurt that he had been so good to them especially regarding Matthew. I knew that he had already bought a plot. I just hadn't realised where it was."

"He's in the same cemetery as Matthew?" asked Sophie.

"Yes, but even if he hadn't made any plans then he would still have been buried there; it's one of the main cemeteries in the area. What some people took against was the location of the graves. But again, it depended where they had plots free."

"Oh my God," said Sophie "He bought a plot near Matthew's grave."

"Yes, the plot is next to him."

The room was silent as Tom and Sophie tried to digest what Lauren had just told them. Tom was still struggling to take in what Noah had done to Alice when he was still alive but this was something else.

"Why would he have bought a plot? He was still only young," said Tom

"A few months after they had been seeing each other, I suppose it must have been when the trouble had just started, he called me up and said could we meet. When I saw him, he was agitated.

He told me he had been to see a solicitor regarding a plot in the cemetery. I asked why he was thinking of it now. He said that he loved Alice and that he knew they would be together for ever; whatever happened in this world they would be together in the next. So he had bought a plot for them in the cemetery. I know it sounds stupid now but I got upset and said what about me; wasn't I the only family he had? He said that he had thought about that and if I didn't meet anyone there was room for the three of us. It made me go a little cold that he had thought about it so much. He said he had made a few plans, depending on who went first. I said that wasn't it a little early in the relationship to be thinking about eternity together. He looked at me then and said that he loved her and would for ever and they would never be apart either in this world or any other. I suppose the inscription didn't help either. Look, I know Noah had his faults but he really loved Alice; she was the closest he ever came to being happy."

"What did the inscription say?" asked Tom

"As I said, don't shoot the messenger."

"What did it say Lauren?"

"It said 'Noah Watts 1980–2011, beloved son and brother. Partner to Alice. We may have been separated in this life but we will be together for all eternity.'"

"So, if he couldn't continue tormenting her in this life he would threaten to be waiting for her in the next," said Sophie.

"Where is the cemetery?"

"You want to go there?"

"Yes, Lauren we do. Don't you think if she was contemplating doing anything she would want to say goodbye to her brother?"

"OK, I'll get the address for you."

They watched as Lauren went to the kitchen. She returned with a scrap of paper on which she had neatly printed the address and postcode. Tom didn't know if it would help but they had no other avenues so at least it was something.

"I hope it helps."

"Do you?" said Tom.

"Of course. I'm not a monster, and neither was Noah, not really, and he did really love Alice."

"That wasn't love, that was obsession and hate."

"Aren't they closely entwined?" said Lauren.

Tom looked at her with disgust; she was almost as bad as Noah. She had these different personas which she would take on depending on which the situation required. Tom had an awful feeling she may even be worse than Noah.

"If for some strange reason Alice calls you or comes here, this is my mobile number. Please call me immediately."

"Of course, I will," said Lauren reaching for the card Tom handed her.

Tom couldn't think of anything more to say to her. Sophie followed him out of the grey room, down the grey hall and out of the house. They were both silent as they got in the car. Tom put the postcode in the sat nav and they pulled away from the curb. Tom looked in his rear-view mirror and saw Lauren waving as if they were old friends who had just spent the evening together. He wondered how Alice had managed to carry on for as long as she had knowing now what she had been through. He felt scared that somehow their falling in love had pushed her to the edge. His illness couldn't have helped. Sophie reached over and squeezed his hand. Words were redundant.

They pulled up at the cemetery just as the light was beginning to fade. It looked spooky in the dusk with shadows playing hide and seek with the headstones. It felt colder inside the gates of the cemetery and he tried not to think of all the cold bodies. They weaved their way through the graves. Lauren had given rough instructions as to the position of the graves. The cemetery was empty apart from him and Sophie and its residents. Had he really thought that Alice would be here? He still felt compelled to see for himself the two graves. Sophie stumbled on a stone and cried out. Her voice echoed across the cold stones. Tom grabbed her hand and held on to her. They had arrived at the graves.

They weren't right next to each other but slightly set back from each other. But she was right that there were no other graves in between them. It was the final insult to Alice, cloaked in the misapprehension of love. Tom felt a fury build up inside him as he read the inscription.

"Tom, what do we do next? She may have been here, but if not, I doubt she will come now."

"To be honest Sophie I don't know."

They walked in silence out of the cemetery. On the wall to the left of the gates was a small brass sign giving the opening times. During the winter months it closed at 4pm, it was 3.50pm. She would, he guessed be aware of the times. He looked at Sophie; she looked worn out, it had been a long day.

"I'll ring Lauren and tell her that no-one was here. Maybe she has had a chance to think of something else."

Sophie nodded as she climbed into the front seat of Tom's car. He pulled out his phone and called the number Lauren had written on the paper. He hoped it wasn't a false one but given that they knew where she lived it wouldn't make that much difference. It rang only once.

"Tom, is that you?"

Lauren sounded upset. He guessed she was dressing up in another of her personas, more than likely to try and make him feel sorry for her. She didn't wait for him to confirm it was him.

"She's here. She arrived about twenty minutes after you both left. She is in the living room but she is very agitated. I don't think I can make her stay."

"We are on our way. Do not let her leave or I will hold you personally responsible. Lock the bloody door if you have to."

He cut the phone and started the car. He pulled off ignoring the angry beep of a motorist behind him.

"Slow down, Tom; let's get there in one piece."

He didn't slow down but he did drive more carefully through the narrow lanes. It was rush hour now and the traffic was heavy. He tried altering his route to gain some time but to no avail. Everyone wanted to get home on a dark winter's night.

It was almost an hour later when they pulled up outside Lauren's house. He felt so afraid suddenly that she may have already gone that he didn't wait for Sophie; he left the car door hanging open as he rushed to Lauren's front door.

Alice

Nothing is lifeless
When the moon writes its screed
On the silvern sand silence

From *The Universe in Blossom*
Munia Khan

She had a choice now; a simple decision between two outcomes. She always hated it when it was fifty/fifty. She preferred it when there were more options because then if she chose the wrong one, the right one wasn't the only one left accusing her of her mistake. She looked over the edge as small pebbles tumbled down the mountainside. She was a brave coward; she knew that it was an odd description but only she knew the battles that raged inside her every single day. She was tired of feeling scared, tired of running away. She knew that it would never end. She missed her parents so much but she knew she had done the right thing by refusing to see them. They had suffered enough; she couldn't put them through any more pain. She hated that they had turned against her but she supposed it was an inevitable outcome given what they had all been through. She thought of

Matthew; she could still remember the smell of him, the feel of his chubby little hand in hers when their parents took them to the park. He hadn't liked the thought of the swings but as long as she sat in the swing beside him and held his hand he loved it. She couldn't really blame her parents for the way they had reacted. Death followed her like a loyal dog.

She took a deep breath and held it. The last letter from her parents had almost finished her there and then. Always the coward she had moved away from the source of the pain. She knew now that there wasn't anywhere on earth far enough away for her to leave the pain behind. She leant forward. The wind rushed towards her as though it was holding her back. She could easily have pushed forward; it would have been so easy.

"You've had it too easy, Alice. That's not your fault but it's why you are so unrealistic about life. If you'd experienced half of what me and Noah had to contend with growing up you wouldn't look at life with those rose-tinted glasses of yours."

Lauren had given her this speech when she and Noah had split up the first time. She had been so cross, especially since Lauren still had her brother and she had lost hers. It had made her a little wary of Lauren after that.

Then she had killed Noah but she hadn't meant to. Even in light of the fact that he had almost succeeded in strangling her she hadn't wanted to really hurt him just stop him. Lauren knew her; she knew that she couldn't pass a homeless person without emptying the contents of her purse into the cap laid on the ground in front of her. Lauren knew that she was kind and considerate to others. Her parents too had been proud of her; they had told her over and over again, but they had walked away from her because of the shame she had brought on their family. She wanted to stop running but it meant having to face Lauren. Maybe if she explained why she had gone back that day then Lauren would finally understand. She had made a promise to herself that she wouldn't use it in court, but even though she hadn't she had still been found not guilty. Maybe it was time that Lauren knew the full story. She had two choices now: she could either give up or she could tell Lauren the truth. She had let Lauren judge her without knowing the full story. It was time to tell her the reason she went back to see Noah that night. Then maybe she would finally understand.

She made her way down the mountain; first she wanted to see Matthew. It would take about two hours to get there; she would just make it before the light went.

Tom

The front door was ajar; his heart sank. Had he missed her? He pushed the door and there in the black and white hall stood Alice. She was much thinner than the last time he had seen her and her eyes were red and sore. She didn't seem to recognise him for a moment. Then it was as if realisation dawned and she smiled.

"Alice. Are you OK? We've been so worried about you."

"Tom."

She didn't elaborate. Lauren came out of the living room behind her and placed a proprietorial hand on her shoulder. Nobody said a word for a few seconds.

"I am so sorry, Tom. I should never have gone for that coffee with you. I knew that day that it wasn't fair to drag you into all this and now I have to make amends for it all."

"Make amends for what? You are the victim here. None of this is your fault."

"No Tom, that is where you are wrong. I took away someone's life; the decision was mine. I didn't mean to but the reality is I killed him and in doing that I left Lauren without any family."

"But he tried to kill you, Alice. What else were you supposed to do?"

"I shouldn't have gone back that night. I did it for the right reason but it was such a stupid thing to do. I have to live with my actions although for a long time I didn't think that I could."

"Why did you go back, Alice?" said Lauren.

Alice turned to stare at the woman behind her; she looked long and hard and then the tears came. Tom watched as she hugged herself as Lauren stood ramrod straight at her side. Sophie moved forward to comfort her but Alice shook her head. Tom wanted to go to her but he knew that she had to do this on her own. They waited as the tears flowed silently down her face.

"I had to, Lauren. Even now in hindsight I'm not sure that I could have stayed away. He was like a wounded animal; the death of your father caused him so much pain it was pitiful. I wanted to help him, but he lashed out at me. I knew then that we would never be able to stay together so I left. However, I had something to tell him, he deserved to know. So I decided to go back and see him. I hoped that he would have calmed down by the time I went back. I knocked the door but there was no answer. I was a bit worried that he might have done something so I used my key. He was sitting in the living room in the dark. He was so very quiet. I should have seen the warning signs; he would always go quiet just before he lashed out. But I wanted to make him feel better, tell him that he was going to—"

Alice stopped and let the last word hang in the air around them. She didn't continue; it was as if someone had flicked a switch that caused her to stop. They all stood silently until Sophie couldn't bear it any longer.

"Alice?" said Sophie.

Alice was almost trance-like; she stared across Tom as though he was an apparition, a ghostly being who wasn't actually there. The hall was silent.

"Alice?" said Sophie again.

"I took a life, didn't I? I know I didn't mean to but I still did it and there are consequences for that. I don't mean jail or anything like that but there are consequences inside of you, in your soul. People have accidents all the time, things they didn't mean to do, but they still pay for them in some way.

"That night I went to see Noah, the night I killed him," – Tom flinched – "I knew it was a risk. We had ended the relationship and I knew he wasn't coping very well. He was still raging about the death of his father. He talked about death all the time. He said that even as a child he had known he wouldn't live to a ripe old age. He said that meeting me had made him want to change the future. He wanted to be that normal person with a house and 2.4 children, but only girls. He loved you so much Lauren; when I asked him why he only wanted girls he said look how you had turned out compared to him. He was so proud of what you'd achieved. In fact, it was his dream to have a little girl just like you."

Tom was getting an awful feeling in the pit of his stomach; he knew why Alice had gone back.

"Alice?"

"Hope Lauren Watts – that was what I called her even though legally she wasn't a person. I wanted to tell him, Lauren, that he was going to be a dad and that he was having a little girl, what he had always wanted. I would have let him be a part of her life; I just couldn't be with him any more. It was my fault. I should have waited until he had calmed down, but I wanted to help him. He was like a wounded animal; I wanted to release him from his pain.

Martha

Your dreams are your solid rock;
All other dreams are sinking sands!
Recreate Your world and I believe you can!

Shaping the Dream
Israelmore Ayivor

Martha dropped her sports bag in the hall. She was exhausted but happier than she had been in months. After years of playing badminton with Pam for fun the two of them had finally joined the local league in the doubles category. Tonight they had won their first cup. OK so it was only after three rounds and it was in the over-fifties group but still she was delighted – a cup was a cup. She placed it on the mantelpiece in her living room. Pam was more than likely photographing hers, as she said to be ready in case the local reporter wanted to do a piece on them. She smiled. Poor Pam, she was a frustrated celebrity. As she had said she wasn't good at anything and she wasn't rich but it didn't stop her wanting to be something more; it didn't stop most of the celebrities she read about.

Marha walked into the kitchen fully intent on having a cup of tea. She picked up the kettle then changed her mind. To hell with it; she was a local champion and she had just registered to finally complete her English degree. She would have to start again but that didn't bother her; she had done it more than once before – she could do it again. She remembered that she had a bottle of prosecco that her neighbour had bought for her birthday last month. It wasn't chilled but she didn't care; she poured a generous glass and then added a few cubes of ice. She replaced the ice tray and carried the glass into the living room. She looked in the mirror. She was red in the face, her auburn curls lay damp on her forehead – she looked like an angry version of Betty Boop. There was a knock at the door. She looked at her watch. It was almost nine. She guessed it was more than likely Pam keen on continuing with the celebrations, although she had said she needed to be home for something.

Martha opened her front door and in front of her was a tall man roughly her age, maybe a little younger. He looked vaguely familiar.

"I'm sorry to disturb you. My name is Martin Harris and I'm the manager at the leisure centre."

"Oh yes."

Her mind ran ahead. Had he come to congratulate her for her sporting success? How did he even know where she lived? Maybe he was a serial killer who picked up lonely middle-aged woman at badminton matches.

"I know what you're thinking."

"I bet you don't. I was wondering if you were a serial killer."

He laughed and looked a little more comfortable with the situation. She wasn't sure if it was a good idea to give him the heads up on him being a serial killer if he did turn out to be one, but then if he was a serial killer she didn't have much defence short of throwing her sports bag at him.

"Someone handed this in; it was on the floor in the Ladies' locker room."

He handed her a plastic bag; inside was her purse. Mystery solved – his career as a serial killer was over.

"Oh, thank you. I hadn't even noticed it was missing."

"I took the liberty of having a look for your address and name only so that it could be returned to you as quickly as possible. Congratulations by the way. I saw some of the match; you played very well."

Martha could only imagine too well the shade of deep crimson her face was. She wasn't used to compliments from strange men, or even normal men for that matter.

"Thank you."

He smiled at her; she smiled back. She was now in possession of her purse so in effect his mission was accomplished. Still he stayed on her doorstep and smiled. He was fairly attractive and wasn't wearing any rings, wedding or otherwise.

"Would you like to come in for a cup of tea or coffee seeing as you went to all the trouble of bringing my purse back?"

"Yes please, that would be nice."

He had practically answered before she had finished her sentence. He could still be a serial killer even if he did have her purse. In fact, he could have deliberately taken it from her bag when she wasn't looking. Then again, he did have a lanyard with a badge featuring his photo and name and the local council logo. Either way it was too late; he was in her hall. She settled him in the living room and, after discovering he actually lived only two streets over from her, accepted the offer of a glass of wine so he could join in her celebration. She poured out a second glass and had just handed it to him when the phone rang. She left him admiring her over-fifties cup and took the call in the kitchen. It was John, which she was quite glad of as if Martin did turn out to be a serial killer then John would be able to tell the police that he had known his mother had been alive at 9.10pm.

"Hi Mum. You know that man Edward that you told me about?"

"Yes. Actually John can I ring you back? There is someone here at the moment."

"Is it him?"

"Is it who?"

"Is it Edward?"

"No of course not; why on earth would it be Edward?"

"Because, he has just been here to see me. He somehow tracked me down but couldn't get an address for you. He begged me to give him your address, so I have. I just thought I'd better ring you to warn you. Mum, are you OK?"

Martha was laughing uncontrollably; it was probably to do with the bubbles – she wasn't really used to drinking – or it may have been the fact that men were like buses: you didn't see one for ages then two came along together. She hung up the phone after telling John that she was fine and that he had done the right thing. She needed a clear head but she had drunk most of the glass of prosecco when she had poured out Martin's drink just to give her a little Dutch courage. Now she needed some for the whole of the Netherlands. She poured out another glass just as she heard a knock on the door. She wondered, as she called to Martin that she was just getting the door, if it would have been better if she had never started any of this and had settled for the quiet life she had been heading for. She opened the door and decided that, hell no, this was all far more fun.

Tom

My body is filled with sand.
The heavy grains flow from my eyes
And seek somewhere to fall.

Jay Woodman

Tom woke with a sore head; he ached all over. He looked at the clock. It was a few minutes shy of 7am. He had been asleep for less than four hours; yet again he wished that he could get a full night's sleep. He pulled on a t-shirt, went to the bathroom for a pee and then padded downstairs to let Febus out. Once they had both answered the call of nature, he made a coffee. The dog looked up at Tom and whimpered. Tom stroked the dog's head. They were both feeling low. The last few weeks had been miserable without Alice; the dog missed her as well. He rubbed his eyes. He was glad now that he had taken a few days off work.

He took his medications and drank his coffee, going over and over what had happened the week before. He had wanted to bring her home with him but she had refused. Sophie had said she could stay at hers but again she had refused. She had promised she would be in contact and that she wouldn't do anything stupid in the meantime. He hoped she meant it. The dog cried again, almost as if he knew what was going through Tom's mind.

He rang her for the second time that day. Once more it went to voicemail – he left a message.

"Alice it's Tom. Please talk to me; you need to talk about what happened. None of it was your fault. I love you, please talk to me."

The dog groaned as if he wanted Tom to say more but there was nothing more he could say to convince her. Hope Lauren Watts. The name played in his mind and he felt sorrow for all the potential that had been wasted because Noah refused to listen to the reason that Alice had come back to see him. As soon as she had started to speak Noah had cut her off by punching her in the face. Once he had started all his energy went into taking out his anger and hurt on her. He had never known that as he pummelled her tummy he was taking away the only thing he had ever really desired. Alice had said that Hope Lauren Watts was eighteen weeks when she delivered her alone in hospital, once she had been let out on bail. She had hidden her blood-soaked underwear in her handbag as the police had questioned her. She had known Hope was dead; she said no baby could have survived the final kick that he had delivered. Lauren had asked her gently why she hadn't told anyone, maybe there wouldn't even have had to be a trial. But she had shaken her head sadly and said that she had let Hope down once; she wouldn't do it a second time by using her to defend her actions. She had only had the scan that morning confirming that the baby was a little girl. It was when she had named her Hope.

The phone rang. Tom grabbed it, hoping that it was Alice.

"Alice?"

"Hi Tom, no its Sophie. I guess you haven't heard from her then?"

"No, I haven't heard from her at all. I've left text and voicemail messages but not one word."

"I still feel there is something that we've missed. The last piece of the puzzle, as it were. Even after all she has been through I still think that she would have reacted differently and I think it's to do with her parents. After all, why doesn't she speak to them? Surely after all the family have been through they would have become even closer."

"I agree and to be honest I think that it's something to do with Lauren. Even though I haven't heard from Alice, Lauren has rung me almost every day. She started by sending me a few texts under the pretext of enquiring about Alice. Then she started ringing; she was chatty to the point of flirting."

"That's interesting, Tom. Keep up the conversations, even ring her yourself. I think our little Lauren has an ulterior motive."

"I have something else to tell you Sophie. A couple of days ago Mum phoned and asked if I could come straight over. She had been crying."

"Your mum never cries!"

"I know. I rushed over there; I didn't like to even think what might be wrong. Anyway she told me something, and to be honest I can't believe she left it until now to tell me. I don't want to tell you over the phone. Let's just say that I'm not who you thought I was."

"You can't keep me waiting after making a statement like that, Tom!"

"Why don't I pick you up after work and we'll go for supper to the little café? Then I can tell you everything."

"I'll bring my notebook; it sounds as though it could be front page news."

He cut the call and looked at the time. It was still only 8am. He needed to get out of the house; he was a bit stir crazy. He dressed quickly; he would take Febus for a long walk. As he laced up his walking shoes, the window in the hall changed from black to gold. The morning light transformed the hall; it looked as though someone was spinning golden threads to hang over every surface. The dog had dozed off in his basket in the kitchen but as soon as Tom shook the lead the dog was out of the basket, delighted at the prospect of a walk.

The sun shone brightly; it was fairly warm for the end of April. He unzipped his jacket and let the warmth of the sun penetrate his shirt. He always felt nearer to Alice on the beach – not just because it was where they had met but because they had spent so much time coming back when they had been together. The beach was deserted apart from a group of school children doing some sort of survival training. A few were rubbing sticks together to start a fire. This was a delight to Febus who made the sudden and autonomous decision of helping by running over and stealing the sticks. Tom grabbed him and put him on the lead until they were far enough away not to cause a problem.

They walked towards the sand dunes where Tom let the dog off the lead once more. The dog scarpered off, barking his joy in life as he went, Alice forgotten for the time being. Tom wished he could feel that carefree. He looked up; where was the dog? He called; nothing. This was all he needed. He called again and this time a sandy head popped up from behind one of the smaller sand dunes. Febus decided he liked this game and continued to play hide and seek in the dunes. Tom wasn't sure whether it was to entertain Febus or if the dog was doing it to cheer him up.

Suddenly he remembered that he couldn't meet Sophie later. He pulled out his mobile and rang her. Before he had chance to explain, Sophie said,

"We can't meet tonight at the café as we have to dress up and go to Genaro's to meet Edward's new partner."

"You read my mind. When did you remember?"

"About half an hour ago when Dad phoned to see what time I was picking him up," she said.

"I'll pick you both up and then maybe Mum can drop your dad off afterwards."

"Yes, OK. That should be fine although you know what Dad is like when Susan is driving. They nearly came to blows the last time."

They agreed a time and Tom made his way upstairs to get ready. He tried Alice's mobile but again there was no answer. He would ring Lauren tomorrow as Sophie had suggested.

He picked Sophie up first and then her dad, who only lived a couple of streets away. They would have to discuss the ramifications of Lauren and Alice later on. Sophie's dad Frank was a pleasant man with a positive outlook on life even though he had been widowed less than a year ago. It probably helped having the whirlwind that was Sophie as a daughter.

His mother was excited and she was winding Roz up. Tonight was going to be about making a good impression on the new woman in Edward's life. He felt sorry for the poor woman;

she wouldn't know what had hit her when his mother and Roz begin their overpowering campaign of befriending.

He walked with Sophie and her dad into the room. The rest of the group including Edward and his new lady were already seated. Tom felt an atmosphere as they entered which he couldn't quite put his finger on. Edward stood up and introduced the woman seated at his side.

"Tom, I didn't realise till yesterday that I have you to thank for my recent happiness. I would like you to meet Martha."

The whole room erupted into applause. What was going on? He felt it was more about him and this lady rather than her and Edward. What was it with him and Genaro's!

"I can't believe you went to all that trouble for me," said Tom.

He and Martha were in the small lounge area of the restaurant. As she had said, they needed to talk.

"I suppose it had been building in me for years – all the lost opportunities, the wasted time. I realised I regretted what I hadn't done more than the mistakes I had made. It's funny, Tom, how like him you are."

She reached into her bag and handed him several black and white photos.

"Wow, you could take us for brothers."

"I know it's uncanny. At the time I was convinced that you were my son."

"I can see why. It's strange, I still feel humbled that you would go to all this trouble for me. I understand that I'm not who you are looking for but even so it sort of makes me feel..." He stopped, unable to think of the right word.

"Wanted," said Martha quietly.

"Yes, exactly."

"That was what I needed him to know; that he was wanted so much."

"Will you keep looking?"

"Yes, I hope to. Edward has said he will help me."

"He's a man of his word. It seems to be a time for revelations, – your search for your son, my mother's bombshell."

"I know. Have you managed to talk to Edward?"

"Yes, we met up yesterday. It was very surreal for both of us. I have known him all my life and admired and loved him. When my father left us he and Olivia helped my mother so much, especially in the early days. Then when Olivia died Mum was there for him. We have been very close all of my life."

"And now?"

"Now I can't believe that Mum duped my dad for all those years. It is almost as if she exacted her revenge for his behaviour before the idea had even formed in his mind."

"Will you tell him?"

"I don't know; I haven't had long enough to sort through it all to be honest. It seems at one point this week I almost had two sets of parents. I suppose I'm not quite ready to let any of them go."

Martha smiled and squeezed his hand.

"It's strange how things all fall into place. Apparently Mum had been trying to find a good time to tell me about Edward but kept putting it off. Then when Edward saw the photo of me and Alice on the beach obviously he recognised me straight away. He had gone to Susan to ask her advice. I suppose it was the fact that she had secrets of her own that finally made her tell him. Then of course she told me.

"Edward said that she felt guilty about not saying anything when Olivia was alive but when she and Edward found out they couldn't have children Mum felt unable to tell him.

"They didn't cheat on Olivia though; Mum and Edward had been going out for a few months but they both knew that it wasn't what they wanted so they split amicably. Then she found out two months later that she was pregnant. By then Edward had started seeing Olivia; they had clicked straight away and got engaged the day Mum found out she was pregnant. She was adamant she didn't want to mess up all their lives. She knew that Edward would have insisted on doing the right thing. As Mum had her own money she wasn't worried about the financial aspect of raising a child and, as for a male influence, she was happy to see what happened. She didn't love Edward so she let him go. As for my dad she said that he needed money and she needed a husband to give me stability, although as she said that didn't work out how she had wanted. That was the bit I couldn't understand; if she was simply looking for someone to raise me with why hadn't she just told Edward? She told me that they loved each other. Why would she want to make all of them unhappy? My mum can be snobbish and calculating but, do you know what, she worked out the best possible outcome for everyone without putting herself first. Then Olivia and Edward found out they couldn't have children. Of course Mum knew that Edward was fine; Olivia and Edward never told anyone why they couldn't conceive so it put Mum between a rock and a hard place. It was too late to tell either of them. It would certainly have broken Olivia's heart, so Mum kept it to herself until now."

"Do you wish Susan had told you earlier?"

"No, we can't ever go back. Mum did what she did rightly or wrongly but with the best intentions at heart. For now, I am blessed to have you all around me."

"Have you heard from Alice?"

"No, not since I saw her a few days ago. So many secrets Martha, if only she had told me."

"It's easier said than done, Tom. We all have our demons."

Tom saw Susan coming towards them. Edward caught up with her, smiling broadly at him and Martha. His parents. He would never have guessed in a million years. Not for the first time, he wondered if he was in the right job – between Alice and his mother, his investigative skills were leaving more than a little to be desired.

Tom

Take my hand and…
Feel the sand
Beneath your aimless feet
Towards the sparkling waves.

Munia Khan

Once the meal was over Tom and Sophie made their excuses and left, heading for the local pub. Sid had made a not so subtle comment about Susan's driving capabilities but she had been in such a good mood that she had let it pass. Tom wasn't surprised at anything any more, particularly after the evening's revelations.

"I can't believe she went to so much trouble," said Sophie.

"I know."

"How do you feel about it?"

"To be honest, Sophie, my head is bursting with everything that is going on at the moment."

"But you must feel flattered in a way that she went to so much trouble."

"Yes, I do and actually I really liked her. It's just that at the moment all I can think of is Alice. I am so worried about her,

Sophie. Although on a positive note at least I now know that I won't turn out like my father. I know this sounds bizarre but I sort of admire Mum for what she has had to deal with. I am absolutely delighted though to find out that Edward is my dad. I used to pretend that he was when I was growing up. It's all a bit overwhelming though."

"I know, it's like a story from *The Jeremy Kyle Show*. Fancy Susan duping your dad into marrying her."

"Please don't ever liken my life to *The Jeremy Kyle Show*!"

Sophie laughed. They both knew that Susan would hate being compared to someone on *The Jeremy Kyle Show*.

"OK you're right, sorry; your Shakespearean tragedy of a life. Anyway, I really liked Martha and she seems to be good for Edward. All from one photo."

"I know. Alice had spoken to the kids when I was getting the coffees; the boy had asked her to take some photos of them so she had chatted to them for a while. It's amazing the effect one photo has had on us all."

"I think it's called the butterfly effect. Look Tom, I know it's all been very complicated but the main thing now is to help Alice. I have done a bit of digging about our friend Lauren and to be honest I don't trust her one bit. I think she has manipulated the whole situation from beginning to end. I think she is even more controlling than Noah; it's just that hers is more subtle and less obvious but I bet she is just as dangerous as he was."

"I agree. From the first time we met her we saw one persona and then different ones depending on what she wanted us to see. I dropped her a text just now and she got straight back to me, suggesting that we meet up this week under the pretext that she had become scared of what Alice may do to her."

"Another change of personality then."

"Absolutely, she has more alter egos than Mr Benn."

"Who is Mr Benn.?"

"Mr Benn, the man in the bowler hat who used to go in the changing room and come out as different characters? Never mind; anyway the last time I spoke to her she dropped into the conversation that Alice had slapped her once when they had had a minor disagreement."

"You think that she is trying to muddy the waters?"

"Exactly."

"The madam is trying to worm her way into your life, Tom. It's almost as if everything that Alice had she wants."

"I know, and I don't know if it's to punish her for taking Noah from her or if she wants to destroy Alice for the fun of it."

"I am starting to get a horrible feeling that she has somehow managed to isolate Alice's parents from her. I have no idea how she may have done it but it would go a long way to explaining why she has no contact with them."

"I know they've already lost their son so why would they not want to have any contact with their only remaining child?"

"It doesn't ring true does it? OK she may have horrible parents but my gut feeling is that there is far more to this than meets the eye."

"Is that your reporter's intuition?"

"To be honest lots have things have been bothering me about this whole thing. I didn't get a chance until last night but I had a look through the archives in work and found an article in one of the national papers about Matthew's death. Alice had been with him that day. She was nine and he was three. Her mum had fallen ill and the dad had rushed home from work to take her to the hospital. A neighbour agreed to come and sit with Alice and her brother while their parents were at the hospital. The neighbour put the children to sleep and then checked all the doors were locked. Except that the back door hadn't locked properly; the catch was faulty. Alice had taken Matthew in to sleep with her as he had a habit of sleep walking. He had woken up and went looking for his parents. Alice didn't wake up. The neighbour didn't wake. He opened the back door looking for them. It had been icy and the path was frozen; it had a steep incline and the little boy not realising had run out of the back door. Alice's father found him on returning from hospital after a frantic search by him, Alice and the neighbour. The boy was taken to hospital and pronounced dead on arrival. It was awful for all concerned. The neighbour, an elderly woman, passed away less than six months later; her daughter said that she had never forgiven herself for what had happened. Alice had counselling for several months after his death. In the aftermath they all struggled but they tried to make something good come out of it. They raised funds for a scheme in the little boy's name to help to provide respite for families who had parents or siblings with medical conditions. It was called–"

"Minute by minute – the Matthew Hodge Foundation."

"Yes, exactly, how did you know?"

"She told me about it once, she just didn't tell me that it was after her brother," said Tom.

"What about the surname being different?"

"I only know that her biological father died when she was only a few months old. Her mother remarried when she was two and that he was the only father she could ever remember."

"So they must have had Matthew a few years later. I think she must have harboured guilt about his death and then when she had the misfortune to get involved with Noah's family it came to the fore."

"Of course, and I think she would have opened up to Noah so that he and Lauren would have known about the potential difficult dynamics in the family and they exploited them."

"Are you saying that Lauren has used this to isolate Alice from her parents?"

"Of course. She has just taken over from where Noah left off."

"We need to find out what she has done, and then hopefully it will help Alice?"

"I don't know. I think they have pushed Alice to breaking point."

The following morning Tom had another call from Lauren. This time she said that she wanted to meet up with him sooner rather than later as she had found out some information about Alice that she didn't want to discuss over the phone. He played into her hands, initially intimating that if Alice didn't want to see him then he had to accept that and move on. It was enough for her tone to become more conspiratorial; she said that what she had found out may make him change his mind as to just how innocent she was regarding Noah's death. He gritted his teeth and said that he could come to London the following day; she said that she would try and finish early and meet him in the pub at the bottom of her road. She chatted for a few more minutes. They said their goodbyes and he replaced the phone. He was glad he had taken a few days off work; he wanted this finished before Lauren hurt Alice anymore.

Febus needed a walk so he grabbed the lead and poo bags. As he clipped the lead onto the dog's harness there was a knock at the door. He dropped the lead and opened the door. Standing in front of him was a tall, slim man with silver-grey hair and dark brown eyes. Tom had never seen him before.

"Hi, can I help you," said Tom.

He didn't have the patience today for any time wasters; he wanted to take the dog for a walk and think through how he would handle Lauren the following day.

"Hello, my name is Phillip Hodge. You don't know me but…"

"You're Alice's father," said Tom.

"Yes, I am. How did you know?"

"The surname, the London accent and a leap of faith I suppose. The question is, how did you find me?"

Tom looked around the empty pub for Lauren – he couldn't see her. It was still early so he ordered a whiskey and settled himself in a corner table. She had texted him a few times since their conversation so he knew that she was ramping up her campaign. If only she knew what was about to happen. He was shaking slightly which was why he had ordered the whiskey. It wasn't because he was nervous but because he was furious and in order for this to work perfectly he needed to be as cool as her. The pub was beginning to fill up but there was still no sign of Lauren. He wondered if he had been rumbled. Then, just as he was about to ring her, in she walked through the door. She had had her hair done and was dressed to kill; for a split second he felt sorry for her but it quickly passed as he remembered the conversation with Phillip.

"Tom, so lovely to see you again."

"You too, Lauren. Can I get you something to drink?"

He wanted her to relax and be off her guard.

"I'll have a white wine please."

He returned with the wine and placed the glass in front of her.

"So, what did you have to tell me?" said Tom.

"Well I've been wondering why Alice didn't tell anyone about the baby during the court case. If she had only told the police straight away then she would have had the sympathy vote and the reason she had gone back that evening. We spoke about it this week and she said that she didn't want to use Hope as an excuse. She said she didn't know what to do with her as she wasn't sure that she would be free to bury her. Anyway, legally before twenty weeks it is not considered as a person so in the end she asked the hospital to see to it. I thought that she would have told her parents; after all they were at the trial every day without fail. She couldn't see how devoted they were to her – she was so lucky – but after the trial had ended she refused to see anyone. Then she had her breakdown. I went to see her and she gave me a letter to give to her parents. So, I started being a sort of go-between for her. She was adamant about not seeing them she said that she had brought shame on the family. Anyway, I'm going off track a bit my point is that I'm not sure that the baby was even Noah's."

Tom clenched his fists under the table. He wished he'd had another whiskey when he had bought her wine.

"Why do you think that?"

"Because I think that if it had been Noah's she would have told the court; I don't believe this nonsense that she thought it would tarnish the memory of Hope. I think that it was possibly her boss's baby. Noah had always suspected that she was having an affair with him. It was why they spilt up the first time."

"Yes, it sounds plausible. I guess you may be right. I'm so glad you told me, Lauren; I think I may have just had a lucky escape. Do want another wine?"

She nodded. Tom was glad of an excuse to get away from her and gather himself. He ordered a double whiskey for himself and another wine for Lauren. He wanted to loosen her tongue even further.

"Lauren, I think this may be the start of a rather interesting friendship."

She smiled at him and placed her hand on his knee.

"The only thing about this whole sorry mess that I don't get is why Alice's parents didn't keep in touch with her. Especially seeing as they had already lost Matthew. Wouldn't they want to keep in touch with Alice? After all, as you just said, they were at the trial every day."

Lauren took a gulp of wine and smiled at Tom; it made him feel a little sick. However, he smiled back at her encouraging her to elaborate.

"Well seeing as we are a bit of an item now…" She paused, waiting for Tom to agree or disagree; he did neither "I think I should let you into my little secret. After the trial, when Alice had her breakdown, I went to see her; I genuinely felt sorry for her. She looked so awful. She had lost a lot of weight, she was skin and bone. She didn't want to see any one particularly her parents. She said that she had put them through such a horrible experience she didn't want to hurt them any more. While she was in the hospital they had to respect her wishes. So they came to see me, as the hospital had told them that Alice was only allowing me to see her. They had written her a letter and they begged me to hand it to her; they didn't want to take the chance of it getting lost in the system. I gave it to her but she still refused to see them. For the next few days I became their contact with her, but I was becoming so fond of them. Her mum would bring a freshly baked cake for me as thanks for trying to get Alice to listen to them. She was being so stubborn; what was she trying to prove? So, I got fed up of being the pig in the middle. I opened the last letter and read it. It was so heartfelt and full of love and support. Each time they had sent her a letter she had just ignored it, so I decided to mix it up a bit. I wrote my own version. I said that, given her refusal to see them, they had come to the conclusion that she wanted nothing more to do with them. They wouldn't contact her or try to see her until she was ready. They didn't know though, so they kept coming to see me with their stupid letters which of course I had stopped giving her."

"Wow that was quite something, Lauren. Did she never write back to them?"

Lauren looked sheepish and Tom wondered how he could persuade her to make the final confession. Up to now, her arrogance had forced her to confess her plan, but she seemed to be weighing up if she could trust him or not.

"I think that Noah would have been very proud of you," said Tom hoping that it would give Lauren the final push.

"I wrote one last letter from them to her. I said that…"

"Go on, Lauren."

"I said that they blamed her for the death of Matthew, that she should have been looking after him, and that if she had he would have been alive today."

There was a scream as a man came as if from nowhere and grabbed her by the throat. Tom grabbed the man and pulled him off, still restraining him as the other customers in the pub tried to decide whether to intervene or not.

"You evil little bitch! We trusted you, we believed what you said! We thought that you had Alice's best interests at heart. You sent that last letter to us, she didn't write it did she?"

"What letter Phillip?" said Tom, still holding him back.

"She wrote to us. We thought that it was from Alice saying that she blamed us for Matthew's death, that we shouldn't ever have put her in that position and now she would have to live with it for the rest of her life. It was so shocking to see it in black and white. Both of us have always felt guilty about the way it affected Alice, so to see all our fears confirmed was too much. It was why we took a step back. It was a wonderful ruse Lauren; it kept us apart from her for all these years. Why did you do it?"

"I had never had parents like you and Melanie. I would have been a different person if they had been more like you." Lauren was screaming at him. "I wanted you for myself. I deserved you, she didn't. She took the only family I had left; she didn't deserve to have any family."

There was silence in the pub as Phillip fell to his knees and sobbed for all he had lost.

Tom

When angels carry you
They leave no footprints in the sand.

Maria Dorfner

Tom called Febus to heel but as usual the dog totally ignored him. He sometimes wondered if Febus was under the misapprehension that he was taking Tom for a walk. It was the third time this week that they were walking on the beach. The dog was delighted although a little tired by the long walks. It had been several weeks since the showdown with Lauren. She had disappeared; no-one had heard from her since. Phillip had threatened to get the police involved; the pub landlord had asked her if she wanted to call them seeing as Phillip had tried to attack her but she had probably weighed it all up in her calculating mind and realised that she probably would come off worse.

After the showdown with Lauren, Tom and Phillip had gone straight to Noah's old flat where Alice was staying. Tom had desperately wanted to see her but he knew that it was more important for the wounds between Alice and her parents to heal. Phillip phoned him to tell him he was taking Alice home with him and that they would be in touch. That was almost a week ago. He had spoken to Phillip almost every day to see how she was getting on. Phillip said that she was improving every day but the Lauren thing had done a lot of damage. They had gone to the hospital where she had given birth to Hope. She had said goodbye to Hope properly this time, as Phillip had said it was his granddaughter. Tom never asked where he stood, he just wanted to know she was being looked after.

Tom called to the dog who had decided it was much more fun to pretend he belonged to someone else. He bounded across the wet sand back to his master, his new owners forgotten in the rush of love for his current owner. Tom knelt down to stroke him, his fur damp from rolling in the sand. As he brushed away the sand a figure came to stand by the side of Febus, who had started barking like a crazy dog.

"You really need to keep that dog of yours under control. Although it's good to see him fairly dry for a change."

"Alice."

"I have something for you."

Tom swallowed hard.

"You do?"

Febus, much to his credit, had stopped barking and sat watching his two favourite people talking politely to each other as though they had just met.

"It's a dry-cleaning bill."

"For your cardigan."

"My very expensive cardigan if you don't mind, the one knitted by a closeted order of nuns on a remote Scottish island."

"Yes, I remember."

"There has also been a fair amount of – how did you put it? – "therapy" to pay for as well."

"Alice, I am so sorry, I never knew."

"No, you didn't because I wasn't strong enough to tell you. I should have trusted you but I didn't."

"And now, do you trust me now?"

"You saved a girl's life, bravely adjusted to a possibly life-limiting illness and then scoured the country to find me because I couldn't open up to you. To be honest, Tom, I don't know if you've done enough."

She was laughing, but it was more than that. For the first time since he had met her, she sounded free.

"I would have done anything for you. I will do anything for you," he said.

"I have a question to ask you then."

She knelt down in the wet sand and took his hands in hers

"Sometimes it's the princess that slays the dragon and saves the prince."

John
England, 2018

Everyone makes mistakes.
If everyone fell into the sand after making a mistake
We would never get anywhere.
We'd all be washed away in the sea, lost forever.
Do you understand?

Celia McMahon, *The Book Eater's Daughter*

John had decided that he needed to clear out some of Evie's belongings. He had been putting it off for far too long. When he had come back from Swansea after the first anniversary he had started the painful process but he had only skimmed the surface. It was time to sort out the rest of her things. There were several items he would never get rid of but he needed to be less sentimental about the rest of her things. It had been the hair cut that had spurred him on to make the decision. Seth had asked a few days ago if he could have his hair cut. It had been a bone of contention for so long but he hadn't wanted to push the boy, so John had been delighted that Seth had finally made the decision himself. He took him to the local barbers and sat reading the paper as they shaved his son's head. On the journey home Seth had asked John if he had wanted help sorting out Evie's clothes.

John had been shocked that Seth had even noticed but then he had always been like Evie, noticing the finer details. Then he had told John that he hadn't wanted to cut his hair because it was the same hair that his mother had stroked every night in the last few months of her life. He had said having it cut was like losing the last part of her. He had looked at John and had said that it was time for him to do the same. Unable to speak John had nodded as he rubbed his hand over his son's shorn head.

On that last Christmas he had given her the charm bracelet; she had scolded him as they had agreed not to exchange presents. It had been so difficult for them both. He realised now he had made it so much harder for her by refusing to talk about her dying. Even so Christmas had been a good one, maybe one of the best. They had all had to wear wigs, a directive from Peggy who had insisted that it was Santa who had the idea. Seth had been horrified at first and then secretly delighted when he had realised he had the complete Blackbeard costume. John's wig had been long and dark and Evie had smiled and said he looked a bit dangerous. Martha had willingly participated, wearing a wig of bright pink much to his children's delight. Darwin had even suffered his own humiliation by having a short blond wig which had ear holes cut out so it wasn't as easy as his usual reindeer antlers to remove.

A few weeks later Evie had said she had a little surprise for John. They had been lying in bed on a Sunday morning making the most of the peace and quiet. Both children had slept at Martha's for the night. Evie had been excited and happy. He was glad to see her like her old self; she had been very depressed through January – he had even thought of calling the doctor at one point. He had made them breakfast in bed. Freshly ground coffee, orange juice and hot buttered toast with peanut butter and jam brought up on a silver tray with a single rose in a tiny vase. She had been delighted. She was weak though and it upset him to see her struggling to eat even the smallest piece of toast. She had asked him to fetch a box from the bottom of the wardrobe. He padded across the warm carpet in his boxers. It was an old shoe box; the writing showed Clarks sandals that had been on sale. The box was heavy, much heavier than he had anticipated, and the weight inside shifted as he lifted it out. He had placed it on her side of the bed and sat by her side as she opened the box. Nothing had prepared him for what was inside.

Nestled in layers of cream tissue was a battered red brick, old and dusty with a split at one of the edges. Beneath the split was an engraving which he could just about make out. It wouldn't have mattered if it had been so badly damaged that the engraving was illegible; he still would have known what was written on it. JM AND GE were inscribed in the middle of a heart. It was only then and on official paperwork she had used her proper name Genevieve. They had scratched their names a month after he had asked her out. He had known then that they would be together for ever. But forever hadn't been nearly long enough. Was that why he had handled her illness so badly? She had been the opposition, the one who had accepted her fate. He had refused to accept it until almost the end. She had forgiven him on her death bed but he had never forgiven himself for it. He was struggling to move forward and he knew that it was unhealthy for the children if he didn't. He had held the brick in his hand after Christmas as she had laughed at the expression on his face. She had said that she was glad that she could still surprise him even after all their years together. He hadn't been surprised at all though; it was in fact typical of her to find something so meaningful that money couldn't buy. It had her written all over it.

He sat on the soft cream carpet. It had been expensive and when they had bought it he had tried to argue with Evie that it wasn't very practical. She had been right; the carpet was still pristine. The only mark was when Peggy had helped her mother do her make-up during the last few months of her life. It was a small smudge of beige on the edge by the dressing table. It made him feel that she was still with him whenever he looked at it. Since she had died he had moved into the spare bedroom, finding it too painful to sleep in the same bed that he once shared with her, but now it was time to find a new normal. Also Peggy had been hinting at taking over her mummy's room for herself; it was larger than her own and had two bay windows. Peggy still harboured the wish of having a window seat or two in her bedroom. Only last week, John had had to call in a carpenter to fix one of the kitchen cupboards and Peggy had practically strong-armed him upstairs to see if he could make the elusive window seat in her mummy's bedroom. She had even told him that the room was no longer in use since her mother had left home and moved in with the angels. John had felt sorry for the man who had not known the etiquette in this sort of situation.

He opened the large wardrobe; the smell of her perfume still hung in the air. He breathed it in; it soothed him. She was still here helping him with the task at hand. He took a handful of dresses out of the wardrobe and placed them on the bed. He looked at the three dresses laid out. He could remember each time she had worn them. He closed his eyes and let the memories flood in.

He looked at the time. Hours had passed without him realising. No more trips down memory lane, he needed to take the items he had selected to the charity shop before the kids came home. He grabbed a black bag and filled it with her clothes; he tied the yellow strings at the top and placed it by the bedroom door. He closed the wardrobe door but it wouldn't shut properly. He pushed the remaining clothes to one side then closed the door; it still wouldn't close. He opened up the other door and looked around the dark interior. Evie had always wanted one of those wardrobes where a light came on when you opened the door. He smiled; she was right about things even when she wasn't here any longer. He hadn't sorted through her shoes yet. She had loved shoes – it had been her only weakness. It was why he hadn't tackled them yet; there were at least thirty pairs lined up neatly on a sort of American bleachers-type frame. There were several pairs of boots and he could now see the reason the door wouldn't shut. Her favourite tan knee-length boots had flopped over and the top of the boot was jamming the hinge. He was surprised as she was fanatical about using the boot trees she had bought on eBay. He pulled the boots out of the wardrobe and the door then shut easily. He felt the soft leather, saw the nick by the toe, a scratch on the leg of the left boot and little patches of discolouration when she had taken the kids out in the snow. He didn't know if he would ever be able to get rid of them. He rummaged in the back of the wardrobe and found the boot trees. He pushed the first into the left boot and then proceeded to push in the right one. It wouldn't go down all the way. He tried again; it still would only go so far. He pushed his hand into the boot. The whole of the foot part was crammed with paper secured with an elastic band. He pushed his hand further into the boot and was able to pull out the stack of paper. They were letters: a thick pile, almost ten in all, ten letters all addressed to Evie. He pulled the elastic band off them and with a shaking hand turned the top one over. He pulled the letter out and instead of reading the contents he immediately looked at who had been writing hand-written letters to his wife.

He indicated and pulled out onto the motorway. It was a horrible day, grey and overcast with the threat of rain hanging in the air. He still wasn't sure if it was a good idea to drive but it had all been such short notice he just wanted to get it over with. Martha was picking the kids up from school; he had told her he may be late home. He hadn't told her he had taken time off work or the reason why he may be late home. They had promised each other not to have any more secrets from each other any more. He had seen first-hand the effect it had on Martha but he had no choice; he needed to protect her until he knew the full story. He had tried to play out the possible scenarios in his head as to why his wife would have letters from a complete stranger. That was the problem though, he obviously wasn't a complete stranger to Evie. The letters were seared in his mind as though the man had taken a branding iron and permanently marked him with every word.

The letters had started formally enough and in the first instance it was obviously purely to secure a meeting. Then they had changed to a more familiar tone but they were still fairly light- hearted. Again, there were references to them having met up and going through some "paperwork" which made little sense to John. Then they changed dramatically and it was obvious she had discussed her illness with him. The man seemed to have a black sense of humour and would write little jokes at the end of each letter. As John had carried on through them he realised that the man had known details of Evie's illness that he hadn't known. It had made him feel so angry and then it had made him feel ashamed that he had refused to listen each time his wife wanted to discuss her death. Had he been so unsupportive that she had to find it in someone else? The penultimate letter was dated a few days after the most devastating diagnosis, the one John had refused to accept. John had dropped the letters onto the floor and had put his head in his hands and sobbed.

As he drove he wondered if he was doing the right thing. Neither of them could bring her back; each of them would only have their own opinion about how she had felt. In a strange way it made him feel as though a part of her had come back to him, a part that this man had and John was going to reclaim as his own. When John had phoned the number on the first letter he had firstly been surprised that the number was still in use and secondly that it was answered on the third ring. He had sounded familiar but John hadn't been able to put a face to the voice. The man hadn't appeared surprised to hear from John. In fact, he had said that he had been waiting for his call. Neither mentioned Evie, they just both accepted that they needed to talk face to face. They were meeting halfway at an impersonal motorway service station. John needed answers to all the questions that he had and only Nathan Devore would be able to answer them.

John sat at the table and waited. He didn't know if he actually wanted to meet the man or would be happier if he didn't turn up. As usual the services were busy; a break en route to their destination for most of the other customers. John did feel that he was starting along a road and had no idea where it would eventually take him. He desperately wanted to talk to Evie and ask her who this man was, why she had been writing to him and obviously meeting him.

"John?"

John looked up to see a tall dark-haired man standing in front of him. The man was more nervous than John and was fidgeting with the seam of his trousers. It made John relax a little; it was a habit he himself had when he was under pressure.

"How did you know it was me?" asked John.

"You gave me a good description of yourself and the fact that you look almost as nervous as I do."

John tried to smile but he knew that his body language radiated hostility. He needed to get straight to the point, otherwise his children may end up as orphans as he was experiencing a severe pain radiating across his chest.

"OK so do you want to explain what your connection is to my late wife?"

"My connection isn't with your wife, John. It's with you."

John looked at the stranger in front of him, confusion tempering his hostility.

"I don't understand."

Nathan leant forward and put his hand on John's shoulder, John stiffened but left it in place.

"You're my brother."

Epilogue

Martha took a deep breath as her name was announced. She got up to thunderous applause as she made her way to the stage. After thirty-five years she had achieved a first in English. As she shook hands with the dean and accepted her degree, she fancied the applause for her had been the loudest so far. She looked at her little group as she made her way back to her seat. Edward, John, and her father were beaming as though she was the only person who had ever achieved a degree. She had only been allocated two guest tickets but as her tutor had said it was the least they could do in view of the fact that it had taken her three and a half decades to finish it. The rest of her family and friends were waiting at the restaurant that Edward had booked. It made her think of the search for her first son which had started the whole thing. She still hadn't been able to find out anything about him even with the help of her nosey and tenacious new friends. It still made her incredibly sad but she had gained so much she felt she was ungrateful to demand more. And, as she had explained to Edward, she had gained a husband the first time she had tried to find him. Did he really want to run the risk of her finding a replacement husband if she looked again? So they had finally decided to take the trip that they had delayed because of her studies. As Edward had originally wanted to do, they would hire a boat for six months. They would point it at the horizon and see where it took them.

The meal had been wonderful and she had felt she may burst as Edward had given a heartfelt speech about how proud he was of her. She felt Edward reach for her hand; they had found an easy rhythm to life since he had moved in with her after the wedding. They had kept his flat in Langland and had split their time between the two countries; it had worked well for both of them. Peggy and Seth had stayed with them there several times. John had said that Peggy had told her friend Chelsea that she "had a little place by the sea".

On the table was a large hand-made congratulations card that the children had made. She remembered then that the postman had handed her some cards before they had left for the ceremony. She picked her bag up from the floor and unzipped the top; she felt inside and found the cards. She pulled the three small envelopes from her handbag. She opened the first; it was a congratulations card from Tom and Alice. They were sorry that they hadn't been able to come and celebrate with her but Alice had an interview as a partner that afternoon with the practice she had been working in; the elderly vet had finally retired. They wished her well and promised to call in and see them all soon; Peggy especially was excited to see her new uncle again. She had developed the idea that her grandmother meeting Edward and Tom becoming her son had all happened because she had taken a photo. She was going to be a detective when she grew up. Seth had said that if he hadn't asked Alice to take the photo it wouldn't have happened. The two children argued tirelessly on this subject. It was good and healthy and Martha was delighted that Seth no longer treated his sister like she was breakable. The second card was from Susan she wished Martha well and said that hopefully when Martha came to Swansea again they could meet up. At the moment she was far too busy to go anywhere as she was standing as a local councillor and was canvassing hard. Martha laughed. She couldn't imagine anyone refusing to vote for Susan whether they wanted to or not. She carefully opened the cream envelope of the last card. Again the card was one congratulating her on her success. She opened the card wondering if Pam had sent it from her Mediterranean cruise. The message simply said: "Well done on your success, best wishes Nathan". She turned the card over in her hand to see If there was any other message but the rest of the card was bare. She didn't know a Nathan.

"You OK Mum?" asked John.

"Yes love, I'm fine. I've had a card from a Nathan Devore. The address is right and it's a congratulations card but I don't know anyone called Nathan."

"The name seems familiar," said Edward.

"Yes, to me too," said John.

Martha couldn't explain it but she felt that there was a power surge in the room. The air became heavy, viscous; she felt a pressure on her chest. Roz had taken the children to get an ice-cream which had seemed an odd thing to Martha given that they had only just finished their meal.

"Martha."

The voice was John's but it was coming from a different man. He walked towards her pausing only to shake John's hand. By the side of John he was taller but more muscular, broader in the chest and the shoulders. He had black wavy hair and piercing blue eyes framed with eyelashes that most women would kill for. It was the walk, the way he fidgeted with the seams of his trousers, betraying his nervousness just as John had always done. And in that second, she knew.

Acknowledgements

Where do I start? There are so many people without whom this book would never have left the confines of my mind.

Firstly, to Lucy Lewellyn at Head & Heart, for encouraging me to send in my rough draft, and to Cressida Downing, her editor, who saw the possibility of a book amongst all the confusion. It was so lovely to work with Cressida and the culling was definitely necessary, so thank you so much for that. She was very supportive but also honest, perfectly balanced to facilitate the process.

A huge thanks to Anouska Mendzil, from Swansea University, my real life sedimentologist. She answered a random e-mail from a complete stranger and then had the patience and kindness to meet with her and explain what it was a sedimentologist did. The information that you sent me was invaluable; there is some poetic licence and of course any mistakes are of my own making.

To the brave people who took home a binder full of pages and read them knowing that they would have to say something to me once they had read it. You're all braver than you realise. To my dear friends Jackie Millen and Judy Munro and a special thank you to Dr Roger Munro for reading it several times! Thank you, Roger for your tenacity in trawling through the manuscript.

To my IT department, otherwise known as my husband, who calmed me down on many occasions when I shrieked "I've lost it all!" when apparently I had just moved it somewhere else. I promise for the next book I won't have twenty-four final versions!

To my family your love and support throughout this long process was appreciated more than I can ever tell you.

To my friends, especially my magnificent seven. Every one of you has given me the compassion, wisdom and encouragement to see this through.

To my son, Luke, over to you kid.

A big thank you to all the cafes, coffee shops and hotels. I took my laptop and set myself up sometimes forgetting that I had a cold cup of coffee in front of me as the words poured out of me. I promise to buy a cake the next time. The caramel apple pie in my local "loaf" is highly recommended!

Finally, I would like to thank Samantha Jayne.

About the Author

Alison Blanche was born in 1966; three months later she was adopted by her beloved parents.

She attended several primary schools due to her father being a prison governor which saw him taking up different posts all over the UK. She often joined schools mid-term which made her develop a natural interest in people's stories as she hadn't grown up with them.

She trained as a biomedical scientist and works part time in one of the local hospitals. She started writing during a period of ill health after trying knitting which really didn't work out well!.

She lives in the award winning town (Wales in Bloom 2018) of Ystradgynlais, with her husband, son and elderly mum. The house though is ruled by a badly behaved Bassett hound who knows better but doesn't care.

Throughout her life she had often wondered what her story was so she decided to write one instead.

Printed in Great Britain
by Amazon